An
ANTHOLOGY
of the ESOTERIC
and ARCANE

Magic

Edited by
JONATHAN OLIVER

SOLARIS

Magic

Edited by
JONATHAN OLIVER

**FIFTEEN NEW STORIES
OF THE SORCEROUS ARTS BY:**

Audrey Niffenegger
Sarah Lotz
Will Hill
Steve Rasnic Tem and Melanie Tem
Liz Williams
Dan Abnett
Thana Niveau
Alison Littlewood
Christopher Fowler
Storm Constantine
Lou Morgan
Sophia McDougall
Gail Z. Martin
Gemma Files
Robert Shearman

First published 2012 by Solaris
an imprint of Rebellion Publishing Ltd,
Riverside House, Osney Mead,
Oxford, OX2 0ES, UK

www.solarisbooks.com

ISBN 978-1-78108-053-5

Cover by Nicolas Delort

A CIP catalogue record for this book is available from the
British Library.

Designed & typeset by Rebellion Publishing

Printed in the UK by CPI Bookmarque, Croydon

CONTENTS

INTRODUCTION

JONATHAN OLIVER

THE WORD MAGIC, for many, will conjure up images of gentlemen in dinner suits pulling rabbits out of hats and producing bunches of flowers from their sleeves. For sure, you can find the popular image of the magician here – the entertainer reveals himself in both Alison Littlewood's 'The Art of Escapology' and Robert Shearman's 'Dumb Lucy' – but you will find much about the magical arts that may not be familiar to you within these pages.

Genre fiction has had a long and complex relationship with magic. Horror fiction has often featured diabolists and their dealings with devils, cults pervade the works of pulp pioneers such as H.P. Lovecraft and Robert E. Howard and magic is an integral part of fantasy fiction as a whole. What I am seeking to do with *Magic*, however, is not to fulfil your expectations but exceed and confound them. This is a collection of unusual fiction; indeed an anthology of the esoteric and arcane.

One question that you'll find repeated throughout is, *what is magic for?* The uses to which the arts of sorcery are tasked are often concerned with human desire. In Alison Littlewood's poignant tale we have the child's desire for magic and a magical existence come up against the realities of the world as experienced by adults. In Gemma Files' story, 'Nanny Grey' we have a darker side of desire, where magic is used to lure a young man driven by sexual need into a horrific encounter. 'First and Last and Always' by Thana Niveau (a magical name if there ever was one) shows us how we can want something too much and how playing with magic, without true understanding, is a very dangerous undertaking. As it is in Will Hill's story 'Shuffle', the structure of which is something of a trick in itself.

The thing about magic, is that it often confounds understanding. And, of course, when we write about magic we are often trying to express impossibilities. Sophia McDougall demonstrates herself to be more than capable of this in 'MailerDaemon' in which a computer programmer finds herself with a gift she's not sure she asked for, and Robert Shearman's beautifully apocalyptic tale shows us the possibilities of an impossible love. In Audrey Niffeneggers's story, 'The Wrong Fairy', we are given a glimpse into an impossible world through the eyes of the father of a very famous writer. While in Liz Williams' 'Cad Coddeau' we are taken back into the time of legend, where myth and story grow into something impossibly beautiful.

Of course, one of the most common uses for a spell is to help another. When the motivation is pure, this can bring about a positive change, as demonstrated in Storm Constantine's story 'Do as Thou Wilt.' Lou Morgan, too, shows us an act of magical sacrifice in 'Bottom Line' that throws new light onto a morally ambiguous character. Sarah Lotz's comic tale 'If I Die, Kill My Cat' shows the consequences of leaving an altruistic magical act unfinished. In Gail Z. Martin's 'Buttons' we have a group of esoteric investigators whose mission it is to help people through the use of magic. In effecting magical change, however, the moral may not always be pure, as is clear from Dan Abnett's politics-meets-magic story 'Party Tricks'. Help sought also has a sinister side in Christopher

Fowler's story of magic gone wrong, 'The Baby.' Sometimes the magic user may not realise how far they have gone, as we can see when Steve Rasnic Tem and Melanie Tem introduce us to a mother who may not have her children's best interests at heart in 'Domestic Magic'.

While these tales show many aspects of magic, it is worth remembering that the act of writing has its own magic. I hope, then, that you find as much enjoyment in reading the works of the prestidigitators herein as I had in gathering them together.

Jonathan Oliver
August 2012
Oxford

THE WRONG FAIRY

AUDREY NIFFENEGGER

Madness and creative inspiration aren't very distantly related. Here, Audrey takes the father of a very famous writer and explores the nature of his 'illness'. There is magic in the creative process and there is the magic our mind can conjure in order to help us cope. This is a rich tapestry of a tale by an extraordinary writer that shows us a glimpse of another world.

THE MAN SAT on the bed and looked about him. There was a wash stand, a pink china bowl with its chipped pitcher, a wing-backed chair by the small barred window, a worn carpet, a small bookcase, a desk, an ashtray, a waste basket, a wardrobe and a lamp. The bed had whitewashed iron fittings, like a servant's. His own things were piled in a heap at the foot of the bed, his clothing and his painting materials, his books and his pipe; all he needed was there except the bottle, the most important thing.

"You're trying to kill me," the man said to his son. His son stood in front of the door, as though to prevent the man from leaving, or perhaps in order to slip away more efficiently.

His son was a substantial young man with an impressive moustache. He looked prosperous, even sleek, but also very unhappy. "No, Father," he replied. "We're trying to help you." He didn't sigh, though he wanted to.

The man appeared much older than he actually was, and this was certainly because of the drink. The drink had brought him here, had compelled his family to commit him to the care of this dreadful place. Now he was here and they were going to keep him from drinking. He groaned.

"You can't imagine."

"I can," his son said rather grimly. "And you mustn't try to escape again. We were lucky to find you a place here. Foudoun won't have you back after the way you behaved."

"Where am I, then?"

"Montrose Royal Lunatic Asylum. They call it Sunnyside; there used to be a farm of that name on the property."

"A lunatic asylum?" He felt faint. "Is everyone here insane?"

"No, the staff are very sane indeed. And the patients look mild enough. You've got a private room; no one will bother you here."

The man stared at his son. "Will you ask your mother to come and visit me?"

The son shook his head. "Better not."

The man stood up and the room reeled. His son steadied him, helped him back to the bed. It was a long time since he had been so physically near his son. He gripped his son's arm and felt him recoil slightly, involuntarily.

"Please," he said.

"Father–" his son began to reply.

Someone knocked on the door and then opened it. His son straightened and stepped away from him. The matron looked in at them impassively. "Your driver was asking if you'll be much longer, Dr. Doyle?"

"Tell him I'll be down in a few minutes, Mrs. Brewster."

The matron continued to stand there.

"Give my love to the girls. And Mary," the man said with an effort at a smile, conscious of the matron's gaze.

His son said, "I will," and "Be well, Father." Then he embraced the man and stepped through the door after the matron. The key turned in the lock. The man lay back on the bed and waited.

THE HORRORS WERE upon him. He was infested by insects that marched across the underside of his skin like directionless armies. He could feel each tiny foot as it touched each nerve. He was hot, hotter, he was going to burst into flame. *Water,* he thought he said, but no intelligible word came out. Every sound in that unfamiliar place was amplified. Footsteps in the hall, cool wet clothes wrung into the basin, the tap of metal against glass. People stood by his bed and whispered. Someone said, "...seizures." They put something cold and hard in his mouth and they restrained him. Crawlers massed at the edge of his vision, their etiolated limbs waving and gesturing at him. Great storms possessed him, then blackness. Nurses came and went, sunlight crept into the room and then it was night. He thought he was at home. His family sat at the table eating oyster soup. His daughter Ida seemed about to recognize him, but then her eyes slid across him and fixed on her mother. He spoke to each of them in turn and in turn they ignored him. He wept. Later he stood on a stony beach and saw birds, small and massed at the horizon, multitudes of birds, all kinds, flying toward him slowly. As they came close, he saw that it was a host of angels and that one among them was Death itself, his own Death, red and magnificent. "Take me," he said. He closed his eyes, lifted his arms and waited. Nothing happened.

He opened his eyes. The beach was empty and quite silent, the waves rolled and the wind blew without a sound.

"I have been watching for you," a lady said.

He looked about him but saw no one.

"Here I am," she said. He turned. A lady stood near him. She was young, but regarded him with a serious, even severe expression. Her short brown hair was loose and cut a bit wildly, as though she had been recently ill. She wore a white tunic and her arms and feet were bare.

"Aren't you cold?" he asked her. He was shivering, himself. He noticed that there was a tortoise the size of a Hackney cab standing near the lady. It was looking at her with adoration and nodding gently.

"No, I'm not cold at all; it's you, you've got the chills." The lady snapped her fingers and the wind died. He felt better at once.

"Charles Altamont Doyle?" she asked.

"Yes," he replied, somehow not surprised. "You know my name?"

"Of course. We know a great deal. Everything."

He did not like to think what *everything* might encompass. "And – have I died?"

"No, don't be silly. I sent him away."

"I wanted to die," he said. "I was quite ready."

"The Queen prefers that you live. She enjoys your paintings of us and she wishes you to paint according to her own specifications. She will send you instructions once you have recovered your health."

"Yes," he said, without comprehension. He blushed and wondered how Victoria had heard of his work.

"Not that queen. The real Queen," said the lady.

"Of course," he said. He was about to ask the lady who this other queen might be when he heard a loud noise and found himself in his bed at the asylum. A char stood by the fireplace, one hand to her mouth in alarm, the other holding an empty coal scuttle. The door opened and Mrs. Brewster entered in a fury.

"Milly!" she hissed. "What on earth was that noise? And oh, dear, look at all this coal all over the floor! Pick it up at once!" She glanced at him and her expression softened.

"Mr. Doyle, good morning. How are you feeling?"

"Better," he said. He raised his head to look at her and the room spun around. "Still alive."

"Yes," she said. "We nearly lost you."

"I was sent back," he said. "I'm supposed to make some paintings for the Queen." Too late, he realized that he sounded like a lunatic.

Mrs. Brewster was used to this. "Well, let's get you washed and you shall have some nice beef broth and then we'll see about those paintings. I'm sure the Queen can wait until you're steady on your feet again."

THE FITS CAME and went and his hands trembled so much that sometimes he could not hold a spoon. But his health did improve and on a good warm day he could sit on a bench in the sun on the grounds; he could sit in the common room and watch the other inmates watching him. He studied the habits of the staff. He adapted himself to Sunnyside's routines. Some of the other patients were alcoholics like himself, and of these he made friends with two Irishmen and talked politics happily with them for hours. Time passed slowly at Sunnyside.

Weeks went by before he attempted to draw. The nurse had laid out his watercolours, pencils, sketchbook and brushes neatly on the desk, as though he might perform surgery with them. He noticed that they had taken away the little knife he used to sharpen his pencils.

He wrote his name and the date, 8 March 1889, on the first page. On the second page he made a drawing of the lady he had met on the beach. He sketched the huge tortoise behind her, roughed in the waves and the shore.

"That's not a very good likeness," the lady said.

He turned to find her sitting in the wing chair looking prim.

"How did you get in here?" he asked. The door was kept locked.

She smiled. "I have a knack." She looked around. "It's rather shabby, isn't it?"

He shrugged. "It's not as grim as some places I've been."

"No," she said. "That's true." She was silent for a long while. He waited politely, unsure what hospitality he should offer. At last she said, "Are you ready to take up your position at Court?"

"I'm sorry," he said, "but I don't understand. I'm not allowed to leave."

"Oh, pish, you needn't worry. You'll be back before teatime." She stood up and handed him a small branch of fir. "Keep hold of that. And bring your painting things." He gathered the paints and other supplies. The lady clasped his hand, and immediately the room vanished and they were walking very quickly down a long tiled corridor with a crowd of strangely dressed people.

"Please!" he said, "Please could we walk more slowly?" He was dizzy and gasping for breath. "Where are we?"

"Paddington Underground station." The lady stopped by an unmarked door. "Here we are. Close your eyes." He did. He felt the lady tug at his dressing gown and he opened his eyes to find them both standing in a meadow. The ground was damp under his slippers. He felt a fit coming on. "Oh, bother," he heard the lady say as the storms overtook his brain.

HE WOKE IN his bed, trying to remember his dreams. He felt blank. There was a stick in the bed with him. He held it up. A fir branch. Well, he had kept hold of it, at least.

HE BEGAN DRAWING every day. He drew heraldry, elves, birds. He drew a giant squirrel holding a screaming baby. He drew people with absurd facial hair, Mrs. Brewster's tea kettle, the maids at their work. He drew the lady being menaced by a massive pole cat.

"I suppose you think that's amusing," said the lady.

"Yes," he said. "Do you?"

"I don't have much of a sense of humour," she said. "You would do well to remember that."

He nodded.

"How are you feeling?" she asked, almost kindly.

"Not well," he said. The insects-under-the-skin feeling had been troubling him all morning.

"Ah. Then perhaps we should leave our journey till another day."

"If it's not too much trouble..." He faltered. "Could I make the paintings for the Queen here in my room? I should be glad to paint anything she likes."

"Oh, but she particularly wanted portraits made of all her children."

"How many does she have?"

"Thousands."

"Dear me. That's... prodigious. But I'm sure I will be dead before I can make so many portraits."

The lady smiled. "You needn't worry. We can keep you alive for as long as you like. Nearly forever. We are quite long-lived ourselves, and it's no great trick to loan you a little extra."

He thought of his death, which had been so near, so inviting. He wished he could ask the lady to hasten death toward him. But he thought that must be wrong. "Thank you," he told her. "But I don't wish for anything that isn't mine."

"What do you wish for, then? For you must have a reward. The Queen would have it so."

He thought carefully. "Perhaps... something for my son Arthur? Good luck?"

The lady nodded. "We will watch over him. But for yourself?"

He hesitated. "Do you have any strong drink, at your Court?"

The lady laughed. "We have wonderful spirits, much nicer than anything you have had."

He stood and held out his hand. "Lead me there, and let me have a drink, or two, and I'll paint all Her Majesty's children."

"Done," said the lady. He gathered up his painting things and she gave him another fir branch. Then she compressed him until he was seven inches tall and she put him in her pocket. He felt marsupial, but it was much more comfortable than going along on foot. They rushed through Paddington and across the meadow. The lady opened a hole in the ground and they made their way through narrow caves. She stopped, took him out of her pocket and said, "Now you have to walk." She made herself seven inches tall so they were again the same height. The caves opened into caverns. Light was always just ahead; he could not see the source.

They came to a room which had a table laid for a feast. "Stop and rest," said the lady. "And have your drink." She poured a dark, syrupy liquid into a glass. He drank it and felt restored; he felt better than he had in many years. "One more?" She refilled his glass and he drank up. His brain seemed to heal. The fog lifted. He grinned at the lady and she smiled back. "Now, here we are," she said, and she led him into the next room.

The room was enormous. He could see the ceiling but not the walls. There were a great many things in the room, too many for him to make sense of at first. When he looked carefully, he could see piles of things. Each thing was spherical, illuminated, each one was in motion. He drew near to one pile and looked into a sphere. Some children were building a snowman. They were in a city. A large shiny vehicle passed by the children, moving under its own power, like a train. One of the children threw a snowball at it. In another sphere there was a war going on, something exploded and he turned away quickly. Lovers embraced in strange clean white bedrooms. Water gushed from pipes into bathtubs, no servants had to carry the water. Bodies were stacked naked in mass graves. Machines. Murder. Magic. He saw things he had no words for.

He turned to the lady, who was standing in an empty space looking depressed. "How do you like it?" she asked him.

"It's overwhelming," he said. "What is it?"

"The Queen's children. The future."

"This? I thought... I imagined that fairies were..."

"Small and pretty with little gauzy wings?" The lady shook her head. "I'm sure we were, once upon a time. The Queen is nostalgic, and she likes to think of her children the way we used to be. She thought perhaps you would be able to see us that way. She hoped you might reimagine us."

"For that you need a genius. Or a lunatic. I'm only an artist and a drunkard."

The lady looked at him carefully. "At least you're honest about it," she said. She held out her hand. He took it and they began the long walk through the caves.

BACK AT SUNNYSIDE he applied himself to his task. He filled the sketchbook with incorrect, out-of-date fairies. Fairies riding on the back of a pheasant, fairies flying through the night sky. Fairies feasting, frolicking, courting and scheming. The lady came whenever he ran out of paper. She peeled each fairy off the page and tucked it into her pocket. "How many more?" he asked her. "Lots and lots," she always said.

One day she pocketed the last fairy. She leaned over Charles Doyle and took his pen in her hand. "Here is a drawing for you," she said. In his own style, she drew a full-length portrait of him, standing in profile with one hand outstretched in greeting. Facing him, she drew his death. They shook hands.

Charles Doyle smiled. He slumped forward; his death was a simple, quiet one. Under the drawing the lady wrote *Well met*. She laid down the pen and left the room.

IF I DIE, KILL MY CAT

SARAH LOTZ

There are things in the following tale that are true. I'm not going to tell you what they are, but let me assure you that it's none of the mundane stuff. After reading Sarah's brilliant and witty story, I did wonder whether the UK government could look to the arcane arts to solve a few problems. Or maybe they already do that, and none of us realise.

"THERE'S GOING TO be maggots," Lindiwe sighed, batting at the blowflies bobbing around her breathing mask. Others gathered in clumps around the light fixtures and swarmed over the single mug upturned on the draining board. Save for the flies, the house was a typical Sea Point rental property: parquet floors, white walls, cheap appliances and minimal furniture.

I dumped the chemicals in the kitchen and joined her in the hallway. I was already sweating like a bastard under my protective gear, but I'd rather melt than take a chance – hepatitis is no joke. "How long before the body was discovered?"

"Four or five days," Lindiwe said. "Apparently he died in bed, nothing suspicious, suspected heart attack. Client said the cops took him away yesterday."

"That long in this heat? Then maggots are the least of our worries."

"Yeah," Lindiwe huffed. "There's going to be maggots *and* goop. My favourite combo."

My phone vibrated in my jeans pocket. I ignored it; no way was I going to strip off my coveralls to answer it. Probably just my sister again. She'd been calling me non-stop since she got back to Cape Town. She could wait.

We clumped down the corridor, pausing to peer into a dusty bathroom, a spare room containing nothing but a daybed, and then, in startling contrast to the rest of the house, an office space stuffed with clutter.

"I think we've reached New Age central," I said, checking out the astrological charts tacked up on the walls, the dream-catchers hanging from the ceiling and the shelves heaving with polished stones. Leatherbound books and catalogues with photos of crystals on their covers were stacked in piles on every available surface. Judging by the titles, most seemed to be in German.

"Check," Lindiwe said, nodding at a woollen robe draped over the corner of a shelf. "You think he was a Jedi?" I knew what was coming next. "Search your feelings, Rachel," she said, breathing heavily into her mask and putting on the Darth Vader voice she uses at every opportunity. "I am your father. You know it to be true."

I snorted. I've heard it a million times, but it always cracks me up.

I opened the door at the end of the corridor, a cloud of flies gusting out to greet me. Ground Zero.

The room contained nothing but a pair of mismatching side tables and a double bed, overfed maggots squirming lazily in the duvet's folds. The bed linen was black with decomposition fluid, and I was relieved I'd remembered to change my mask's filter and couldn't smell the aftermath of what had to have been a lonely death.

Lindiwe lifted up the duvet to assess the extent of the damage.

"Wait," I said. The corner of what looked to be a passport was peeking out from between the mattress and the base. As I pulled it out and flicked through to the back cover, a piece of paper fluttered out of the centre pages and drifted onto the floor. Lindiwe retrieved it while I stared at a photograph of a middle-aged man with watery blue eyes. "Dead guy was Austrian," I said. "Named August Schuller."

"Yeah? Whoever he was, he clearly had problems."

She passed the piece of paper to me. The words, 'If I die, kill my cat,' were scrawled on it in shaky handwriting.

"What the hell does that mean?"

Lindiwe shrugged. "Maybe he wanted to be buried with it or something."

"You see any sign of a cat?"

"Police might have taken it away."

"Yeah, well I hope they didn't follow his instructions. You want to start bagging the linen? I'll go get the rest of the stuff."

I headed back towards the kitchen, pulling off my gloves and hood to wipe away the rivulets of sweat trickling down from my scalp. I piled the chemical bottles on top of a hazmat box, freezing when I heard a faint noise. That couldn't be right – it sounded almost like a baby crying. I held my breath. It couldn't be coming from outside; the flats that flanked the house were still under construction. No – it appeared to be emanating from behind the door on the other side of the kitchen, one we'd missed when we'd done the recce.

I yanked it open, yelping as something shot out towards me. I retreated, looked down and into the eyes of a small black cat. It mewled at me. It was super cute, but also super thin, the ridges of its spine and ribs clearly visible under its coat.

"Rach?" Lindiwe yelled. "You okay?"

"I found the cat."

Lindiwe swished her way towards me. "Where was it?"

"In here." I peered through the door, fumbling on the wall for the light switch. Strip lights hissed into life, revealing a small garage, empty but for the remains of a ripped bag of cheap dry cat food. I spied a small bathroom and toilet nestled in an alcove. If the cat had been trapped in here since its owner died, at least it'd had water. The cops probably figured it was too much of a schlep to deal with it. Bastards.

It snaked its body around my legs and I picked it up and carried it over to the kitchen counter. "Shame," I said. "She must be starving." I found a tin of tuna in the cupboard and unearthed a tin opener and a bowl.

"How do you know it's a she?"

"I checked."

"We'd better call the SPCA."

"You ever been to the SPCA, Linds? It's like Belsen for four-leggeds."

"So what do you suggest? Shall I call the rental agency, get them to deal with it?"

"They won't give a shit. Maybe the dead guy's family will want her." I could try contacting whoever was listed in the 'in case of emergency' section in the back of August Schuller's passport. It was worth a shot. If not, I could call a cat sanctuary that had a non-euthanasia policy.

While Lindiwe started shoving the soiled bed linen into incinerator bags, I searched the house, looking for a cat box. Nothing. Not even a cat bed. Using a screwdriver, I stabbed holes in the lid of a hazmat box, and stowed the cat inside it with a bowl of water.

WHEN WE SHUFFLED out of the house, arms full of equipment, two guys dressed in identical slick suits were leaning against the side of our van. Their gold jewellery glinted in the afternoon sun; Ray-Bans hid their eyes.

"Not again," Lindiwe sighed.

The taller of the two, a fellow with faint acne scars and a disarming grin, stepped forward. "Madam," he said to me. "I hope you are having a fine day. I represent a certain party who would be interested in conducting some business with you."

He bent down to inspect the hazmat cat box.

"Don't touch that!" I snapped.

For the thousandth time I cursed Lindiwe's insistence on displaying our 'Crime Scene Cleaners' logo so prominently on the side of the truck. It's a magnet for unscrupulous muti sellers who believe that adding body parts to herbal remedies will enhance the power of the 'medicine' they sell to promote wealth, luck and better erections. It was the second time that week we'd been approached by agents eager to purchase the biological waste we collect. They weren't fussy – anything would do: brain bits, fingers, even teeth.

"You're wasting your time," I said. "We're not interested."

Undaunted, the guy increased the wattage of his smile. "But madam, this is an opportunity for you to–"

"You're sick, you know that?" Lindiwe jabbed a finger in his face. "Now fuck off before I call the cops."

The muti agent's smile snapped off and he and his sidekick slunk away. A minute later I saw them roaring past in a shiny black Mercedes sedan, an Orlando Pirates sticker on its bumper.

I whistled. "Nice car. We're in the wrong business."

"They make me sick." Lindiwe glanced at me. "You haven't told your sister pricks like that are stalking us, have you?"

"Are you crazy? She already thinks I'm infested with evil spirits as it is. Keeps nagging me to go for a cleansing."

"So have one. How could it hurt?"

"Are you serious? Since when did you start believing in all that ancestor crap? I thought you were into Jesus."

"Whatever." Lindiwe turned her back on me and stalked back into the house to fetch the rest of the gear. Me and my big mouth. Religion is one subject we tend to avoid, and for good reason. Lindiwe is well aware of my hardcore agnostic tendencies and rarely discusses her own beliefs. Mopping up after murders, hijackings and suicides takes its toll, and I suspect her weekly church visits are her way of coping with the horrors we encounter on a daily basis.

I deal with it in my own way: vodka and mindless reality television.

The atmosphere between us still frosty, we heaved the ruined mattress into the van to drop off at the incinerator, and set off towards Kloof Nek Road, air-con cranked to full power.

We'd barely driven a kay, when the traffic in front of us slowed to a crawl.

"Rush hour?" I asked.

"Accident," Lindiwe said, as we inched past the cops setting out cones along the side of the road.

A policewoman signalled for us to stop. A tow truck hauling a concertinaed mass of black metal pulled off the hard shoulder in front of us. As it shuddered away, I caught a glimpse of an Orlando Pirates sticker stuck to a dented bumper.

"Think it's the same guys?" Judging by the state of their car, they couldn't have escaped uninjured.

"Instant karma," Lindiwe said. But she looked shaken just the same.

Victor, one of the Nigerians who lived in the flat directly below mine, appeared in his doorway as I struggled past his flat, juggling the hazmat cat box, a litter tray and the cat food I'd bought en route home from the incinerator. The delicious aroma of spicy stew wafted out his doorway, reminding me that I hadn't eaten all day. "Yo, Rachel," he said. "There is someone waiting for you outside your flat. I let her through the security gate. Strange chick." He shrugged. "She said she was your sister."

Great. As if the day couldn't get any shittier. I slogged up the stairwell, found Naomi sitting cross-legged outside my door, wrapped in a colourful blanket. She looked every inch the white sangoma: barefoot, dreadlocks threaded with beads and goat-hair bracelets looped around her wrists.

"What is that?" She nodded at my makeshift cat box.

"Hello to you too, Naomi."

"Sorry. How are you, Rachel?"

"Fine. Bit tired." I decided not to mention the dead Austrian Jedi, and I definitely wouldn't be bringing up the probably dead muti guys.

I unlocked the door and gestured for her to follow me inside. She started in on me straight away. "Why haven't you returned my calls?"

"Been busy."

"I know you don't want to hear this, but it's important that we talk about your spiritual–"

"You're right, I don't want to hear it. Can we please just have a conversation that doesn't involve any witchdoctor bullshit?"

She flinched, and I instantly regretted snapping at her. Accusing a sangoma of being a witchdoctor is pretty much the worst insult there is. But since Naomi received her calling from the ancestors and started dreaming of goats and chickens, I just didn't know how to act around her. I didn't get it. Two years ago she was a straight-laced accountant from the suburbs who didn't speak a word of Xhosa, and practically had a heart attack if she missed a Pilates class. It's not that I think she's appropriating African culture or anything like that, it's just that I like to think of myself as an equal opportunities agnostic. I don't buy into any faith, be it Christianity, Hinduism, Buddhism, Islam, African spirituality or the New Age crap the dead guy was clearly into. And I'd always assumed Naomi felt the same way.

I forced a smile. "How about some coffee?"

"Fine."

I filled the kettle, sniffed the milk to make sure it wasn't too far out of date. She peered at the box. "Is there an animal in there?"

"Yeah. A cat. I need to find her a home. You interested?"

"Where did you get it?"

"Abandoned at a scene."

She shook her head. "You must get it out of here, Rachel. I have told you before about the bad spirits your work attracts—"

"Jesus, Naomi. It's a cat, okay? A *cat*."

I angrily unclipped the lid, and the cat leapt out onto the kitchen counter, padded over to me, and pushed her face into my hand. Naomi backed away from her, murmuring to herself.

"I don't *believe* this shit, Naomi."

"I can't stay with that here."

"Then go. I didn't invite you anyway."

The cat shimmied down from the kitchen counter and sashayed off to explore the rest of the flat. I suddenly remembered I'd left the bathroom window open. If the cat got out, she would be toast – my flat overlooks the busy Green Point main road. I raced after her, but I needn't have worried; she was busy making herself at home on my futon.

I heard a door slam. When I returned to the kitchen, my sister had gone.

TRYING TO BLOCK out the aftertaste of Naomi's visit, I poured myself a hefty slug of Absolut and logged onto Skype, typing in the number at the back of August Schuller's passport.

A gruff voice answered on the third ring. "Hallo?"

"Um hi. Is this Mr Schuller?"

"Ja?"

"Do you speak English?"

"Who is this?"

"My name is Rachel Greenberg."

"Who?"

"Rachel. I'm so sorry about..." I took a gamble. "Your brother."

A pause. "Thank you. You are a friend of his?"

"Not exactly... we had more of a business relationship."

He sighed. "For many years my brother, he has a heart condition. His death was not unexpected."

"I see. Um, he had a cat."

Silence.

"I was wondering what you want me to do with it."

"You are from the police?"

"Er... no." Mentioning that I was the one who cleaned up his brother's body fluids probably wouldn't go down well.

"There is nothing I can do with a cat."

"Shall I try and find her a home here, then?"

"Ja. Please."

I knew I was being nosy, but I couldn't help myself. "Mr Schuller... I hope you don't mind me asking this, but what did your brother do for a living?"

A pause. "You do not know?"

"We weren't that close."

Another sigh. "I suppose now it does not matter. He is – *was* – a druid."

Jesus. "A *what*? What was he doing in South Africa?"

He broke the connection. I thought about ringing him back and decided against it. I'd had enough kak for one day.

I took a shower, poured another drink and slumped down on the couch to catch up on *American Idol*. The cat jumped onto my lap, kneaded my thighs with her paws, then curled into a ball, paws cupped over her face.

I stroked the ridge of her spine. "Why would your owner want to kill you? You're so cute." She needed a name. I decided to call her Muti; that would piss Naomi off.

I WOKE WITH a jolt, flooded with panic. Something was pressing down on my chest – I couldn't breathe. I opened my eyes, looked straight into bright yellow orbs. It was just the cat. I brushed her away and sat up, gulping air. My head throbbed, and for a second I was sure I was going to throw up.

Drinking on an empty stomach again. My own bloody fault.

"Sorry, cat." She didn't seem to be at all affected by my rude treatment of her. She sat at the edge of the futon, contorting her body in order to wash her tummy. I scrubbed a hand over my face. I felt like death; my mouth tasted as if I'd been licking a crime scene.

My cell phone trilled and I blearily checked the caller ID. Lindiwe. "What's up?"

"Hey," she said. "You sound terrible."

"I *feel* terrible. Think I might be coming down with the flu."

"Eish. You want me to do this one on my own?"

"What we got?"

"Suicide."

"Hotel room?"

"You got it. The Radisson on Buitenkant Street again."

"Male or female?" I asked.

"Female."

Women tend to kill themselves in a tidier fashion than men. The job shouldn't be too arduous. "I'll be cool. Meet you there in an hour."

I dry-swallowed three extra-strength Disprin, and topped up Muti's food bowl. She rubbed her face against my hand and chirruped at me. I reminded myself to call a humane cat shelter after work. I couldn't get too attached to her. Keeping her imprisoned here would be cruel.

THE SCENE WASN'T as tidy as I'd hoped. The woman had cut her wrists in the bath; a pool of jellifying blood stained the floor tiles and bathmat. The remains of a smashed bottle of Stoli lay at the base of the sink. Every scene tells a story – hers said she'd needed a bottle's worth of Dutch courage to go through with it.

We suited up in the bedroom, and Lindi carried the hazmat box and the goop scoop into the bathroom while I set up the steamer.

I'd barely begun spraying the bedroom when I heard a thump, followed by, "Shit!"

I darted into the bathroom. Lindi was lying on her back next to the bath, holding her left wrist above her head. A jagged piece of glass from the smashed vodka bottle protruded from her arm.

"I slipped in the blood," she said.

"How the hell did you do that?" She was usually ultra careful. We both were.

"God knows. My legs just went out from under me."

Trying not to wince as she pulled the shard out of her arm, I helped her step out of her gore-soaked coveralls and led her into the relatively bacteria-free bedroom.

I dug out the iodine we kept on hand for incidents like this, and mopped her up as best as I could. The wound wasn't deep, but anything could be lurking in the victim's blood. "We can't deal with that here, it's not sterile. I'd better take you to see the doc."

"I can take a taxi. You cool to finish up here?"

"Yeah. I'll cope."

As I HAULED the equipment out of the lift and lugged it towards the van, a shadowy figure loomed out from behind one of the underground parking lot's pillars, making me jump.

"Ms Greenberg?"

"Yeah?"

A balding white guy with a serious beard stepped into the light. I relaxed. He was dressed in colourful shorts and sandals over socks – not the most intimidating of outfits. Besides, as I made my way over to where I'd parked the van, he seemed to be quite keen to keep his distance from me.

"I believe you have something that belongs to my colleague, August Schuller." His accent was thick, Germanic. "I have been out of town. I have just now heard of his demise."

"Sorry for your loss. How did you find me?"

"Your associate said you would be here."

What the fuck was Lindiwe thinking? "Right. Did you work with Mr Schuller?" Another druid, perhaps? Apart from the dire fashion sense, with that beard he looked the part.

"I believe you have his cat."

"Yeah."

He beamed. "I will be happy to take it off your hands."

There was something off about the way he was staring at me – the expression on his face reeked of desperation, his bulbous eyes unwavering as he waited for my response. "I don't have the cat here. Text your contact details to my office and I'll get back to you."

I turned away, expecting him to get the message and walk away. He didn't. He cleared his throat. "May I ask... how much contact you have had with it?"

I blinked. "Why, is the cat sick or something?" Shit. Maybe it wasn't a hangover after all. I hoped I hadn't caught something from her – rabies or cat AIDS or whatever. *If I die, kill my cat.*

"No. It is not diseased." He smiled again. Definitely fake this time.

I chucked the gear into the back of the van; I suspected I might need to make a quick getaway. "Why did August Schuller want the cat to die?"

He frowned. "How do you know..."

"I found a note."

"Ha," he said, waving his hands in the air. "August could be eccentric at times."

"I figured. His brother said he was some sort of druid."

"Did he?"

"If you take the cat, how do I know you'll look after her?"

He cleared his throat. "I do not understand."

"How do I know you won't follow through on Schuller's last wishes?" I took a step towards him and he skittered back as if he was afraid I was going to touch him.

"Please, I have to have the cat. You must trust me. If you do not, the consequences will be bad."

"Is that a threat?" He was starting to get panicky; I was starting to get pissed off.

"No... please, Ms Greenberg, you have to –"

"I don't have to do anything. Look, what is this all about?"

"If you won't give me the cat, then please, destroy it yourself."

"You need help, you know that?" I climbed into the driver's seat, gunned the engine, and reversed without checking to see if anyone was behind me.

"Please!" I heard him calling after me.

I WAITED UNTIL I was back at my flat and safely slumped on the couch before I called Lindiwe. Muti mewed from her nest on my futon, leapt over to me and snuggled into my lap. She didn't look sick, but I gently pushed her away just in case.

"How's the arm?" I asked when Lindiwe answered.

"Fine, thanks. Didn't need stitches after all."

"You tell some dude where I was?"

"Yeah. He was asking about the cat. I thought you were trying to find it a home?"

"He was a weirdo of note."

"Sorry."

"Listen. That Austrian guy. Who are we invoicing for that?"

"The rental company. First Rate Rentals, I think."

"Can you find out from them who was paying Schuller's rent? You're good at that sort of thing. Make up a story or something."

"Why? This about the cat?"

"Long story. Please, Linds."

"Hang on."

She called back almost immediately. "Debit order from SARA."

"What's SARA?"

"The South African Roads Agency."

This was getting weirder and weirder. What the hell did the roads agency want with a druid?

On a whim, I fired up the laptop, typed druids + roads + Austria into Google. I was gobsmacked when a slew of hits popped up. I clicked on a *Daily Mercury* piece, headlined: 'Austrian Government Uses Druid Magic to Combat Traffic Black Spots.'

Holy crap.

I scanned the article, which was written in a mocking, 'those crazy Austrians' tone. According to the reporter, Austrian motorway officials had secretly hired a team of druids to unearth and dispel the negative energies they believed were the cause of otherwise unexplained traffic fatalities in certain areas prone to accidents. The pilot project had been so successful that the Austrian government was considering extending it to the rest of the country.

I scrolled down to a photograph of a bearded guy in a Jedi robe, posing next to a traffic cone. I recognised him immediately – it was the sandalled fellow who'd cornered me in the hotel parking lot. The caption said his name was Reiner Meyer.

I now thought I knew what August Schuller was doing in Cape Town, but that didn't explain the cat situation.

I Googled Cape Town's SARA offices, dialled the number, and listened to a "we're too busy to take your call" message.

I checked the time. Three-thirty. If I wanted answers, and if I put my foot down, there was another option.

I PUSHED MY way into SARA's air-conditioned building with five minutes to spare. I'd been held up at an intersection – a bakkie in the lane next to mine had been rear-ended by a taxi, and I'd been forced to hang around while the bakkie's elderly driver painstakingly tapped my details into his ancient Nokia.

The stone-faced security guard looked me up and down. "We are closing."

"I need to speak to someone in charge," I said.

"You have an appointment?"

"No."

"Then I cannot help you, sisi."

"Tell your boss it's about August Schuller."

"August what?"

"He or she will know what I mean."

I waited while the guard ducked his head and mumbled something into his radio. "Third floor," he snapped at me.

A fortyish man wearing the tailored suit and bland grin of a politician was waiting for me when I exited the lifts. "Do you mind giving me your name?" he asked, without offering his own.

I handed him one of my business cards.

His smile didn't slip as he scanned it. "What is it that you want, Ms Greenberg?"

"I need to get hold of Reiner Meyer – August Schuller's sidekick. It's important."

"I cannot help you."

"Fine. My boyfriend works for the *Cape Times*," I lied. "Maybe I'll give him a call. It'll make a good story, the roads agency using taxpayers' cash to fund druids and magic and hokey shit like that."

"Please." He ushered me into a large office, the walls adorned with framed maps and 'Arrive Alive' posters, and waved me towards a chair in front of his desk.

I sat down, crossed my arms. "Do you seriously believe this druid stuff works?"

I was treated to another bland smile and a slick non-answer: "Have you any idea what a drain traffic accidents are on our resources, Ms Greenberg?"

"But why use Austrian druids? Why not use sangomas to dispel the bad energy or whatever? Proudly South African, local is lekker and all that shit." I thought of my sister – she'd probably love nothing more than hanging around by the side of the road dressed in her beaded finery.

He shifted in his seat. If I wanted answers, now was the time to shut up. But as usual, I couldn't stop my mouth doing its thing. "Whoever's in charge got a kickback, didn't they? A bribe." The smile snapped off. "Am I close? It's the South African way, after all. We're outsourcing everything these days. Clothing manufacture to China; armaments to Germany. And now, magic to Austria."

His phone started ringing. We sat in silence until it stopped.

I tried one more time. "Look. I don't care what you're doing. I seriously don't. Tell me where to find Reiner Meyer and I'll be out of your hair. Won't say a word."

He held my gaze for what felt like hours. I still couldn't read his expression. Then he dug wordlessly in his desk drawer and handed me a map.

IT WAS GETTING dark as I pulled onto the N2. I stuck to the slow lane, gung-ho mini-bus taxis and luxury sedans with blacked-out windows zipping around me en route to Gugulethu and the airport. Table Mountain shrank in my rear-view mirror as I crawled past the endless shacks that flanked the highway. The irony of SARA bankrolling bizarre druid rituals in the heart of so much poverty didn't escape me.

According to the map, Reiner should be doing his stuff a couple of kays past the airport turn-off. Blinded by the lights on the opposite side of the highway, I had to slam on my brakes when I finally spotted a silhouetted figure behind the buckled safety barrier. I flicked on my hazard lights and pulled over.

Reiner barely acknowledged me as I approached him. Dressed in the same robe he was wearing in the newspaper photo, he was waving a U-shaped metal contraption at each car that roared past us.

"I know what you're doing here," I said.

He shrugged and pointed towards a cell phone transmitter in the distance. "The bad signals, they must be dispersed."

"What's this got to do with the cat?"

"The bad energy we collect has to go somewhere. It is poison."

"Hang on. Are you saying you transferred this bad energy into a *cat*?"

"I prefer to use chickens, but August did, ja. He kept it alive for far too long. After so many sessions, he should have destroyed it, burned its body. But as you know he died unexpectedly before he could do this."

"You're insane."

"Am I?" His hood shadowed his eyes, but I could feel the weight of his gaze just the same. "You have experienced no consequences?"

I thought about the incidents I'd witnessed: the muti guys wiping out; Lindiwe slipping in the suicide scene blood; the fender bender en route to the SARA offices.

Just coincidence, right?

Right?

I cleared my throat. "Say someone *had* been close to the cat and this bad energy stuff. What could they do about it?"

He shrugged. "They would have to wait for it to disperse."

"And how long would that take?"

He sighed. "You should not be here. I have worked hard to clear this area. It is too late. I cannot help you."

I climbed back into the van. My hands were numb, and it took several attempts before I managed to fit the key in the ignition. Driving as if the van was made of glass, I took the first off-ramp, turned around and began heading back towards Cape Town.

I almost screamed as the approaching shriek of emergency sirens filled the air.

It was the last straw.

I pulled over, locked my doors and fumbled for my cell phone. It might all be bullshit; it might just be coincidence, but I was past caring.

When my sister answered, all I said was: "You win."

I hoped she knew how the fuck to cleanse a cat.

SHUFFLE

WILL HILL

There's an element of sleight-of-hand in Will's story, and not just in the content of the tale itself, but in its structure. As this is a story about cards, this is somewhat apt. But it is also a story about gambling and about what makes a gambler. In particular, it is a story about a gambler playing to lose, in order that he can be free.

WATCH CAREFULLY. THAT'S what I always tell them.

You know the game. Three cards, my hands, your money. The red backs of the cards moving in tight little circles, quicker than your eye can follow, no matter how fast you think you are. No way for you to win, we both know it. You pay your money and I show you what's beyond you. What's beyond anyone.

No way to win. Unless I let you.

Watch carefully.

THE ARM AROUND my waist is warm and soft as it guides me up the stairs and out of Johnny's basement. My head is pounding and there's a blanket around me and I'm holding my clothes in my hands and I can't stop crying. My hands and forearms and stomach are soaked with blood and the policeman looks at me like I'm an animal as the paramedic straps me down onto the stretcher.

That night the thing inside me speaks for the first time.

THE PIT BOSS in The Grosvenor casino doesn't look like one.

He's a small, thin man with round silver-framed glasses perched on his nose. The eyes behind them are dark blue, almost black. He patrols his section of the floor slowly, stopping to chat to the regulars, to summon waitresses for the drunk tourists, his demeanour light and friendly and welcoming. But what he's really doing is watching the tables, looking for the people winning too much, losing the small hands and winning the big ones, looking for silent movement of the lips, for tension and nervousness revealed by the untrustworthy bodies of men and women trying to cheat the house. He's looking for people like me, people who aren't playing the game straight. His gaze lands on me every few minutes, but I'm not worried.

I'm exactly what he's looking for, but there's nothing he can do.

I'm untouchable.

"NICE INK," SAYS a pretty mark in her late teens.

I follow her gaze down to my forearm, and let out a short laugh. I consider correcting her, but decide against it. Instead I say thanks.

She nods, but her eyes remain on my arm. I can see she's counting, so I save her the time.

"Forty-three," I tell her, and she looks up. "All the spades, ten hearts, twelve diamonds and eight clubs. Forty-three."

"Nine missing," she says.

I tell her I know.

* * *

"WHAT HAPPENED?" ASKS the policeman. He's pale and he keeps twisting his hands in his lap.

"I don't know," I say. "I can't remember anything."

He doesn't believe me. It's written all over his face. But there's no way he can prove me wrong. No one who came up out of the cellar is talking. Erin and Adam are catatonic, Chris is on life support somewhere in the hospital, and Johnny and Alice are dead.

My word is gospel.

NEVER TOUCH YOUR chips unless you're making a bet.

Halving and re-stacking, arranging into equal smaller piles, lifting a stack and letting it clatter through your fingers back onto the felt; all signs of nerves. Nerves aren't your worst enemy, but they're close. They make you do stupid things, they narrow your attention down to the cards and the dealer, reminding you that there is money at stake. You should never think about money when you're gambling. The game is a game, nothing more, to be won or lost. The money is secondary.

I watch the dealer's hands. He slides cards from the shoe with well-practiced smoothness, with studied nonchalance. He is presenting indifference, relaxation, projecting openness and welcome, while he makes calculations in his head, while he reads the players at his table, assessing intoxication and mood and fatigue.

He plays his role well. A worthy opponent.

I GET BACK to my flat some time around midnight. There's a bed and a desk and a chair that I never use. The wardrobe has my clothes in it, but they barely fill half the rail. It's functional. I sleep here, and that's all. There should really be a photo on the bedside table, so that I could stare at it every night as I fall asleep and remind myself why I do what I do. But there isn't.

THE DEALER FLIPS the ten of spades over in front of me, lays out the nine of hearts and the eight of diamonds to the other players at the table: a platinum blonde woman wrapped in dead animals and drunk on endless refills of champagne, and a frightened-looking man in a cheap suit and dirty shoes. Desperation rises from him in a cloud so thick it's almost visible. The stack of chips in front of him is tiny, and he fingers them endlessly, as though trying to convince himself that they're real, that they are all he has left, that somehow it has come down to this. The woman has six tall stacks in front of her, and pays no attention to them whatsoever. The money isn't hers, and she doesn't care if she loses it. As a result, she's winning. The man is losing, his stacks disappearing slowly, inexorably. He wears the expression of a drowning animal.

I SET MY stall up outside Liverpool Street station just before the rush hour starts. It's simple, a folding table and a small printed sign:

Three-Card-Monte
Find the Queen
£10 to play, WIN PAYS £50

As always, within about ten minutes there's a good crowd gathered. The world is a smaller place than ever before, with information available on everything at the press of a touchpad. So few secrets left. The crowd are looking for the scam, looking for the strings behind the puppets. None of them think they can actually win, but for the sake of a tenner, I know full well that eventually someone will try, just to see if they can work out how I do it. Their eyes scan the crowd, trying to identify my plants, watching my hands, trying to discern a Mexican drop or a bottom deal as I move the cards round and round and round.

THE TEN OF clubs is flipped over in front of me. The blonde woman gets the king of hearts, the man the four of spades. He groans. He knows what's coming, we all do, it's inevitable. The dealer turns over his card. Seven of hearts.

I split my tens, moving a second stack of chips onto the table. All of a sudden, I've got twelve thousand pounds riding on this hand. I feel a flutter of excitement and push it away. It's not nerves, not exactly – I don't care about losing the money I have, but I care about losing the pot I should be about to win. I care about losing the hand, of having good play punished, more than I care about the chips. The woman purrs appreciatively, either at the money the chips represent or the courage of my play, I don't know which. She leans forward, two bags of liquid silicon threatening to spill from the narrow straps of the dress that are supposed to be holding them in place. She wants me to notice, wants me to look, wants me to approve of her, but I keep my eyes on the cards. The dealer slides a card from the shoe and flips it onto my first ten.

Jack of diamonds. Twenty.

He flips another.

Ace of clubs.

Blackjack.

I SEE THE two men in the shiny black suits long before they think I do. But that's OK. I want them to see.

THE FIRST TO pluck up their courage is a man in his twenties in a sleek grey suit. He steps forward, places an expensive brown leather satchel between his feet, and takes a ten pound note out of his wallet. He places it on my table, and I nod without a word. I flip the cards over and show them to him; the queen of hearts, the four of spades, the nine of clubs. I flip them back face down, and begin to move them. Within three rotations of the cards I know there is no way he still knows which one is the queen. In a straight game, his odds of winning would now be one in three, pure luck with the odds in my favour. In a bent game, a usual three-card-monte game, his chances would now be essentially zero. If he somehow managed to identify the queen, there would still be no way I'd let him see it; I would double flip one of the black cards, or one of my plants would shout that they saw the police. Either way, the very worst case scenario would be my returning his tenner and announcing that the game was void.

JOHNNY BLOWS THE candle out. At least, I think he does. Erin giggles as the cellar is plunged into darkness, but it's not a giggle that sounds full of fun. It sounds nervous, it flutters as it emerges from her mouth.

It's the last thing I remember hearing before the screaming started.

THE DEALER PAYS the blackjack out immediately, pushing chips across the table. Nine thousand pounds, fifteen with my chips. Six thousand still in play on twenty.

The woman waves her hand. The man taps the felt so softly his fingers make no sound. The dealer flips over the queen of spades that we all knew was coming, and the man lets out a strangled sigh that sounds close to a sob before gathering up the last few of his chips and leaving the table.

One card left. The woman and I pretend not to care, the dealer pretends the same, pretends he doesn't want to turn a four and a ten and fuck us both over, wipe the smiles from our faces. The chips on the table are more than he earns in a year, and all three of us know it.

He flips the card. Eight of diamonds. He draws another from the shoe and turns it over. Nine of spades.

Bust.

THE THING INSIDE my head's voice is light and playful. It tells me not to worry, that they won't be able to prove anything. Then it tells me what it wants to do, and I lean over the side of the hospital bed and vomit onto the white linoleum floor.

THE DEALER SLIDES me another six thousand in chips, and then more than thirty thousand to the woman, who smiles at me with open mischief, her dress riding high up her thighs, her breasts straining for release. "Drink?" she asks, her lips wet and glossy.

"No thank you," I say. Her smile falters, but only for a second.

"Your loss," she says, then slides her chips into a cup and disappears.

I lift my chips with both hands, and make my way to the cashier. The pit boss watches me all the way, his eyes trained on my back, but there's nothing he can do. I'm not wired, I'm not counting cards.

I'm something else.

I pass over my chips, and receive forty-nine thousand pounds in fifty pound notes. They offer me a cheque, but I decline. Cash is what I need.

IT WAS ADAM's idea. It really was. He'd seen something on TV and he wanted to try it. I don't think he ever thought it would work. To this day, I'm still not sure whether it did. I felt something sharp dig into me when I sat down, and pulled the deck of cards out of the back pocket of my jeans. I carried one with me everywhere that summer. I'd discovered poker and I was always looking for a game. I put the cards down next to me before we got started.

I still don't know whether that's why what happened happened to me. I'll never know. The thing inside me doesn't answer questions.

I ACCELERATE, MY hands moving the cards into a blur, and I see the moment where the connection between his eyes and his brain fails, where the speed of the information input overwhelms his ability to process. I slow the cards, then line them up before him. The queen is to my left, his right. He considers for a second, a look of grudging admiration on his face at the quality of my performance, then points to the middle card. I slide the queen under the middle card, and flip it over. As far as he knows, I've turned over the middle card, the one he chose. But I haven't. I've let the queen flip and slide over the top of the middle card. I lift it up and away, revealing the queen of hearts. For a moment he says nothing, then a little smile of triumph begins to emerge on his face. He's beaten me, he thinks. In front of the watching crowd, he's beaten me.

"Well done," I say, and pull a fifty pound note from the pocket of my jacket. I hand it to him, along with his tenner, and he looks slightly incredulously at the money. Then his usual demeanour returns, his master of the universe arrogance, and he tucks the notes into the inside pocket of his grey suit jacket.

"Better luck next time mate," he says, and tips me a wink. "You're pretty good. Bit more practice, that's all you need."

He struts away, and a silver-haired man clutching a black travel mug, his eyes wide and hungry with greed, immediately takes his place.

* * *

46

I SLOW DOWN and let them come. They're strolling through the crowd, not even trying to stay hidden. They look like bouncers, which is what they are. They're wearing dark suits that don't really fit them, high-necked black T-shirts, flat black shoes with rubber soles. They should be wearing earpieces, but they've taken them off in what seems to be their only concession to blending in.

I leave the crowds of the West End behind and head towards the river. Here the streets get narrower and darker, the buildings crowding in above the cobbles, and the air is quiet and still. I continue to stroll. Two figures lurch out of the shadows at me, but I let them pass by. The man leers drunkenly at me as he drags a semi-conscious girl towards the taxis and buses of Trafalgar Square.

Near the end of the street there's an opening in the wall. It's a pitch black rectangle, that I know leads into an alley with a dead end. I can almost feel the excitement of the two men behind me, feel them hoping against hope that I make the turn.

WE DID IT in Johnny's cellar.

His mum and dad both worked so his house was empty during the week, and it was where we spent most of our time anyway. There were six of us, the same six that had been hanging out all summer; me, Johnny, Adam, Chris, Alice and Erin. Chris and Alice started fucking that summer, and didn't think the rest of us knew about it. But Erin had read Alice's diary when she was in the shower one evening, and told the rest of us. We'd taken to dropping lines from her breathless, feverish descriptions of their couplings into normal conversation, and watching the colour rise in her face. She never confronted us about it, so we kept doing it. As a result, there was tension in the air the morning we made our way down into the basement. I still wonder sometimes whether that was partly to blame for what happened.

We followed Johnny downstairs, and looked at the arrangements he had made. The rug in the middle of the basement had been rolled back against the wall, and a pentagram had been drawn on the concrete floor in red chalk. Candles stood at each point of the shape, and a small bowl sat on the floor to one side.

"Spooky," laughed Erin, but the laughter didn't quite reach her eyes.

She looked nervous as we sat in a circle around the chalk outline, forcing small talk, trying not to appear scared. I was scared. I can remember that much. I was scared from the second I saw the pentagram. It was cold in the basement, and the shape seemed unpleasant, almost threatening. I knew I was projecting, that there was nothing scary about the chalk lines themselves, that I was thinking about the things I had seen them used for in films and TV programmes, none of which were real.

Johnny passed a box of matches around the circle, and we each lit one of the candles. There was now a greasiness to the air, a thickness that I didn't believe had been there before the yellow flames flickered into light. Then Adam picked up the bowl, put it in his lap, and unwrapped a razor blade.

"Let's do this," he said, grinning.

WHEN THE POLICE eventually turn up and move me on, I've managed to lose just over four thousand pounds, and the crowd waiting for their turn has swollen to almost a hundred.

THE DEALER GIVES me a curt nod as I sit down. I've had him before, but I don't think he remembers me. Hundreds of faces pass before him every night, most of them creating no impression. The drunks, the screamers, the ones who throw punches and spit threats, they're the ones who get remembered. I'm none of those.

The pit boss glances in my direction. He keeps the recognition from his eyes with practiced restraint, but he looks for just a millisecond too long, and I know I'm on his radar. I shouldn't be here, shouldn't be back in the same place so soon after I was last here. But I'm desperate. The yearning, the need to atone is wider and deeper than it's been in years, and it's Christmas and most places are closed. Even the most debauched, degenerate places like to close for a day or two over the holiday. It makes them feel a little more respectable, a little more dignified, rather than the open, running sewers they really are, whirlpools of filth and one-way lust that suck in the hopeless and the helpless.

THE THING INSIDE me tells me I did well. I thank it through gritted teeth, and wait for the police to let me leave the hospital.

I TAKE THE dealer for four thousand quid in about forty minutes. I'm not counting the cards, not really. I could be, could tell anyone who wanted to know that the true count through the decks was positive nine, but that's not why I win. I can't explain why I win. The thing inside me might be able to, but I don't let it out. I never let it out, not voluntarily. I bet and double and split and I win and win and win and it waits and waits and waits.

That's the deal. The deal I never agreed to.

I WAKE UP and the flat is cold. I paid the man who owns it a year's rent to leave me alone, and he's held up his end of the bargain admirably. I pay the bills even though I rarely use the gas or the electricity. I shower in the morning, and I turn on the lights at night for about ten minutes when I get home, but that's all. I eat breakfast in a café around the corner, and that's normally the only meal I sit down for each day. I grab something in the evening if there's time, or I get a waitress to bring me a sandwich if I'm working one of the shiny casinos on Park Lane.

They'll bring you anything they want, especially alcohol. Nothing tips the odds in the house's favour quicker than getting the players drunk. It doesn't matter how many free beers or gin and tonics they give you, as long as in the end you lose your chips. It's a mutually beneficial system; the player feels like they got something out of the house while they played, and the house gets your money. Seems fair, although it obviously isn't.

Most people are just too stupid to see it.

An hour and ten minutes at Fenchurch Street and last night's money is all gone. Sixteen thousand pounds given away in just over two hours.

It's not enough though. It's never enough.

I stroll into the alleyway, and I feel their excitement spike. The possibility of violence is close now, and they know it. As I walk down the alleyway, my heels drumming on the stone beneath them, I feel the air shift and the light change as they follow me through the opening. I keep walking, my eyes fixed on the damp, dripping wall in front of me, and then the thing inside me speaks, its voice soft and lazy, the voice of something that has just woken up.

It asks me the question, the same question as always, and I answer it as I turn around to face the two men in suits, a wide smile on my face. The smug expressions on their faces falter as they look at me, as they see something they don't like. They stop, ten feet away from me, and for a long moment there is no sound at all. Then the thing inside me emerges, raw and growling, and everything turns red.

*   *   *

"NICE TATTOO," SAYS a girl with two metal bars through one of her eyebrows.

I don't correct her. She starts to count them, like they always do. I let her get to the end of the first suit, watching her eyes flicker across my skin.

"Forty-five," I tell her, and smile. "There are forty-five of them."

She smiles back at me, and I shuffle the cards.

DOMESTIC MAGIC

STEVE RASNIC TEM AND MELANIE TEM

Steve and Melanie Tem's writing utilizes every trick the genre has to offer, and more. I urge you to seek out their autobiographical novel, The Man on the Ceiling, *in which you can witness the full range of their powers. The story that follows shows their talent for literary prestidigitation and demonstrates why they are amongst the most exciting writers working today.*

FELIX DIDN'T HATE his mother, but got so mad at her so often she probably thought he did. Sometimes his anger scared him, that she might be right when she said thoughts could make things happen.

That was what made him so mad – that she said and believed ridiculous stuff and she almost got him believing it, too. And she didn't take care of Margaret right. Why'd they have to get a mother like her?

He'd skipped school again today to run errands with her. She'd never ask him to miss school, she was worried he'd get behind like she had when she was a kid. But she just let him do it. What kind of mother let her son skip school? Wasn't that against the law? What kind of mother made her son worry about her so much he didn't want her leaving the house without him? At his age you were supposed to be thinking about friends and music and video games and sex, not whether your mother was capable of crossing the street by herself or taking care of your little sister. He was almost grown now; it was too late for him. But Margaret was little.

He couldn't remember his Mom ever saying no. He was the good kid, which was kind of sickening but it was easier than doing stuff that made his mother cry and chant and cook weird stuff in the slow-cooker that stank up whatever crappy apartment or homeless shelter they were living in at the moment.

Margaret was not a good kid. Felix tried to tell her what to do because somebody had to, but she just ignored him or laughed or threw a fit. When she was a baby she'd cried all the time because her world wasn't perfect, and Mom had fussed and worried and chanted and rubbed goop on her chest and the soles of her feet.

When Margaret had started crawling and toddling she got into everything, Mom's stuff and Felix's stuff, dangerous stuff and stuff you didn't want ruined. One time because of a hunch he looked into the dirty playroom of the shelter and she was coloring in his school books, copying one of Mom's so-called secret designs over and over again in the margins, crossing out words and underlining other ones, and he had to pay for the books. Another time when they lived in a studio apartment he had a feeling and found her on a chair reaching into a cabinet and dipping into Mom's jars of herbs and tinctures and sticking her fingers into her mouth, and he grabbed her and yelled at her and she threw up all over everything.

Mom would explain why she shouldn't do whatever she'd just done, and Margaret listened and then did the same thing again or worse because now she had more information. Felix yelled at her but it didn't make any difference. The minute she'd started talking she'd been whining, sassing, lying, chanting, telling you her dreams whether you wanted to hear about them or not which he didn't.

So he had a crazy mother and a bratty sister who was probably crazy, too. It was like living with aliens. Everywhere else Felix felt like the alien, but he was the most normal one in this family, which was scary.

Mom patted his shoulder and said in order for powers to be most efficacious we have to meet people where they are and not wish they were somebody else. What about somebody meeting *him* where he was for a change? The only thing Felix ever got from his mother's advice was knowing what words like 'efficacious' meant in case they showed up on some standardized test.

Practically the minute Margaret could run she'd started running away. Not like she was going somewhere; more like she was just *going*. Mom would chant and throw cards and do divinations until she thought she knew where Margaret was. Then she'd send Felix to get her. Felix got mad when she was wrong because she'd wasted his time. He got mad when she was right because Margaret was such a pain and Mom wouldn't punish her. She said it was Margaret's nature and the rest of the world, including him, would just have to get used to it. Well, what about *his* 'nature'?

Wasn't that child neglect? Was there somebody Felix could report it to without having to tell everything else about his nutso family? Like that Mom really was a witch? She preferred 'seer' or 'person of powers,' so he made a point of thinking 'witch' in case she could maybe read his mind.

So far today there'd been no calls or texts from the school that Margaret had escaped. So here Felix was with his mother in a thrift store doing his best to act as if he'd never seen this crazy lady before. Being anywhere in public with her sucked. The older she got the weirder she became, and if anything bad happened to her he'd be stuck with Margaret by himself.

She talked to junk. Out loud. Who does that? Now she was holding up some old jar thing and speaking to it. "What have you held inside you? If I put some quarters for the laundromat into you, will you help me make them multiply?"

Great. Felix had been saving quarters for a couple of weeks so he could wash his and Margaret's clothes. He almost had enough. Maybe the jar would cough up a couple more. If they walked around much longer in dirty clothes somebody would surely call Social Services. Maybe that would be a good thing. Maybe not.

When the tone of Mom's voice told him she was about to start chanting, he walked over to the other end of the store and pretended to be looking at men's shoes. He needed shoes. So did Margaret. But who knew where this stuff had been, who'd touched it, what they'd used it for? Felix didn't believe in evil spirits but he did believe in germs. Donated clothes like from churches and clothing banks were safer but still embarrassing.

His mother bought the jar for herself – for the family, she'd say – and a long curved knife for Margaret. A knife for an eight-year-old? One more thing he'd have to get rid of, preferably before Margaret saw it and thought it was cool. Nothing for him. He didn't want anything, but it was another reason to be mad, along with the fact that she'd wasted $2.78 they didn't have. Sometimes people paid Mom for tomatoes or rhubarb, spells or potions or readings, and she got food stamps and checks from the government, but it still seemed there was never enough money for good food. Nobody should live like this, especially a kid like Margaret who didn't have a choice. But Felix was almost old enough to have a choice.

Next stop was an organic grocery where everything cost a fortune. Mom had been sick a lot lately, and she said it was because she had to wait for money to come in before she could buy what she needed. But obviously it was the crap she ate from places like this and from her garden and the woods and streets. He wasn't going to put any more of that crap into his body no matter how Mom tried to hide it in orange juice or disguise it as real food. Give him burgers and fries any day. "The government removes essential nutrients from our food," she told him cheerily for like the thousandth time as they went into the store. "Who knows what they replace them with?"

It was one thing to practice voodoo medicine and hoo-doo eating on yourself. But not getting real food or health care for your kids made it other people's business. What would've happened if he'd told the school counselor that time Margaret had a fever for days that made her blue eyes shine like wet lilacs and Mom had refused to take her to the ER but she'd made her dolls dance?

When Felix came home from school that day every doll in Margaret's room, every figurine, every picture of a human or beast, even stuff that only vaguely looked like it had a head and legs was gyrating, hopping, waving, dancing. Margaret was laughing, and then she was out of bed and trying to make them dance the old-fashioned kids' way, moving them with her hands and pretending. She got frustrated and Mom wouldn't do it again because she said it wasn't right to be frivolous with your powers, and Margaret threw a fit. To shut her up, and because he was happy she wasn't sick any more, Felix played puppets with her and showed her how to put life into them or pull it out of them or whatever. The puppets had tugged at his hand and Margaret's hand, and she'd hugged him and said he was the best big brother in the world and he had to teach her how to do that, and he did his best but she never did learn.

So maybe Mom had cured her, but maybe Mom had made her sick in the first place. Felix never got around to telling the school counselor and pretty soon they'd moved anyway.

Margaret had the only clean, relatively nice room in their new house. Every other space, including half of his basement man-cave, was full of the witch's projects. Her clay sculptures and things that looked like body parts floating in colored liquids had mingled with and seeped into his ships in bottles and crushed leaves and sketches of things he knew about but couldn't name yet, couldn't quite make move, and everything got ruined. He'd given up having projects after that.

Seeing her plop another grape into her mouth, he whispered, "Mom!" She raised her eyebrows. The produce guy was heading their way (again) to tell her to quit shoplifting. What kind of role model was this for Margaret? Felix hurried around the corner and pretended to be interested in free-range eggs. More than once Mom had explained to him what 'free-range' meant, but he refused to remember it and picturing the top of a stove full of brown eggs running around free like hamsters out of their cages made him laugh.

Mom chatted away at the bored checkout clerk. Felix just wanted to get out of there before she did something else embarrassing, and he almost made it. He had picked up the grocery bags – why was it his job to carry the bags? – when Mom reached over, stroked the bananas, and sang out, "Thank you, my little curved friends, for letting us eat you." The clerk stared at her, then stared at Felix, the poor kid with the crazy mother. Maybe somebody would call the authorities. Could you lose your kids for talking to bananas?

Mom wouldn't quit until she'd checked out at least one used bookstore. Felix wanted to tell her to carry her own damn groceries, but her back or shoulder or arm was giving her trouble. He thought about leaving her there and going to what they were calling home this week in order to be there when Margaret got out of school. Wasn't it illegal to leave a little kid alone? But when he compared who was more likely to get into trouble on her own, Mom or Margaret, Mom won by a landslide. He thought about pulling a Margaret and walking away as far away as he could get.

But he'd never do any of that because he was a wimp and a mama's boy and her enabler, and somebody had to watch out for Margaret, which made him mad at both of them. Too bad he couldn't just think Margaret into a safer place. Mom could probably do that, so why didn't she? Personally, Felix didn't have any magic.

Mom and the bookstore guy said hi to each other like they were buds, except that Felix heard the OMG! in his voice. She got out her list, longer every time because nobody could ever find any of the books she wanted. The bookstore guy tried, or pretended to try, until a couple of actual customers came in. Then Mom wandered around. With the bags Felix couldn't fit between the shelves unless he turned sideways. The plastic handles dug into his hands. There were chairs but they all had books on them, and even though the bookstore people always said it was okay to move the books if you wanted to sit down, Felix couldn't bring himself to do that, and it would be embarrassing to sit on the floor. He leaned against the end of a bookcase, willing it not to roll, and tried to think about things other than his mother or his sister.

She'd be here for a while, looking up weirdness like the fourteenth word on the sixty-seventh page in twenty-one different books. She'd write those words down in a tattered notebook and study them for weeks. She never bought anything – on her way out she'd grab some random book out of the freebie bin. When he edged around the towering books crowding the apartment he'd pretend to cast a protective spell so they wouldn't collapse on Margaret, but it was just making fun of Mom. Every time they moved there were more boxes of books to carry, except you couldn't bring extraneous stuff like that to a shelter, which was the only good thing about being homeless.

Feeling like a homeless person again with all the crap he was carrying, Felix almost wished for a grocery cart. The thrift store bag had the name of the store in enormous letters so there was no way to disguise where they'd been shopping, and the jar was heavy against his leg and who knew what would be released or destroyed or pissed off if he dropped it and it broke. Naturally the natural-foods store wouldn't use plastic so he had to deal with a flimsy cloth bag, and something in it smelled weird. The not one but three books Mom had grabbed out of the free bin without even looking had slick dust jackets and kept sliding out of his grip. He couldn't reach his phone to see what time it was, which at least meant he didn't have to deal with Mom's dumb comments about how cell phones introduced foreign energy into your brain.

"You about done?" he asked her. "Margaret'll be home soon."

But she was communing with the spirit of a piece of trash out of the gutter. Felix didn't want to know what it was or what she thought she was doing, but as she gently deposited it into the bookstore bag he couldn't help hearing its voice and seeing that it was a piece of broken pink plastic with sharp edges that would probably tear the plastic so everything would fall out and he'd be the one who had to retrieve it all and figure out how to carry it. "What is that?"

"That's Tinkerbell. A piece of Tinkerbell. You know how your sister loves Tinkerbell."

He had no clue what Tinkerbell was or if his sister loved it. "What's it for?"

Mom smiled. "I don't know yet. But it told me it could help us."

"Right." He didn't sound half as sarcastic as he wanted to.

She reached up and actually patted his head. He hated when she did that. She was the one who didn't understand the world and had to be taken care of and have things explained to her but wouldn't listen. He might be the kid, but he was the grown-up around here. "If you have a talent you should use it," she told him, like he hadn't heard that a million times. Like she was talking about a good pitching arm or being able to fix cars. "Sometimes there's just a thin line between survival and disaster. Sometimes it's so thin you can't even see it. Remember that, son. My abilities help this family stay afloat."

"Terrific, Mom. That's really nice. Can we go? Margaret'll be home and I gotta take a leak." The second part was very true. He hoped the first part was.

If he started off first there was a good chance she'd get distracted and stop following him and he'd have to go looking for her and Margaret would either be at home alone or not at home and wandering around somewhere by herself. Finally they were heading more or less toward the apartment. Felix sometimes worried that Margaret would forget where they lived today, or that he would. Mom seemed at home everywhere, which was really annoying and kind of creepy.

He was tired of walking but most of the time they couldn't afford bus fare and he couldn't get a job to buy himself a car because he had to watch out for his sister and his mother. When he complained Mom just twirled her fingers at him and said walking was good for your mind and your soul. She had her arms stretched out and her head thrown back, singing high and loud, and people on the sidewalk were detouring around her, even the homeless people. She actually squatted by one of them and invited him to sing with her, and he swore at her and walked off. Too crazy for the crazies. Felix trudged along, lugging her bags of junk and worrying about Margaret and hating it that he had to lug and worry.

They could be wearing decent clothes, eating good food, living in a nice house – still living in that house where he'd actually had a little space of his own. But no. She'd rather shop in thrift stores and wear smelly old clothes and eat obnoxious things and mumble under her breath. "Why can't we have a better life?" he'd say.

"It's a resource," she'd say. "Like clean water. You have to be careful or you might use it up."

"Why do you let people think you're crazy? Just *show* them what you can do – it'll shut them up!" Never mind that she *was* crazy.

"It's an art, that means it's personal, and nothing you can really explain. You don't know why it works, it just works. And what may work for me may not work for you. That's what people don't understand. They try it out, it doesn't work for them, and they stop believing."

"Why do we have to live this way?"

"It's all about luck. You try to line everything up proper, and the luck runs your way. But when it runs your way, you got to remember that means it runs against somebody else. So you have to be careful. You have to be responsible. You don't want to hurt people, but sometimes you have to just to survive, just to make do for you and yours. And sometimes maybe you let go of the luck so that it'll work for somebody else, because that's the right thing to do. You'll figure it out, Felix. I have faith in you." Just what he needed.

Could you go to the media with a story about a mother who was a witch and had special powers but wouldn't use them for the betterment of her children? Devising what he'd say and quietly rehearsing the interviews he'd give to the press occupied his mind so he could tolerate the rest of the walk back to the apartment.

Where Margaret was not.

Felix knew she wasn't there before Mom opened the door. Something about the energy. He didn't like noticing energy. He also knew Margaret was in danger. He didn't know how he knew that. Maybe he was wrong. Maybe he was just imagining the worst, and that would not make it happen. He wasn't the witch of the family.

Just as he dropped the bags onto the already-full couch, the handle of the health-food bag broke. It wasn't his job to chase after the bottles that rolled across the floor. Mom talked to them as she gathered them up. She didn't seem worried about Margaret. She seemed kind of excited or something. He didn't have time right now to try to figure her out.

On Margaret's bed in the corner, her lunch bag was open on top of homework papers. So she'd been home after school. She hadn't been doing her homework, though. Toys were out of the trash bag she kept them in. Crayons and colored pencils were scattered around, and papers with drawings on them of her stuffed animals and dolls with legs going this way and that, kicking at the big empty spaces on the page.

"She didn't eat her sandwich." Mom was digging through the bag.

He took the neatly-wrapped sandwich away from her. "Mom, she *never* eats her sandwich. And nobody will trade with her. She throws it away at school or on the way home. Maybe today she was – distracted." Maybe she was kidnapped. Maybe she was–

"Why not?"

He unwrapped it, took it apart, spread the halves like a biology lab dissection. "Look at this – broccoli, grapefruit slices, and what's this paste made out of – honey and hummus? And I used to think this was bean sprouts, but it's that weed from the backyard, right? Gray bread, like chunks of paper mache. Who eats like this, Mom?" He thought about keeping it for evidence.

"It's full of essential nutrients! What has she been eating, then?"

"I give her money. From little jobs I get. And sometimes I just take it from your purse."

"Stealing is bad karma." She was looking at the floor.

"Like you never steal. And starving your kid – I bet that's bad juju too." He'd heard that word in an old Tarzan movie on TV and had just been waiting to use it on her. "She's gone, Mom. We've gotta go find her."

She didn't try to pretend Margaret might be at a friend's. Margaret didn't have any friends, because she didn't want anybody coming here. Felix had been the same way, so by now he didn't know how to make friends. Once Margaret was back safe, he might just point that out to Mom.

Mom said suddenly, "You look around the room, think about where she might have wandered to. You're smart, you'll figure it out before I can. I'm going out to get a tattoo."

Felix stared at her. "Mom. Margaret's gone *missing*."

"And we'll find her."

When she rolled up her left sleeve Felix realized it had been years since he'd seen her bare arms. It was covered by a series of mostly geometric tattoos, some maybe professional, a lot of them obviously amateur – it wouldn't surprise him if she'd done it herself with a sewing needle dipped in plant-based ink. Gross.

"Look." He didn't want to, but he looked. There was a tattoo of a sailing ship. "Look," and there was a fairy with a wand. "I've been tattooing pieces of your and your sister's lives, your passions, your dreams, maybe a lot of things you aren't even aware of, onto my body since before you were born. It's my map to my children. Once I add her disappearance, I'll know right where she is."

He found himself focusing on her tattoos, or they focused on him. They were changing, developing, growing longer and thicker, joining and crossing over to display twisted passages and dance-like movements.

He jerked his gaze away. "Aren't there some practical things, more *normal* things we should be doing? Like walking down the street, searching the park, knocking on doors? Maybe even calling the police?"

"No need for that. Don't you understand that the authorities poison us against the natural magic of the world? But go ahead and do that 'normal' stuff. Watch and listen. Pay attention to your feelings and let them guide you. I have great faith in you, Felix." She hurried out.

For the next few minutes he searched the room. He picked things up gently and put them back where he thought they'd been. Tearing things apart would've just made him more scared, and Margaret would be furious when she came home. Books facedown to hold her place didn't tell him anything. None of her zillion unicorn and castle and enchantress and Harry Potter posters had anything to say to him, either. Real magic was a sham – hard to access, hard to control, crazy and arbitrary and unfair. It promised everything but never gave you what you really needed.

In her lunch bag he found a slip of paper. Mom used to leave notes in his lunch, too – stupid advice like YOU CAN DO

IT! and REACH FOR THE STARS! This note had a silly fairy sticker on it that said Tinkerbell, plus a lot of weird designs, circles mostly, with various spokes in them, and scribbles connecting them. If he glanced at them a certain way the circles turned and the scribbles danced. Right beside Tinkerbell, under the glow of her tiny wand, was GO FIND THE MAGIC! in Mom's one-of-a-kind handwriting.

Tinkerbell told him what it meant, which was a clue to how upset and out of it he was. Mom had sent Margaret away on some impossible quest.

One of his sister's drawings crinkled under his hand, tingling his skin. He pulled the drawing up against the light and watched as the lines of the furiously dancing doll vibrated.

Felix had no idea what he was doing. Like his mother always said, he let himself be led. With various pencils, pens, crayons, he extended the lines on the paper so that they wrapped, cocooned, buried the dancing doll in a hard shimmering tunnel. Then the spiral spread off the paper to contour the folds of sheets, comforter, pillow, until he dropped everything, hands shaking, and stood back.

Vaguely he recognized the park by that shelter they'd stayed in for a few weeks last year, elaborate slide system with a tower where kids waited their turn. On the wall of the playground was a mural he couldn't see in the drawing, wizards and fairies, gnomes in fur coats like rats escaping a sewer, that had always creeped him out when he'd taken Margaret there. So had all the old guys hanging around like wizards who'd lost their powers, or who'd just hallucinated them, now convinced all the tasty magic was there in the bodies of the playing kids. Margaret had always wanted to say hi, and Felix hadn't let her. The lines didn't show anything but the dancing of the kids and a space of no-dancing, no-motion, watching.

The deep-shadowed tangle behind the playground hid the entrance to a secret cavern, or something more everyday. The sewer. He'd yelled at Margaret to keep away.

When Felix got into the park it felt like dusk although he didn't think it was that late, hoped Margaret hadn't been left alone that long, didn't stop to check the time on his phone. Homeless guys were sitting on the wall. There was the mural, more faded and dirtier than he remembered, layered in a graffiti of filthy, hysterical requests. The opening of the sewer pipe was huge, protective mesh broken into fringe. It quivered like it was singing.

Margaret was in there. Looking for a magic place. Because she was a kid, and magic could be anywhere her mother said it was.

Felix dropped onto hands and knees and, without allowing himself to think about it, started into the pipe. Then the darkness detached into a ragged bulk of shadow backing out. The man grunted, hit his head and swore. The seat of his pants was muddy. He had Margaret. Her pale face popped up on one side and then disappeared.

Felix's first impulse was to block the exit, trap the guy inside the pipe and call the police. He fumbled for his phone. Then he thought he might have a better shot at saving his sister if he moved out of the way. The guy kept coming, dragging Margaret, his fist swallowing her hand. Felix grabbed at the guy's shirt and was about to throw himself at him when Margaret yelled, "No! Felix! He's my friend!"

The big, red-faced, dirty guy was all the way out, and he reached back into the pipe with both hands and pulled Margaret out. She hugged him before she hugged Felix. The homeless guy growled, "You better tell somebody, dude."

Into Felix's neck Margaret said, "I'm scared, Felix."

"Of him? What'd he—"

He felt her shake her head. "Of Mom. She makes me do stuff. She doesn't take care of us. My friend says it's not right, kids shouldn't be treated like that."

"Felix, you found her!" Mom went to hug Margaret but Margaret turned away. "I knew you could do it — I've always had faith in you." To the homeless guy she said, "Thanks, Woody," and kissed his cheek.

"You sent her out here, right?" Felix didn't care who heard. "A test for me."

Mom looked at Margaret and lowered her voice. "She loves magic but she didn't inherit my abilities. You did."

"I want it!" Margaret wailed. People were looking at them. Woody patted her head, told Felix again to tell somebody, and shambled off to find saner company. Felix finally found his phone.

"You have great talent, son. And if you didn't find her, I was your back-up." She was actually proud of herself.

She'd think he hated her, but he didn't. He just didn't have anything more to say to her. He waved his hands once, twice, and the lines danced around them. He didn't know if Mom couldn't see them, but she definitely couldn't see him or Margaret. He called 911.

CAD CODDEU

LIZ WILLIAMS

Liz Williams is somewhat familiar with magic, running, as she does, a witchcraft shop with her partner Trevor Jones in that most magically evocative of places, Glastonbury. I first encountered Liz as a science fiction reader, with her brilliant novel Empire of Bones *(2002) and have since also enjoyed her terrific short stories. Liz seemed like a natural choice for this anthology and the tale that follows is steeped in ancient magic and myth.*

THE STORM BROUGHT the warriors, and perhaps the girl as well. I know that it was not I who conjured her, and at first I did not understand how they had drawn her forth. I first saw her as she ran through the groves of birch, a swift doe, and though she was not in her human form, I knew her for one of the Changing.

The warriors followed her as far as the lake, but then she lost them. I, floundering behind, did not see where she went: perhaps into tree or water, or dissolving into mist. Hidden among the briars, I watched as the warriors splashed along the lakeshore: big men, with armour the colour of oak bark and hair like a fox's coat. They searched around for a little while, but then gave up and stumped back the way they had come. When they turned, and I could see their faces, my suspicions were confirmed. They were wood-warriors, with rough features carved in the middle of rougher heads, and soon their movements grew slower and they became a pair of oak stumps. They would not, I knew, stir again until morning, and it was now twilight, with the air heavy after the rain.

The Changing stepped out from a swarm of gnats at the lakeshore. She had left the doe's shape behind and was human now, more or less. Her hair streamed down her back, dappled silver and fawn. Her face was small and pointed, a little pinched, and I could see a prickling beneath her skin as her form congealed. Her eyes were as yellow as a wolf's: pale and cold like piss in winter. There was something familiar about her, but I did not know why. I did not think she could see me, but then she turned and looked straight at my hiding place.

"You," she called. She had a clear voice, and that was familiar too. "Come out from there."

I both wanted to do so, and feared it, but she gave me no choice. She lured me out with the strength of her gaze. I stumbled forward, my legs turned to dead-wood weight. I saw a crease between her brows.

"Don't you know me?" she said.

"No. Yes. I don't know."

Her frown deepened. "Do you know who you are?"

"I am a man," I said. "Not much of one, it's true."

"Don't you even know your own name?"

"No." But I knew what I was: landless and mad. Sometimes I remembered a little of who I used to be, but more often not. I recalled a woman with a fawn in her lap, a castle wall, a bitch with a litter of pups lying in summer sunlight, but it was all snatches and fragments like the ruins of a song. I didn't know whether it was my past, or someone else's. I used to be someone's kin, perhaps, but now I was little more than hair and bones and the skins of others, a reed through which the wind whistled. But I knew the Changing, and that they were other.

"And you are one of *them*," I whispered. She gave me a gracious smile, the reward of royalty.

"Of course."

"And the warriors?"

Her lips twisted. "They say they are my brothers, and thus can do what they wish with me. But they're no kin of mine. They are wood-made, where I am living. *They* are not my brothers." She gave me a strange look.

"Who made them?" I asked.

"An oak-lord, one of Mac Derga's men. Skilled, I suppose, if you admire that sort of thing." She spat. "Ash-born, split from the wood. Not born of anything female." Her form shivered in a sudden wind and I thought she would go. There was no reason for her to be talking to me, after all.

"And yourself?" I said.

"I am of the deer." She was proud of that, I could tell. Beast-born, then. A small voice from the tatters of my memory told me that there weren't many of them, and those that there were came out of bloodshed and war: the havoc of magic men. But I did not want to tell her that, and risk her anger. Besides, mad though I was, she was still the most beautiful thing I had seen for a long, long while. It struck me as an odd thing, then, that I knew so much about the Changing, and so little about myself.

"Well," she said next. "I must go now."

"What of the wood-warriors?"

She laughed. "What of them? They will be back, no doubt. But they will never catch me." The surface of her skin boiled and bubbled. Next moment, there was nothing more than a cloud of gnats, skimming across the surface of the lake.

I DID NOT expect to see her again. The Changing may be a part of nature, but their creation means that they can never stay long apart from the world of men, and that is not my world any more. My world is the woods, the lakeshore, the caverns beneath the earth, and sometimes it is none of these, but the world in-between, the dragonfly world of the dead. It was in that world that I saw her for the second time.

My madness is tied to the wheel of the stars and the moon. When the moon goes dark, and is eaten by the great beast, then my madness reaches its peak. I was scuttling through trees and bones when I saw her. The lake had turned to blood. I felt that something vast had been slain and there was a squealing inside my head. She stepped out of shadow and moths to place a hand on my brow. Her skin felt cool and prickling, like the skin of a toad. She said, "You are running mad."

I said, or thought I did, "What does that matter to you?"

"Hush. You are disturbing things. You should not be here. This is the wild, not the home of men."

"It is *my* home." But the pressure of her hand increased until all I could see was the castle wall, yellow with lichen, and the bitch yawning in the sun. My mother was standing before me. I fell to my knees.

"The trees are coming," my mother said with a fearful glance, and was gone into a haze of black air.

IN THE MORNING, just as the dawn's light touched the lake, I woke. There was no sign of the Changing. My head felt cold and clear, water-still. I stumbled to my feet and looked around for her, seeking her in the gnats and the flickering trout among the cress, but she was nowhere to be seen, or not showing herself. I felt filthy and old. I stripped the skins from myself and washed, for the first time in months. When I came out again from the lake, I felt as though I had been peeled down to the pith.

She was standing on the shore, not bothering to hold her form too greatly. Her face was the muzzle of a doe. She said, "They're coming."

"Who?" I asked. Had she been a human woman, I would have been ashamed of my nakedness, but despite her beauty it was like standing naked before a beast.

"The wood-warriors." Her lip curled. "I need your help." It was not clear whether it was the warriors she despised, or myself.

"What kind of help?" I asked.

"You know the caves, don't you? They have Mac Derga's oak-man with them; he can force my form."

"I don't understand."

"Force me to take one shape and one shape only. If he does that," she shifted from foot to gleaming foot, "it will be easy for them to capture me."

"Why do they want you so badly?" But I already knew the answer to that.

She shrugged. "Beauty. I think they plan to give me to one of Mac Derga's men, perhaps Mac Derga himself. For no more than a night, most likely. He is betrothed already, to a chieftain's daughter."

"Then come with me," I said, snatching up the skins. I felt filled with purpose, for the first time in months. She said nothing more, but followed me through the bramble and briar, which seemed to shrink away from her skin.

Sometimes, the caves were not where I expected them to be. The woods seemed to change with the moon, just as the sea does, or perhaps it was only my madness. I found them with some difficulty, but the Changing betrayed no impatience or surprise. Perhaps the woods really did alter and shift. And the mouth of the cave seemed more overgrown than I remembered it. I stepped through into clammy cold. The Changing followed me and as she did so, she gave a long breathy sigh.

"You'll be safe here," I said, but I wasn't sure if I believed it.

"That isn't why I came," she said. I looked back to see her eyes, a chilly gleam in the darkness.

"What do you mean?"

"I need something. Something that is down here."

I stared at her. "There's nothing here. You can see for yourself. No treasure, no gold."

She gave a shrill little laugh. "Oh yes, you are a man, no mistaking that. Even your mad head is filled with metal, just like all the rest. I'm not looking for gold."

"Then what are you looking for?"

"You will see, if it comes to it."

I did not like the sound of this, but it barely mattered to me any more whether I lived or died. A thin voice at the back of my head told me that there were worse things than dying, but I did not want to listen to it. The cool ghost beside me was the only thing I cared about now. We went on.

I couldn't keep track of time at the best of it, and if I could no longer see the sun or the moon, then I was wholly lost. I took the flint from my skins and struck a bundle of tinder.

"No light!" she said sharply. "Put it out." So I did.

Her own faint gleam lit our way, but we were deep into the cavern, where water dripped and pooled, before she next spoke. "He's here."

I turned to look at her. She had stopped in her tracks. Her face was beginning to lengthen, but then it flattened out once more, back to human.

"Who?"

"Mac Derga's oak-man. I can feel him. He's sent his spirit out to look for me."

"Can his spirit find you, this far below the earth?"

"I do not know. He has allies, many of them. I hoped–" She grew still and trembled. I longed to protect her, but did not know how. Something was snuffling and grunting in the tunnel. Without a sound, the Changing fell apart into a series of water droplets and melted into a nearby pool. Her light was gone. I was alone in cauldron blackness. The grunting grew louder: something grumbling and angry. I blundered against the wall of the cavern, scraped my arm. I smelled blood, briefly, and then I ran.

It was not my thought to abandon her and escape. I hoped to draw the thing off, away from her. I was nothing, and she had become the light of the woods. And even in the dark, I knew the way. I had been down here before and the tunnel led only up and out, without branches. I ran along it as swiftly as I could, with the thing close behind me. I could smell it, too: a thick earth stink.

Teeth grazed my ankle, but I was out. The woods were waiting, still and cool, and there was a slice of new moon above the trees. The power of the oak-men is strongest when the moon is waxing, they grow together. I fell, rolling down a bank of earth, and the thing tumbled out behind me. I glimpsed it, briefly. It was a badger: huge-shouldered, claws outstretched. A gold torc glinted around its throat. And then it shimmered, Changing into a man.

Mac Derga's oak-man was old, perhaps forty or more, a sinewy form covered in the blue. Old markings lined his arms and chest; he was naked. His hair was limed into spikes, black and white like the badger's. I am not a small man, but he swept down on me and picked me up by the throat.

"Where is she?"

I did not care if he choked me. It was almost a relief that the end had come at last. I managed to say, "Where you will never find her," and he dropped me.

"Then that is no place at all," he spat. He raised his arms to the woods. "Rise! She is here."

I thought at first he was talking to Mac Derga's warriors, but it was the woods themselves that woke. He spoke their names, the secret *ogham* names that I had come to know through their own whispering: *fearn, duir, nuin, tinne*. He spoke to the male trees only, the chieftain trees, calling them up, and where they had stood, wood-warriors stood in their place. Holly men, straight as their spears, sharp toothed; alder men, with need-fire flickering around their wet skins; rowan men whose hair was tipped with blood. Their eyes were hollow. They stepped forward. Their spears were levelled at me and I did not close my eyes, but waited to die.

And then there was a voice behind me. The oak-man's head snapped round and I saw a fierce exultation cross it. Whatever his plan had been, it had worked. The voice was hers and she spoke the name of the other trees: the women's trees. *Straif* and *quert* and *beth* and *huathe*, blackthorn, apple, birch, haw – and they too rose from the wood and ran shrieking forward, to where the girl was standing.

"Deire!" the oak-man shouted, "See this, you bitch of a doe?" – and cast a glittering net from his hand. The Changing hissed and fell back, scrambling into the cave. The oak-man cursed and bolted after her: I followed them both, but a wood-warrior blocked my way. He was a holly man. His teeth glittered, even in the darkness. I discovered that I did, after all, care whether I lived or died. Behind me, I heard hisses and cries as the wood-warriors fell upon one another with the rustle of branches. I reached for the flint, nearly dropping it, and struck kindling. It was dry, the spark caught. I threw it. I saw the holly man's mouth open in an O and then he was gone in a rush of flame. The wood-warriors cried out. Clutching the burning kindling, I went into the cave and a rush of wind sent the smoke after me.

I found them down by the pool. He was stalking her, and I wondered whether he wanted her for Mac Derga after all. I could see his erection, strong for an old man. She was merging and changing, too far away as yet for him to cast his net, but his power filled the little chamber. I rushed him. He was not expecting it, and we both fell to the floor. His hand flew out and I saw the sticky strands emerge from it, bloody as they left the skin. But he missed her. She gave a cry and a doe was standing there for a fleeting moment. Then she was back. She struck him about the head, but she was too small and slight to do much damage. And so was I, in my half-starved state. The oak-man rolled me over and hammered my head on the stone floor until the cave spun. His hands closed around my throat. I heard her shrieking, but I was choking, and, I saw dimly, so was he. The smoke from the burning kindling had drifted upward. The air was thick with it. My ears hummed, louder and louder, as the blood rose. I could think only of her. I beat at him, feebly, but it was no use. The humming grew and suddenly, with a great cry, he was off me. I hauled myself to my feet, faint with coughing.

The Changing was nowhere to be seen. The oak-man writhed on the cavern floor, beneath a crawling, moving mass of bees. Wondering, I looked up and saw the paper cone, high in the roof of the cave. The oak-man lay still. There was silence outside the cave. I watched, breathless, as bees became woman again. The clear cold place in my head was growing: no more humming, like the voice of bees. I felt the oak-man take my madness with him, as his spirit fled. She looked at me.

"Well?" she said. "And now?"

I was able to tell her, for I knew. "My name is Suibhne Gelt," I said. "I am the son of Fergal Mac Maigen. I come from Dun Dubh Fort and the People of the Deer. I am your brother." The bitch yawned in sunlight: her name meant Summer. My mother walked smiling around the fortress wall with a pail of milk. My sister stood before me, lately bees.

"It's really you," I said.

She nodded, smiling. "It's really me. I knew I could get you back. I just needed the right form. Gnats and deer weren't enough. I do not have the power to take a wolf's shape. So it had to be something little and dangerous."

"I remember him," I said. I looked down at the motionless, bloated face of my enemy: Mac Derga's high druid Coann, who had sought to kill my father's only son and so take Dun Dubh. But he had not slain me, and my sister had come to take me home. I reached out and took her hand and led her from the cave, through the quiet morning wood, past holly and blackthorn thicket and the songs of birds, to the high land and home.

PARTY TRICKS

DAN ABNETT

Dan Abnett is a writing machine, producing vast amounts of work in many different genres and many different mediums. Unlike a machine, however, Mr Abnett has wit and soul and a quick and clever way with words, all of which he brings to his fiction. In the following tale Dan shows us the benefits of keeping our enemies close.

LOOKING BACK, QUITE frankly, it's difficult to know what to make of it. It's very hard to recall why things happened the way they happened. The PM always said he'd discuss it in his memoirs, but he never did. They say his mind was going by then, and he certainly didn't seem to remember any details when I asked him about it. But the PM was a tough old bastard, and I honestly believe it was the Fleet Street hack he got to ghost the memoirs who decided to leave the whole thing out... For the sake of discretion, I'd imagine, or credibility. There are some places even Fleet Street hacks don't like to go, if you can believe that.

Anyway, the point is, no one took to Rakely to begin with. No one liked him, or fancied his chances. He had no prospects.

I can't even remember the name of his first seat, but it was as safe as houses, and we'd kept it since William the bloody Conqueror. It would have taken an utter prick to lose it. He was just a warm body.

People who'd been up at Merton at the same time as Rakely never had much to say about him. He hadn't made any lasting impression. It seemed so unlikely, one of them told me, that he'd choose to go into what was, essentially, the public service industry. It required charm to do that, because you needed people to like you enough to vote for you. It was a simple enough formula to grasp. You needed, at the very minimum, a decent facsimile of likeability.

Whatever the case, Rakely was a back bencher at the time. He was on a few subcommittees, nothing of note. Basically, he didn't matter. What mattered was the moment. This all began during the Henig-Duncans share scandal. That had just broken. Everyone's attention had been on Europe, and the Health Bill, and no one had seen it coming. God, not even Rosmund, and he was the biggest scalp. They took him to the cleaners. I remember his face on television, at the Grandage Inquiry. He looked as though he'd been violated with a pineapple. I have never seen anyone appear so uncomfortable.

Suddenly, it was sheer shitstorm on all sides. Rosmund and the share thing was the big one, of course, but there was also Peters, and that idiot Doverson, and then that frankly astonishing business with Parkin and the schoolboy at the swimming baths. I don't even know where to start with that. I swear to almighty God I never knew he was the sort. We were at Colet Court together, for god's sake. He was a sound chap. I'd have put money on it.

Except, of course, it turned out he wasn't.

Any one of those things, just Parkin alone, should have taken the Government down. I remember the Foreign Secretary suggesting at a Cabinet lunch that we should fall on our swords, let the Opposition in, and come back in four years when the dust had settled in the hope that the general public would have forgotten, or at least forgiven, our association with liars, cheats, insider traders and perverts.

Maybe it would have been better that way.

The first move, if we were going to strategise any kind of survival, was to replace Rosmund. The Party Chairman and the Chief Whip were both absolutely gunning for someone more capable than Rosmund, and Rosmund – hard though it is to admit in the wake of Henig-Duncans – had been damned good. He'd known how to work the Commons, and the party faithful. Not shares, so much, as it turned out.

So, their list pretty much started and finished with Forster. I mean, he was the only serious contender. We'd known for three or four years he was a party leader or deputy PM in waiting. One of the main reasons we hadn't rolled him out earlier was simply to keep his nose clean for the succession we all knew was coming. The PM had a term left in his legs, at best. Forster was the coming man. And my godfathers, he was good. TV loved him, the constituency party loved him, and he regularly trumped forty-five or forty-six per cent approvals with working mums and job seekers, which made the PM shit actual blood with envy. None of that mattered really, though. What mattered, what I believed mattered, and what the rest of the Cabinet believed mattered, was that Forster was a real professional. He understood the way the House worked. He understood the process in some kind of uncanny, intuitive way. I've never seen horse trading done the way he did it. I've never seen cross-party work like it either. God, the Opposition benches adored him too. You know what it was? He was a statesman. He understood parliamentary craft.

The plan was, we'd bring him in from the Northern Ireland Office, probably swapping him out for Peters initially, get him placed as Special Advisor to Number 10, then do a whole re-shuffle at the start of the next session, which would leave him as Home Secretary by Christmas. He'd be the poster child for our mid-term rebranding. Clean, scandal-free.

I think I slept well the night we settled on that. Forster was on board. I went home, and tried to ignore the fact that every commentator on every channel was trying to burn us at the stake.

Then, as I remember, it was Billy Hutchins who rang me about Rakely. He wanted to have a conversation, that's was what he said. I asked him to be a little more specific, and he said that he thought we, and by we he meant the PM, were being pretty hasty about running with Forster without considering Rakely.

Well, I can tell you I laughed at him. I think I even checked my calendar to make sure it wasn't the start of April. Billy could be a bit of a wind-up merchant at times. But he was dead straight serious. I mean, bloody serious. That gave me pause. I'd known him long enough to recognise the tone.

We had a quiet lunch at Severay's. It's not there anymore, but it was a nice place. Quiet. I wanted to sound Billy out on the Q.T. before bringing the PM in. I suspected Billy might have been doing a little horse trading of his own, and I thought I could keep him sweet with a promise or two.

But he was actually on the up-and-up about Rakely. He said something mysterious about Forster not being the man we thought he was, which I poo-pooed, then he kept on about Rakely. I pointed out that Rakely wasn't really very able, he wasn't very senior, and he certainly wasn't very popular. Billy said to me, "We don't need someone good, Charles, not to replace Rosmund. We just need someone different. We just need someone who hasn't got any baggage. Any blood on his hands."

Well, I didn't think Forster had, but he advised me to look into it, and to do a little due diligence on Rakely while I was about it.

I don't know. There was something about it that stuck with me. I made an excuse to go and see Rakely at his office. I think I pretended to be sounding him out on the Health Bill. He wasn't very much more charming than I remembered, but he had a way about him that I hadn't seen before. It seemed as though he had a sharper political mind than I'd initially given him credit for. From the way he talked, entirely casually, I got the impression that he knew the deeper purpose of my visit. He understood what was at stake and what was on offer. He didn't push it or anything, but he knew. And he was leaving it up to me to make the call.

I felt I had underestimated him. I took a look back through Hansard and the party record, and through his official papers, and there was nothing. Nothing good or remarkable, granted, but nothing even remotely controversial, let alone bad. He was as clean as Billy Hutchins said he was. He was a *tabula rasa*. Then I thought about Forster, and his slight dalliance with the left wing in his student days, and his constant, noble but rather exasperating stance on the nuclear issue. I mean to say, they were minor, *minor* things, just little sticks that the press could use on a rainy day to beat him, or us, with. Nothing significant in the long run, merely niggles.

But Rakely had nothing.

Rather to my surprise, I brought some people in on it: Tom Jeffers, Douglas Barney, Mark Broadbent from Defence, and Hardiman. You didn't make a play like this without Alex Hardiman. We also talked to a few others, like Kinley and Sobers, to take their temperatures. In the meantime, I went to the Whip's office through soft channels and got everything on Forster slowed down a little, just to buy us a day or two.

Jeffers and Barney were pretty easy to convince. I fancy Billy Hutchins might have talked to them along the way. Mark Broadbent was more dubious, but he could easily see how Rakely's declared interests would make him a desirable asset for Defence. Mark knew that if he smoothed the path for Rakely, he'd get his reward in due course.

Only Alex Hardiman was against it. He positively didn't like Rakely. When I gently pointed out that there was nothing about Rakley to dislike, he insisted that was exactly it. Hardiman was old school, a real veteran, and in the main I think he objected to Rakely's sheer colourlessness. He liked

Forster very much. Forster reminded him of Billings, and our last glorious days in the sunshine.

We were stymied, to be honest. We had to make the call one way or another. The PM was on the inside now, and he was waiting for our brief. We had to go one way or the other. What we couldn't afford was a delay, or the impression of dithering.

We all went up to Chequers for the weekend. On the drive up, I was fully braced to throw in for Forster after all, because the party listened to Hardiman. His opinion would be the clincher. When we arrived, we heard the news. We actually didn't realise quite how serious the stroke was at first. All we knew was that Hardiman was in hospital and he wouldn't be joining us.

It was rash, I suppose, and a little disingenuous to Alex Hardiman not to represent his feelings on the matter, which we all knew full well. But we went in like gunslingers, the four of us, and quite dismantled Brian Templestone's cheerleading for Forster.

The PM was swayed. I think we'd taken him by surprise. He needed a deal of convincing, though, because he was reluctant to let Forster go. I called Rakely at home, and told him to be in the Cabinet Office on Monday morning. The PM would drop by for a quiet chat before the afternoon vote on the Freight Tariff Act, which was the next meaty piece of legislation looming in the queue leading to the Health Bill. It was going to be a rough ride, and the meeting would simply look like the PM popping by to glad-hand some of the party faithful and generate a little confidence before the vote.

Rakely was there, ready for us, on Monday morning. He looked good; rested, serious and attentive. He was wearing, it seemed to me, a better suit than usual. He met with me, Jeffers and the PM, and we chatted about stuff, just this and that. We all knew it was a job interview. It was the PM's way of doing it. We went back and forth on Health, and Europe, and kept coming back to the Freight Tariff Act.

Rakely suddenly asked if the PM had fully considered the effect of union support on the vote. The PM was surprised. The unions was not an angle we usually looked at with any real enthusiasm. If nothing else, the composition of our party was not determined by direct union interests the way the opposition's was.

It looked like a terrible mis-step. It made Rakely seem a little naive even to bring it up and waste everybody's time. But he began to stress that we were, as usual perhaps, ignoring the possibility of finding friends where none usually existed. He delicately mentioned the unmentionable, which was that we were in a very dark place, with the polls at an all-time low, and that we really needed a strong result to take the sun out of our eyes. Then he mentioned the union interest in certain aspects of the Health Bill, aspects that, in the grand scheme of things, would be painless sacrifices to make.

He got the PM's interest. Damn it, he got my interest. What he was proposing, informally, was that the Transport and General Workers Union, Collatera (which had been the TBFGU), and the Manufacturer's Union would all come across if we offered them concessions on Health when it came up. They couldn't directly affect the Commons vote, of course, but they could make it very plain to Her Majesty's Opposition how much the withdrawal of their support over the Tariff Act would hurt in the months to come.

I don't think we really believed it. So he took us into a side office. He had them waiting on Skype: Murray from the Transport and General, Richardson from Collatera, Patanjali from the MDMU, and even Colin Babcock from the IGMT. It was done and done in about five minutes.

We took the vote, of course. A huge climb down for the Opposition. A rout. The Freight Tariff Act went straight through the House. I have never seen so many stunned and unhappy faces sitting across from me.

But even before the vote, the PM took me to one side. He said to me, "Charles, it's Rakely. Do what you need to do."

So I did. We switched Forster to Health at the last minute, put McKenzie out to Northern Island, and made room for Rakely by securing for Bob Thomas a very prestigious position with the European Commission. Which, in those days, was as good as saying he was going to spend more time with his family.

Rakely didn't disappoint. He led the charge on Health, got it through on the second reading, then took the lead on Fiscal Policy and the fall-out from the Pepper Report. It was a joy to watch, I have to admit. Suddenly, we weren't so much thinking about Home Secretary by Christmas, we were thinking Deputy Leader by the time the Party Conference came round.

Forster took it badly, as you might imagine. He'd waited so patiently for his moment to come, and now it had been snatched from him. He was sour. We tried to make something of Health, but the big job there was already done, and besides, his heart wasn't in it. He made noises about the Treasury, which I suppose might have been a reasonable consolation, but we didn't want to rock the boat. Things were turning, but it was still choppy. The scandals were still rumbling around the red tops.

Rakely they liked though. He sort of won them over a little, enough so they could tease him but seem affectionate. I also remember a cartoon appearing in the FT around that time, one by Pax, which showed a triumphant Rakely dressed as Aleister bloody Crowley or something, sacrificing a buxom virgin in Parliament Square in exchange for Faustian advancement. In the background, there was Forster as an alley cat, sniffing around some bins marked 'Cabinet scraps'.

I must say I really admired the way Rakely grew into the job. He developed a really deft, light touch with things that I had imagined him incapable of. He just mixed well, and in return, he got results. He played an absolute blinder in support of the PM at the G8 towards the end of that year, and then surpassed himself on both the Amenities Bill and the Public Access Commission. He also proved pretty much indispensable when the Bradbury Report went to committee. Everybody, of course, remembers his speech to the 1922 Committee, which was so hilariously funny, and which left Godbridge spitting feathers, and they still, to this day, replay that segment on Newsnight when he patiently pointed out all the factual errors in that Peston fellow's analysis of the Banking Regulation Policy. The PM started to refer to him as his 'spin bowler'.

It was a little while after Hardiman's funeral in March the following year that I received the book in the post. It came to my office. It was the paperback of a work called *The White Cockerel*, published by some American university. It was really rather an ugly thing, with poor typography and an awful cover. I gave it a look, and realised it was an annotated, academic edition of what was, allegedly, an Italian text from about 1625. It was part political treatise, and part grimoire. I mean, it was absurd stuff. The package was unmarked, but it wasn't hard to work out where it had come from, especially because of the copy of that Pax cartoon tucked inside the cover. It was, all-in-all, a fairly childish exercise.

I wanted to ignore it, simply leave it alone, but Forster was growing increasingly erratic, and the last thing the party needed was a time bomb like him holing us below the waterline in front of the Interest Rate debate. So I went to see him, for a quiet chat, to set him straight and get him back on-side. The man was clearly so afflicted by bitterness he was making poor choices. I had to calm him down. There were still some prizes for him to win, in time, provided he didn't make an utter embarrassment of himself.

He was in a poor mood, positively whiney. I found it all a bit awkward, to be plain about it. He wouldn't let it go, not at all. He kept on about Rakely. The resentment was palpable. He'd lost that statesman-like gloss entirely. I began to wonder what we'd ever seen in him. He blamed me for his woes. He blamed everyone.

He blamed Rakely.

I asked him what he'd been playing at with the stupid book. He looked at me blankly, as though I hadn't understood. He started to tell me about it, in all seriousness.

"That's not the real thing, Charles," he said. "Obviously it isn't. I couldn't get my hands on that, not even a copy. That's just some shitty college edition, entirely bowdlerised and full of fundamental errors. I was just trying to show you what I meant."

"And what did you mean, Andrew?" I asked him.

"Obviously, that's how he's doing it. That's how he's doing it all."

"Doing what?"

I think he realised that I wasn't playing ball. He started to tell me about *The White Cockerel*. He said it had been written by an Italian courtier, called Lucci, at the *Dieci Di Liberta e Pace*. He'd been the man who pulled Machiavelli's strings.

"No one pulled Machiavelli's strings," I said to that.

"That's the point," Forster replied. "That's how good Lucci was. No one ever saw him behind the curtain."

"Andrew, I really don't think you understand who Machiavelli was," I said.

He banged on regardless, and then claimed that the book, and Lucci, had also been a guiding influence behind the rise of some of Henry VIII's key appointments, and had played a significant power-broking role during the Stuart Succession. I finally had to call time on the whole conversation.

"For God's sake, Andrew," I said.

"It's all there, in the book," he declared. "Of course, the commentary in that edition fudges the details a little, especially the specific content and language of the ritual practices. I mean, the rites are the really potent stuff, the stuff that actually influences situations and the course of events. But it's all the basic facts."

"Oh Christ," I said. "These aren't facts at all, Andrew. This is some kind of sub-Dan Brown bullshit. This is, *what*? A *spell book* for securing political advancement? How to achieve power through magic?"

"Don't make it sound so ridiculous!" he protested.

"I don't have to. Oh, Andrew, please. *Please*. Devil worship and black magic? Satanic pacts–"

"It's not like that."

"Whatever. If you're trying to start a rumour that Rakely only got where he did thanks to magical rites, then you're the one who's going to look pretty bloody daft. Come on, this is all bullshit."

"What if it isn't?"

"Okay, quite apart from the various geographical issues involved, don't you think it's unlikely one man could have coordinated the careers of... what was it again? Wolsey, Cromwell, and James 1st and... and... Machiavelli? This Lucci chap would have had to be a *very* old man."

"He wasn't always called Lucci," he said.

"What?"

"I mean, he went on and on. He was different people," said Forster, but his voice was dropping and he sounded less convinced. "He used different names. Wore faces. I think the rites allowed him to live several lives–"

"You're making yourself look ludicrous, Andrew, you really are. A senior cabinet minister can't be seen to be thinking like this. Maybe you need a break. A rest. Perhaps we can move things around a little after the recess."

He glared at me, as if I'd thrown him over, but I think he knew how foolish he looked.

"You should ask about Jenny Carr," he said, then stopped.

I asked him what he meant, but he refused to be drawn, so I said a few encouraging words, expressed a keen desire to see him keep a lid on it, and told him to come to me the moment he felt he couldn't.

He said he would. I left it at that. The next time I saw the PM, I casually mentioned we might have to think about getting someone new at Health. He told me he'd already been thinking the same thing.

And I assumed that was that.

Over the summer, Julia Strachan from Welfare got in touch and said that she'd taken a few odd questions from a journalist at some event, and did I know anything. She said it felt like someone might be briefing against Rakely. I told her I'd look into it, but before I got a chance Ben Worden from the *Times* came to me. I liked Ben. He could be an absolute stinker, but he had a very nice habit of checking sources. He didn't like to run something if it was going to cause a mess for no reason. He said he'd been given a story, and he wanted to sound me out before he went anywhere with it. He said it was about a girl called Jenny Carr. I asked him where he'd got the story from, and he politely declined to tell me, but I knew full well it was bloody Andrew Forster. I thanked Ben for having the courtesy to come to me, and told him I'd look at it and get back to him, but I warned him it was probably an awful lot of smoke damage and zero flammable content. I said I could guess who his unnamed source was, and if I was right we were talking about a man who was becoming a liability because of his desperation to grind axes.

Ben nodded. He'd imagined it was something like that. He left it with me.

I gave it all a look. Within about two hours, I have to say, it had given me a little wobble. I was astonished that something like this could have remained essentially invisible for nearly three years. I went to see Rakely about it. I wanted to get it straight.

"I want you to tell me about Jenny Carr," I said to him. He he had this funny thing he did with his upper lip when he was slightly uncomfortable, sort of folding it in under his bottom lip for a second. I knew the moment I saw him do that I'd got hold of something. But he kept his cool.

Jenny Carr had been his PA the first time he ran for Parliament. A nice, efficient girl. She'd lived in St John's Wood. She'd pretty much been with him from his selection all the way to the by-election.

She'd died about a month before he'd made his maiden speech. She'd been killed at her flat. The police had suspected a burglary gone wrong. Someone had broken in, not expecting to find her there, and then stabbed her eight times with a knife or possibly a sharpened screwdriver. Her body had been discovered in the living room of her home by a friend. No one had ever been arrested in connection with the murder.

It was awful, and clearly he didn't want to talk about it. But there were odd things about it. According to the police report, which Ben Worden had given me a copy of, there had been no evidence of a break-in or a struggle. The front door of the flat was unlocked, as if she'd let someone in, someone she knew, someone she hadn't had any reason to be wary of. Nothing had been taken. The alternative theory, that it wasn't a burglary but in fact a sexually motivated crime, was undermined by a lack of forensic evidence. There was no sign of sexual contact at all, not even any removal or adjustment of clothing or a pose that might suggest some sexual motivation or behaviour. The coroner's report went so far as to say she was *virgo intacta*, in a prim fashion that seemed to suggest it was far more unlikely for an attractive twenty-four-year-old woman to be a virgin than it was for her to be murdered.

Strangest of all, as I said to Rakely, was the fact that we didn't know anything at all about it.

He was very frank in his reply. He told me that the whole thing had been kept quiet for the sake of the girl's parents, who were, understandably, devastated, and had simply refused to allow the memory of their beloved daughter to become a sordid item in the news cycle. Though he'd keenly supported the police investigation, he'd gone along with the parents' wishes. He freely admitted to me that there had been a significant element of self-interest. No matter what, his association with a murdered young woman would have probably crippled his political career right from the get-go. The alternative, which he described as being even more distasteful, would have been to deal with it openly, and risk being seen as trying to make political capital out of her death. The sympathy vote, he said. He didn't want that. He hadn't wanted that to be her legacy.

He'd just wanted it all to stay off the front page, and for her family to be left in peace. He'd had nothing whatsoever to do with her death, but they had gone out, briefly, when they'd first met, and he knew the press would take hold of anything and turn it into something lurid.

"Well, now someone's got it," I said. I told him who, and I told him how. I said I'd have a word with Ben Worden. I told him I couldn't stop Worden running with it, but that I'd try to appeal to his better judgement and get him to see it was a non-story that could only, irresponsibly, do damage to the government and the country. You have to remember, the party was in fine form just then, pretty much due to Rakely's amazing run, and we were going into an election year.

Before I left, on a whim really, I asked Rakely if he knew anything about a book called *The White Cockerel*.

"I don't know, Charles," he said. "What's that?"

I said never mind. But I noticed he did the thing with his lip again.

I spoke to Ben Worden, and he told me he'd probably drop it anyway. After that, we really just yanked and cranked towards the election. The PM's health issues came out, which was a total shock. There'd been no record of Alzheimer's in his family. We accelerated the process of elevating Rakely. We wanted to go into the election with a leader who would win it convincingly.

And we did, in the end, as it turned out.

The plane crash was just awful. Of course it was. It was a terrible blow that I didn't think the party would survive, but I have to say I think we scored a little bit of that ghastly sympathy vote in the end. The PM even offered to stay on, but we had his exit strategy in place, and besides, the public already knew he was ill.

That crash though. I mean, really. Just a routine flight back from the Strasbourg Summit. Rakely, Doug Barney and Eileen Clemmens, plus their aides and several members of the press. Including, and I always remark on this, Ben Worden. The

Civil Aviation Authority never did work out what happened to those engines.

After the election, the landslide, I went to see the PM. The *new* PM, I should say. He was in very fine form. I'll freely admit it. He'd turned things around in the most spectacular way. It was admirable. Hats off to him. He'd really stepped up in our hour of need.

Anyway, we were having a quiet chat over a good malt, and he said this thing to me. I remember it very clearly.

He said, "Charles, sometimes you can only get so far. You have to clear the slate. Just clear everything aside. Sometimes things go past a point where they're useful, and you have to brush them away and start again."

It was a very singular thing to say. I felt he was referring to something that only I might know about.

In a way, he was right. He must have known.

I looked him straight in the eye, and I said, "By the by, Andrew, I wrote to the librarian at Merton about six weeks ago. I asked her if the college had ever had a book called *The White Cockerel* in its collection."

"Did you indeed?" He laughed, as though I'd brought up some embarrassing gaffe from the past to rag him with.

"It took about a fortnight, but she rang me back in the end," I said. "She told me the index suggested that there had been a manuscript of that name in the college library. Seventeenth Century Italian, very fragile. The notes said it was an Italian translation of an earlier Aramaic text, which itself was believed to be a translation of an even earlier work. The manuscript had been in the library at Merton until 1992, at which point it had vanished. She said, sadly, that books were taken from time to time, especially by undergraduates who fancied making a little money on the antiquarian market."

"Oh," he said. "Never mind, Charles. Looks like we don't actually need it now."

Which was an amusing remark, of course.

"Rakely was up at Merton," I said. "1991 to 1993."

The PM nodded.

"What do you think of that, Andrew?" I asked.

He shrugged, and did a funny little thing with his upper lip.

Then we went in to join the others for dinner.

FIRST AND LAST AND ALWAYS

THANA NIVEAU

There's a danger in wanting something too much, and when you couple that with sorcery, the consequences can be grave indeed. Thana shows us what happens when a casual witch takes the plunge into a more complex arcane world than that found in popular books on love magic. Desire has its own kind of magic and in playing with it, Tamsin finds herself on a dangerous path.

TAMSIN PLACED HER hands on either side of her phone and gazed intently at the picture of Nicky she'd taken the day before. Her heart soared as she said his name aloud.

The flickering candlelight gave him the illusion of movement and Tamsin could almost believe she was watching him through a portal, seeing him as he was right at this moment. After a few seconds the picture faded and the screen went dark. She peered into the smooth black surface, focusing on the afterimage – Nicky in negative, overlaid by the reflection of her eyes and the ghostly glow of the flame.

"Nicky."

When the image behind her eyes finally faded, she tried to see beyond the scrying glass of the phone's screen, into whatever dimension the emptiness might reveal. Past, present, future – she didn't care as long as she saw *him*.

When nothing happened she tapped the screen to wake it up, to reveal the photo again and repeat the entire process.

It was just a quick candid shot but she'd captured the vibrancy of the setting sun. Nicky had been on his way to rehearse with his band, Valhalla, and he was smiling at someone out of frame. His head was turned slightly to one side. She'd shot straight into the sun, creating a dramatic lens flare that partially obscured one hazel eye. A lock of black hair fell over his other eye, just reaching his cheekbone.

Tamsin tried to visualise herself in the picture with him, her long blond tresses transformed by the evening light into burnished gold. That was how she liked to imagine she looked to him, anyway. Her hair was her best feature. It fell in lustrous waves halfway down her back and it made her average face a little prettier, gave her the wild, windblown look of a gothic heroine. Nicky had complimented her on it one day when she'd had it down and she'd worn it that way ever since.

"Hey there, Tamsin," he'd said, hearing the click of her camera phone.

His low sleepy voice turned her knees to water. And his smile...

"You coming to our show tomorrow night?"

It was only a half hour spot at a local student hangout but to Tamsin it may as well have been a major concert.

"Of course," she'd said, thrilling to the sound of his voice. It rang in her ears as she cast about for something else to say. Anything to keep him there for another minute. "Oh – I saw the video you guys posted on YouTube."

He'd blushed then, shyly lowering his head as though he had anything to be shy about. She'd played the clip endlessly, imagining that every time he looked into the camera, he was looking right at her.

"Oh, it's just a demo," he said. "Rob said we should build up an online presence before we send anything to the record companies."

"Just a demo? It looked completely professional to me!"

"Thanks."

Nicky smiled again and they shared an awkward silence before he glanced at his watch. "Well, guess I'd better go."

"Yeah," she'd said, dying but not daring to take another picture of him. She'd already copied all the ones on his Facebook profile and even printed some of them out. Her favourite one sat in a little gold frame on the nightstand by her bed. His beautiful pale face in closeup, his eyes meeting hers every night and every morning.

"OK, see you tomorrow, then."

"Yeah," she breathed. "See you..."

The memory of the conversation echoed in her mind as she woke her phone up again and said his name, willing him to hear her in his mind, to acknowledge his true feelings for her. She was dressed and ready for the concert, determined that tonight would be the night. Tonight he would love her back.

But it was not to be.

VALHALLA PLAYED FIVE songs and Nicky was brilliant, as always. The pub was full of students who cheered as though they were at the Glastonbury Festival. Tamsin stood as close to the stage as she could but Nicky didn't look her way once. He seemed completely lost in the performance, singing with his eyes closed, oblivious to everything but the music. Someday he would be a big star. Tamsin had no doubt about it. But she had to make sure he was hers before that happened. Once he was famous he would be hounded by groupies. Girls with tramp stamps and black lipstick. Tamsin was what he needed, what he really wanted. He just didn't know it yet.

After the show he was surrounded by his friends and Tamsin's stomach clenched with jealousy at the sight of all the other girls flocking around him. There was no way she could push her way through the crush of bodies. It was torture to be so close to him, yet unable to reach him. Torture to watch him with all those other girls, none of whom understood him the way Tamsin did.

Tears blurred her vision and she wiped her eyes with the back of her hand, smearing her mascara. She couldn't let him see her like that so she made herself turn away. As she opened the door of the pub she glanced back one last time, hoping he would sense her anguish and signal to her to stay. But wishing only made the reality worse. He hadn't noticed her at all.

That night she sat cross-legged on her bed, staring forlornly at an uninspired Tarot spread. It was her third attempt. Each time she had managed to draw cards that told her nothing meaningful or even relevant. The Knight of Cups hadn't appeared in any of the three spreads. Cups represented the world of feelings and the Knight was the most romantic card of all. But he was nowhere to be seen tonight. Nicky's symbolic absence felt like a sickness, something that would grow and spread until it consumed her and spat out her indigestible heart.

She swept the cards away in disgust. Her chest felt tight, as though her insides were trying to shrink away from the pain. If she closed her eyes she saw his face. Her skin burned for the touch of his hands.

Her flatmates had teased her about him, calling him "goth boy" and other dismissive names. Beth had drawn a cartoon of him as Dracula and Chrissie had once left a pair of comedy fangs in the bathroom for her to find. Tamsin was sure they didn't mean to be cruel; they just didn't understand. After all, neither of them had a boyfriend either.

At least they didn't mock her religion. Beth had got Tamsin a book on witchcraft for her birthday and she had tried both the love spells in it. They were of the 'bad poetry and herbs' variety, probably inspired more by *Harry Potter* than by any real magic. But she'd tried them anyway, feeling silly for doing it and then feeling even sillier when they didn't work. What had she expected?

She'd been so sure he would notice her tonight. Her feelings were too intense to be only one-sided. In desperation, she powered up her computer and began searching online for proper love spells. She quickly found a naff website hawking 'love spells that totally work', along with 'amazingly accurate' astrological charts and other rubbish that was probably just designed by spammers to harvest your email address if you were gormless enough to provide it for a 'personalised' reading. But there must be other witches online, real witches who knew what they were doing.

It was on a forum called *eBook Of Shadows* that Tamsin finally found what she was looking for.

In order to truly love something, you have to make it part of you.

The post was by someone called Osprey and she was relating a story her gran had told her.

There was a young girl who lived with her family on a farm. Times were hard and one year there was a drought, the next year a flood. The crops were destroyed and the family was facing ruin. But the girl was in love with a boy from the neighbouring village and she was terrified that her parents would decide to move. If they did, she knew she would never see her true love again.

So she cast a spell to bind them to the land. She took a spoon and circled the farmhouse, collecting one scoop of soil for each member of the family. That night she sprinkled it into the stew her mother made and mixed it well. She said a few words over it and wished very hard for it to work. Her family complained that the food tasted strange but they ate it all the same.

A year passed and love continued to blossom between the girl and the boy even as the crops failed yet again. Her family was forced to sell all the animals but they insisted on staying with the farm. Friends and neighbours urged them to sell up and move somewhere else, suggesting that the land was cursed. No one could understand their stubborn refusal to stay. No one but the girl, who lamented their poverty but was comforted by the knowledge that now she could never be parted from her soulmate.

Tamsin had no idea if the story was true or not, but she liked to think it was. At least the happy part. She knew she was supposed to be too old to believe in fairy tales, but she couldn't help it; she was a romantic. She wanted to believe that wishes came true, that love conquered all. Most of all she wanted to believe that there were magic spells that worked.

She lay awake in bed for several hours that night, her mind racing.

In order to truly love something, you have to make it part of you.

How could she make Nicky a part of her? The girl in the story had bound her family to the land by physically feeding it to them, although perhaps she should have tried binding herself to the boy instead. Tamsin had tried so many different love spells over the months but nothing had worked. Was it because none of the spells had any physical link between her and Nicky? Gazing at his picture and saying his name wasn't getting her anywhere. She might as well be clapping to keep Tinkerbell alive.

She was always hearing about girls who had date-rape drugs slipped into their drinks. How hard could it be to turn the tables? But the very thought made her feel like a stalker. She didn't want to rape him; all she wanted to do was make him recognise what was already inside him. Surely there was no harm in that. But even as she brainstormed different scenarios, she knew she couldn't spike his drink in a public bar. If he saw her – or worse, if someone *else* saw her – that would be the end of everything.

No, whatever she did had to be done in private. And the only way to do that was to screw up her courage and invite him over for dinner. But what could she feed him? It had to be something she could sneak into the food undetected but most importantly, it had to be something uniquely hers. Uniquely *her*.

The question obsessed her over the following days. Then one night while she was revising for a poetry exam, the answer jumped out at her. It was a line by Thomas Carew.

Those curious locks so aptly twin'd
Whose every curl a soul doth bind.

Tamsin sat before the mirror, her heart pounding. In the joy of her discovery she looked radiant and she brushed her hair slowly, sensuously, as she focused her mind on crafting the perfect spell. She pulled several loose hairs from her brush, wondering how many she would need. But as she looked at them, curled in her palm like a tiny nest, she knew it wasn't right. Those hairs were already dead. She dropped them in the bin and met her eyes in the mirror.

Then she carefully selected a strand of hair from the top of her head. She smoothed away the other hairs around it and tugged. It did not come free at once. She had to pull it several times before she yanked it out at the root. The pain was astonishing. It was only a single hair but it felt like someone had jabbed her scalp with a needle. She cried out as it came free and wasn't surprised to see a tiny drop of blood on the end.

Her voice trembled as she whispered, "First."

With her fingers she combed through her hair on the left until she isolated another strand. It also proved reluctant to come out and when it did it brought with it another drop of blood.

"And last."

She moved to the right for the final strand, taking hold of it firmly and holding her breath. She yanked, hoping it would pull out more easily than the others. But it was the most difficult of all. Only after many painful jerks of her hand did it finally come out. She yelped and had to resist the urge to scratch her scalp, to rub away the burning sensation where the hairs had been plucked.

She took a deep breath and laid the three strands side by side on her dressing table. "And always," she said. "Mine."

The blood held them together at one end and Tamsin weighted them down with her phone while she set about plaiting them together. She found herself humming as she did, barely aware of the warm trickle from her scalp until the blood dripped into her eyes. She paid it no mind. Her hands completed the task as though guided by external forces.

When at last she had a long thin braid she wiped the blood from her face and knotted the ends together to form a circle. It would remain unbroken until the right moment.

She tucked the charm beneath her pillow to keep it close to her while she slept. She knew it would bring her dreams of Nicky, dreams that were about to come true. In the morning her pillow was stained with blood.

SHE SAW HIM the next day, chatting with his friend Rob, and she didn't hesitate. She had dressed up for the occasion. Her athletic frame was showcased in her tightest jeans and a lacy purple top. She'd worn a push-up bra and gothed up her makeup. Smudged black eyeliner and blood red lips. Just enough to get his attention.

It worked. His face broke into an easy smile as she walked boldly up to him before she could lose her nerve. Rob was eyeing her cleavage.

"I saw your show the other night," she said breezily. "It was awesome!"

Nicky's smile broadened. "Hey, thanks! I wasn't sure about that Sisters of Mercy cover. Was it really OK?"

Rob jumped in before she could answer. "Of course it was. I *told* you." He rolled his eyes at Tamsin as though compelling her to agree with him.

But Nicky was still watching her expectantly, waiting to hear what she thought. She hid her exhilaration and nodded as though she had any business telling him whether something was good or not.

"I thought it was brilliant. Better than the original."

His eyes shone with genuine delight and her heart twisted a little at the thought of him doubting his talent. And before the opportunity could slip away she said "Do you want to come to mine for dinner tonight?"

He blinked in surprise but his smile didn't falter. Out of the corner of her eye she saw Rob's face fall a little.

Nicky glanced at his friend and then back at Tamsin. "Sure," he said.

"Great! I'm making a curry. Hope you like it spicy." She knew full well he did, just as she knew loads of other little things about him that he'd never told her. Just to leave him in no doubt about what was on offer she added, "My flatmates are away for the weekend."

He actually blushed. "Brilliant," he said.

Her heart leapt and it was all she could do to maintain the casual act. "Cool. It's a date. I'll text you my address. What's your number?"

It was almost too easy. Just like that, the deal was sealed.

"Well, I've gotta get to class," she said. "See you tonight!"

Nicky waved as she trotted away, pretending to be in a hurry. She felt lighter than air.

Mine, she thought.

SHE SKIPPED THE class she'd pretended to be late for and went to Waitrose to buy the poshest ingredients she could find. Then she spent the whole afternoon making the curry. Soon the aroma of coconut milk and chillies permeated the flat and Tamsin left the meal to simmer while she tidied away the few things Beth and Chrissie had left lying around. She closed the doors to their rooms and opened her own like an invitation.

She placed two red candles on the small dining table and set it as though she were entertaining royalty. A bottle of chardonnay was chilling in the fridge although she suspected

Nicky would prefer beer. Too bad. This was her big night and it was going to be classy.

Choosing what to wear took even more time. Jeans were too casual but a party dress would look like she was trying too hard. She eventually settled on a flirty red skirt and a black velvet top. She admired herself in the mirror and looked at her watch for the hundredth time. She'd told him to come at six and there was still nearly an hour to go. She spent it pacing, checking the curry, making minute adjustments to the place settings, straightening the pictures on the wall and making the bed. With a gasp she suddenly spotted the framed photo of Nicky by the bedside and she hurriedly shoved it to the bottom of her underwear drawer.

That done, she returned to the curry. She would have to wait until the very last minute to add her secret ingredient. The kitchen smelled heavenly and she was sure the spicy brew would disguise any odd flavour. But she threw in an extra chilli and another splash of ginger wine just to be sure.

At ten to six she put on some music and tried to slow her galloping heart as she waited for Nicky to arrive.

He was almost ten minutes late. Tamsin had been just about to text him when she heard the entryphone ring. She took a deep breath and picked it up.

"Hello?"

"Tamsin? It's me, Nicky."

Warmth flooded her face and throat at the sound of his voice. "Hang on, I'll buzz you in."

She hung up the phone and pressed the button to unlock the downstairs door. Then she ran to the bathroom for a last look at herself in the mirror before racing back. She could hear his boots thumping up the stairs and she held her breath until he reached the door, opening it before he could knock.

To her delight, he had worn her favourite shirt. It was a deep silky black with vivid green pinstripes. He always wore black but the green brought out the colour of his eyes. She stilled her trembling hand against the door as she closed it behind him.

"Smells good," he said.

Tamsin smiled. And when he told her she looked nice she thought she would faint. "Want some wine?" she just managed to ask.

"That'd be great, thanks."

They sat side by side on the couch for a while, drinking from the chipped goblets Tamsin had found in a pagan shop. Every time he met her eyes she felt her stomach swoop as though she were falling from a great height. They talked about music, university, films, games, poetry, life. To Tamsin it seemed they talked for hours. She wanted to drown in his voice.

Eventually the talk turned back to Valhalla and Tamsin told him again how awesome she thought his songs were. What he said next made her want to pinch herself.

"I wrote a new song last night. No one's heard it yet. It's just me with no music and it's really rough but..."

"Yes," she said before he'd finished. "I'd love to hear it!"

He smiled shyly and lowered his head as he fished his iPod out of his pocket. Tamsin took it from him as though it were a priceless artefact and swapped it for hers in the docking station. She navigated to the track he directed her to and she sank back on the couch to listen.

It was all Nicky. Nothing but his voice. It sounded slightly husky and out of tune but none of that mattered. The song was called 'Blood Mirror'. And he was singing it just for her.

His hesitant voice sang about what lay beyond the mirror, what could be seen and what couldn't. Black mirror, velvet mirror. A reflection of dreams, of screams. Then nothing at all.

Tamsin felt the words circling her, seeking to enter her and redefine themselves according to her needs. A mirror revealed things. Sometimes hidden things. Like feelings. But try as she might, she couldn't make the lyrics fit. The song ended on a line about fangs and a reflection in blood and she realised that it wasn't about her at all. It was only a song about a vampire.

After a lengthy silence Tamsin opened her eyes.

"You don't like it." He said it with such dismay that she immediately felt guilty.

"Oh no," she assured him, "I loved it! I was just… imagining how the video would look."

She smiled then, picturing Nicky in period clothes, white lace pouring from his cuffs and collar, his razor-sharp cheekbones enhanced by the shadows of the gothic castle he would be prowling as he sang. He would carry a candelabrum, dripping red wax as he leant down over a sleeping maiden (Tamsin, of course), her pale throat exposed and vulnerable.

"Cool," Nicky said, relaxing. "I'm glad you liked it. I just wasn't ready to play it for the guys yet."

"I'm honoured to be the first," Tamsin said and she genuinely meant it. She had recovered from her initial disappointment. It didn't matter anyway. After tonight *all* his songs would be about her. "Are you hungry?"

"Starving."

"Good. Put on some music if you want and I'll get the food."

She left him on his own while she went to the kitchen and divided the curry into two bowls. Her hands shook as she removed the plaited coil of hair from where she'd tucked it inside her bra. She'd wanted to keep it close to her skin until the very last moment. With a pair of scissors she cut through it once to break the circle and then began snipping carefully along its length, cutting as finely as she could and sprinkling the tiny bits into Nicky's bowl. The pieces vanished into the liquid where she hoped they would be undetectable.

She put the bowls on a serving tray with a dish of jasmine rice and carried it in to him. Her hands were shaking but she managed not to spill anything. It seemed like a good omen.

"Here we go," she said. "I hope you like it."

And she could see that he did. He closed his eyes in bliss at the first bite and made appreciative noises throughout the meal.

She first sensed the spell was working when she caught him watching her as she refilled their wine glasses. When she looked up at him he averted his eyes and she heard his spoon scrape the bottom of his bowl. As a test she gathered her hair in her hands and piled it up on top of her head as though it were suddenly too hot to wear it down.

Instantly Nicky's eyes flicked back up to her and he stared openly as she twisted her hair into a loose knot, only to let it fall again. It spilled over her shoulders like molten gold. Nicky didn't blink.

"Still hungry?" Tamsin asked, nodding towards his empty bowl.

He rose slowly to his feet, shaking his head. He didn't take his eyes off her.

SHE WOKE SEVERAL hours later in a tangle of limbs, her hair spilling coolly over her naked skin. Late afternoon light was painting the room orange and she opened her eyes to look at Nicky. He was still deeply asleep. In his bliss he looked like a dark angel.

She tried to turn her head but found she couldn't. Locks of her hair were wound tightly around both his hands, as though she were his lifeline. Tamsin usually plaited her hair before bed but last night she had left it loose and wild for him. Tears welled in her eyes as she replayed the night's countless pleasures. Kisses and caresses, skin on skin, a blur of passion. Her dream come true.

She didn't want to leave him but nature was calling and it took some manoeuvring to finally slip out of his grasp. She took the opportunity to clean her face and brush her teeth, not wanting him to wake up and see her with panda eyes.

How he had loved her hair! She could still see the otherworldly shine in his eyes as he gazed at it in the firelight. His fingers had stroked it reverently, combing through the glorious waves and clutching handfuls of it as he made love to her.

"Beautiful," he'd said, over and over. Like someone in love.

She sighed as she gazed at the girl in the mirror. Her skin was flushed, her eyes dreamy. A girl fulfilled. Her scalp tingled pleasantly as she ran a brush through her tangled curls, each stroke hissing and popping with static. She dropped the loose hairs into the bin and stared down at them, remembering the spell she had cast. It had worked. She was a part of him now, forever.

"Tamsin?"

The sound of his voice made her jump and she shook herself out of her reverie. When she emerged from the bathroom she saw him standing before the window, his body silhouetted against the autumn light.

"I'm here," she said, curling into his embrace.

He kissed her head and then held her face between his palms, staring at her as though unable to believe she was real. "Last night was incredible."

Tamsin sighed as she let the words wash over her. There couldn't possibly be another person anywhere in the world as happy as she was at this moment.

"I have to see you again."

"I'm yours," she said, her voice catching.

"Mine," he whispered, sounding bewildered. He repeated it with more conviction. "Mine." Then he clutched her tightly and pressed his lips to hers so hard it hurt.

HE HADN'T WANTED to leave and she hadn't wanted to let him go. But they both had classes that evening and, frankly, Tamsin needed some time to recover from his attentions. She hadn't counted on him being such a violently passionate lover. Her insides burned with a deep dull ache and she wasn't at all surprised to find bruises on her inner thighs. Even her face felt bruised from his kisses. At times it had felt as though he were trying to force his entire body inside her, to devour her.

When she'd finally persuaded him to get dressed and follow her to the door, his eyes had shone with such fervour as he said goodbye that it became uncomfortable. She'd had to look away as she promised she'd see him again later that night.

Tamsin found it difficult to concentrate. Not even her favourite professor could distract her from the strange disquiet. She was thrilled that the spell had worked and the night had been truly magical. But Nicky's intensity was a little unnerving. There was something alien in the way he had looked at her as she'd shut the door that afternoon. After he left she'd gone to the window and was further unsettled to see him standing across the street, staring intently up at the building, his face a blank, pale oval. Not seeing her, but *searching*.

But then she shook off her misgivings. Of course, he was bound to be acting a little weird; she'd *bewitched* him! She hoped he wasn't wondering too much at his newfound feelings. It should have felt like coming home. But perhaps it would take a little time for it all to sink in. Until then she would have to be patient.

She glanced down at her notebook and saw that she hadn't written a single word. Professor Canning was talking animatedly about Walt Whitman but Tamsin hadn't taken in a thing. With a sigh she closed her book, gathered her things and slipped out at the first opportunity.

Her legs ached as though she'd overexerted herself at the gym and she grimaced as she made her way down the corridor. She pushed open the front door of the building and was dazzled for a moment by the glare of the streetlights. The nights were getting longer and the darkness only reminded her how tired she was. She'd barely had any sleep the night before; Nicky had seemed inexhaustible.

Despite her pain and weariness Tamsin felt a smile tugging the corners of her mouth as she recalled the past few hours. She knew that Valhalla had another gig at the end of the month and she dreamily imagined Nicky coiled round the microphone, his silky voice singing words he'd written for her, *about* her. She knew Rob didn't like her and the others would probably side with him in thinking she was breaking up the band. But Nicky was better than all of them put together. He could make it on his own if he had to, with Tamsin as his partner and muse.

As she made her way home she became aware of a soft crunching behind her, the sound of someone treading through dry leaves. A chill slithered up her back as she realised she was being followed. She braced herself for a confrontation and then whirled round.

"Hey, creep–"

But it was only Nicky. Her surprise gave way to delight, but her smile melted as soon as she saw his face. His eyes blazed, red and bloodshot.

"Nicky, are you OK?"

"I love you," he said.

His wild expression dampened the joy she should have felt. "But why didn't you say anything before? Why were you following me?"

He frowned. "I love you," he repeated, as if that explained it all.

"I love you too." The words came naturally to her. She'd said them hundreds of times on her own. But she said them now out of obligation and a sense of – yes, fear. There was something dangerous in his eyes, something akin to religious mania.

He took a step towards her and she flinched at his outstretched hand. But then a look of puzzlement crossed his features and she softened. She took his hand and kissed it, trying to remind herself that this was Nicky Renwick, the boy she had loved from afar ever since starting university. The boy she had now charmed into loving her back.

He shuddered as her lips touched his hand and he moved closer, winding his arms around her. He pressed his face into her hair and moaned softly.

"Nicky, no," she said, trying to disentangle herself from him. "I was just going home to try and get some sleep."

"We could sleep together," he offered immediately, still stroking her hair.

She forced a laugh. "I'm not sure we'd get much sleep." She cast about for more excuses. "Look, I need to do some major revision anyway. Why don't you come over tomorrow?"

He blinked at her slowly. "Tomorrow?"

"Yes. I'm really sorry but I'm totally knackered after last night. Hey, why don't you try to write a new song? Then you can play it for me tomorrow night."

Her words seemed to be causing him physical pain. His eyes glistened with tears at the rejection, although they widened slightly at the suggestion of a song.

"Tamsin," he murmured, as though tasting her name. "Yes. I'll write another song about you."

She heard the words in spite of her desire to get away from him. Her heart flickered with excitement even as she found the idea unsettling. *Another* song about her. When had he had time to write a first one?

"This afternoon," he said, answering her unspoken question. "While you were in your lecture. I watched you through the window."

The skin on the back of her neck prickled. He'd sat outside watching her, composing a song about her. And then he'd followed her. How long would he have kept it up if she hadn't heard him and turned around?

She forced another smile. "Nicky, that's really sweet. And I can't wait to hear it. But let's wait until tomorrow, OK? I really have to do some work."

For a moment he looked as though he wasn't going to accept her request. But then he nodded slowly and took a step back. "OK" was all he said.

The silence stretched between them for an awkward minute before Tamsin finally said, "Right, then. I'll see you tomorrow." She waited for him to say something and when he didn't, she turned and walked away. She could feel his eyes on her the whole time, burning through her. It was all she could do not to glance back. But she didn't need to. She knew he was still watching her.

She felt flooded with relief when she finally reached the flat. She closed the door behind her and flopped into a chair, exhausted by the strange encounter. Clearly the spell had been too strong, but was there any way to moderate it? She hadn't imagined it would be like this. Still, she was hopeful that it would mellow.

She was too wound up to sleep so she dropped her books on the dining table with the honest intention of trying to do some work. But it was useless. She couldn't concentrate. The dishes from last night seemed to mock her and the candles had dripped onto the tablecloth to form a waxy bloodstain that reminded her of the hairs she had plucked. Suddenly the flat felt close and stuffy and she pushed her chair away and went to the window. She jerked the curtains open and was about to open the sash when she noticed the figure standing by the streetlight.

Nicky was staring up at the building the way he had been earlier. Only this time he saw her. He raised one hand and waved faintly but Tamsin couldn't bring herself to return it. She was starting to get seriously creeped out.

She closed the curtains and edged away from the window. Maybe she should go back to the forum and see if anyone there had any ideas. She had just booted up her computer when she heard the thumping. As she made her way past the kitchen she realised with a sense of dread that she'd heard the sound before. It was the sound Nicky's boots had made on the stairs last night. As he came up.

Either she hadn't closed the outer door properly or someone else had left it open. She braced herself, expecting him to knock, but all she heard was a soft scratching.

The sound unnerved her more than any dramatic pounding could have done. Tears filled her eyes at the thought of him standing out there, too hooked on her to be able to leave her alone, reduced to scratching plaintively at her door like an abandoned puppy.

"Nicky?" she called, trying to keep her voice steady. "Go home, OK? Please? I've got a lot of work to do. Why don't you come back in the morning?"

He was silent for a moment and then she heard a ragged sob. "Tamsin," he said, his voice choked with tears.

Her heart burned with shame and pity and she couldn't bear the thought of the pain she was causing him by leaving him out there. It was her fault he was lovesick and desperate. What was that old saying about being responsible forever for someone whose life you'd saved? Surely the same applied to someone you'd bewitched.

With a heavy heart she turned the lock and opened the door.

He flew into her arms, burrowing his hands into her hair as he whispered fervently that he loved her, he loved her, he loved her.

"I love you too," she said helplessly, all the time wondering what the hell she was going to do.

He pulled away to gaze at her face. "You're so beautiful."

Last night it had thrilled her; now it made her skin crawl.

She pushed him away gently. "I have to use the loo," she said.

His blank expression betrayed no understanding but at least he didn't try to force his way in after her.

She splashed water on her face and stared at her haggard reflection. She suddenly looked ten years older. Maybe Beth or Chrissie had some sleeping tablets. She could knock him out while she figured out what to do. But a search of the medicine cabinet revealed nothing but an empty packet of birth control pills.

With a sigh she dropped the box into the bin below the sink. Then she glanced down at it. Something wasn't right. It took her a minute to realise what was missing. The loose hair she'd dropped into it that morning was gone. With a sinking feeling in her gut she suddenly understood what had gone wrong.

But she didn't have time to berate herself for her foolishness before the door crashed open and she cried out as she saw the look in Nicky's eyes. It was the stare of a starving animal, crazed with hunger.

"I love you," he said softly, his eyes fixed on her hair. He took a step forwards, closing the space between them. Tamsin immediately backed away. Confusion flickered in his eyes for a second and then he moved forwards again and reached out for her before she could move.

She shuddered as his hand settled on her hair and then he was winding it around his hand, pulling it hard.

"Stop it!" she yelped, flailing at his hand. "Let me go!"

He didn't seem to hear her. He continued to wind her hair around his fist, pushing her down onto the cold tiles as he did so.

She screamed when the hair at last tore free from her scalp. Blood poured hot and wet over her face and into her eyes, blinding her. All at once she couldn't breathe. She struggled frantically, her hands flailing against the side of the bathtub, feeling for anything she might use as a weapon. From somewhere behind her came a terrible sound. A wet munching. Sickness rose in her throat and she crawled away, slipping in the pool of blood as she felt for the open doorway.

She only got a few feet before she felt his hands in her hair again. The world went black with pain as he wrenched another fistful from her head.

The last thing she ever heard was his voice. Between hungry mouthfuls he whispered, "Beautiful."

THE ART OF ESCAPOLOGY

ALISON LITTLEWOOD

A large part of childhood is the desire for magic. As children we are drawn to the fantastical – whether it be The Lion, The Witch and The Wardrobe *or* Harry Potter *– and the need to believe in magic is a big part of growing up. Alison's story shows us what happens when we see behind the illusion and the losses that such a reveal can inflict upon us. This beautiful and charming tale will have you believing, but will also teach you a lesson in the consequences of believing too much.*

IT WASN'T THAT Tommy could imagine his dad in a circus. His dad was portly with thinning hair and liked to play Scrabble. He wore a suit and went out all day and did strange things in an office. He looked at Tommy now with a blank expression and blinked slowly, in much the same way a tortoise might.

Tommy shifted in his chair in frustration. He clutched the flyer more tightly, waving it at his dad.

Amazing feats, the flyer said.

Amazing feats and mind-blowing escapades! See the incredible bird woman! Death-defying trapeze fliers!! Acrobats!! Fire swallowers!!! Mysterious warrior monks!!! Magic performed before your very eyes!!!! See feats of wonder hitherto unknown to man!!!!!!!

It was this last that had stuck in Tommy's mind. Feats of wonder hitherto unknown to man: yes, he thought when he saw it. *Yes.*

Now the look in his mother's eyes said *no*, or at best, *maybe*. But Tommy knew what he wanted. He wanted to sit in the big top, with all the other kids. He wanted to hold his breath with wonder. He wanted, if he got scared, maybe just a little, to look aside and know that his dad was there. It wasn't that he didn't want his mum, but his mum always took him places: football, piano lessons. It wasn't anything special, and this was special.

"Dad," he said. "Please." He tried to keep the whine out of his voice, because his dad didn't like the whine, would sigh and turn away. It was there anyway, a little bit. His dad looked at him sharply.

"*Please*, Dad." Tommy waved the flyer again. He saw that the touch of his fingers had smudged the ink: it was already spoiled. He felt disappointment tugging on his lips.

When he looked up, his mum was watching him. She sighed, too.

"Oh, take him, love," she said, and that was that.

Tommy sat back in his chair and turned his attention to breakfast. He tried not to smile too broadly, but he was holding it inside him, a trapped and wriggling thing. He couldn't stop it any longer: it broke out onto his face in a broad beam. He heard his dad's resigned sigh from across the table, but it didn't matter. His mum had made a decision, and when his mum had made a decision, it stayed made.

TOMMY HAD THE flyer in his pocket as they walked from the car park towards the recreation ground. He could see the tops of the tents, one tall white point dominating them all. "That's the big top, isn't it, Dad?"

Dad grunted. There were other people walking all around them, parents with kids, the figures ahead of them outlined by golden evening light. Tommy thought it was magical. Excitement thrummed through his legs, making him skip along. They passed a huge poster with a big arrow on the bottom. *Death-defying feats!!!* it said in big red letters, and there was a picture of an acrobat plunging through the air, not a trapeze or a safety net in sight.

"Look, Dad." Tommy pointed.

"They like their exclamation marks, don't they?" Dad muttered.

THEY DID LIKE their exclamation marks. The ringmaster wore a red sequined jacket and a splendid red top hat. He even looked like an exclamation mark, standing there tall and thin and straight and strident in the centre of it all, and everything he said seemed to end in three or four, falling invisible from his mouth and hanging in the air. All was dark except the glitter of his clothes; he was lit by a single spotlight.

"Next," he said with a sweep of his arm, "we bring you the amazing bird woman!!!"

Incredible, thought Tommy. The leaflet said she was *incredible.* But it didn't really matter. The ringmaster was gone and instead a new spotlight shone, this time high in the air. A woman stood there, bright with feathers. There were white ones and pink ones, but mainly they were blue. She wore a tightly curved smile. The audience gasped as the incredible bird woman launched herself from her perch and into the air; but she wasn't flying. Tommy focused on her hands, where they grasped a small trapeze. She somersaulted and caught hold of another and everyone clapped. Tommy didn't clap.

From somewhere beneath them came the sharp high calls of birdsong. It didn't sound like real birdsong. It was cut through by crackling; it sounded like Dad's old record player, the one that played funny black discs, only louder.

Tommy leaned towards his dad, but he didn't say anything. His dad was staring up, intent on the woman. Tommy looked up too in time to see her do another somersault, a double one this time, and something fell from her and drifted down through the air.

He almost lost it in the dark; then it was in front of him, and Tommy reached out and grabbed it. It was a feather. It was a dirty grey feather, such as a pigeon might let fall. There was a dab of flaky blue paint on it, and a blob of dried glue on the quill.

Tommy nudged his dad. "It's not real," he said.

"Sh. Of course it is, son." Dad was still looking up; he started to clap, enthusiastically, with everybody else. He turned and Tommy saw his dad's wide grin, white and shining in the dark.

THEY WATCHED MORE of the death-defying trapeze fliers, the acrobats and fire swallowers. The mysterious warrior monks feinted with broad swords and dodged them. They were only playing at it, Tommy could see that. He clapped, but only just touching the palms of his hands together. It wasn't what he had expected. The acts weren't death-defying, not really. The trapeze artists even had a safety net. The poster hadn't shown a safety net; it hadn't been mentioned in the flyers. *Feats of wonder,* he thought. *See feats of wonder hitherto unknown to man!!!!!!!*

"It's not real," he whispered again.

His father answered: "Of course it is, son."

Now everything fell quiet. Everything was dark. Tommy waved his fingers in front of his eyes and dimly saw them, shining green. He turned and realised they were lit by a fire exit sign and he sighed.

"Now," the ringmaster said, "we shall see our most daring act of all. We shall travel to the farthest reaches of the earth to bring you – nay, *farther*. For why should we show you an imitation – a mere facsimile of magic, when we may bring you the real thing? Now, for your entertainment and edification, we travel *beyond*"

– he waved his hand dramatically – "Yea, I say to you, we travel even beyond the veil, to bring you – *real* magic!!"

Unseen exclamation marks danced in the air and the ringmaster swept away. Now a new figure stepped forward. This one was cloaked and hooded, but his costume was plain: plain black.

At first, he didn't speak; he simply waited. Then, slowly, something lowered itself towards him. It was a white, twisted thing, lowered on a chain from the top of the tent. He reached out and caught it, held it out for the audience, spinning it so they could see. Tommy realised it was a straitjacket; only that.

"The great Houdini," he said, "was born in 1874 and left this life in 1926. There has never been an escapologist to match him." He spoke softly, but his voice carried around the ring. There were no exclamation marks, but Tommy sat up a little straighter.

"Tonight, for your – *amusement*" – here he sounded contemptuous, even bored – "I shall summon the great Houdini to perform for us again."

Silence. Nobody moved. It seemed to Tommy that nobody even breathed.

"I shall conjure him from beyond the grave, his wonders to reveal. But first, I need a volunteer."

Tommy's hand shot straight up in the air like a... like an exclamation mark.

The man looked into the audience, made a show of shading his eyes. He pointed. "There," he said, and Tommy's heart sank; he wasn't pointing towards Tommy. There was giggling, a hand rapidly withdrawn.

"Very well," the man said. "Then where?" He searched the audience. His gaze lighted – or *seemed* to light, because Tommy couldn't see his eyes, couldn't see his face at all – on Tommy. "Too young," the man said, and Tommy's heart sank. "I fear you would slip straight through the bonds, my boy." Everyone laughed, but Tommy didn't.

"Your father, perhaps."

Tommy froze. His dad shifted in his seat. He would say no; Tommy knew he would say no. "*Please*, Dad," he whispered.

At first, Dad didn't move. Then, slowly, he stood, and the big top burst into applause. "In for a penny," he muttered, and made his way down into the ring.

When Dad was standing in the centre of the arena he didn't look like Houdini. He looked like a man from an office who had found himself in a circus, the spotlights picking out the shine of his balding pate and the sawdust sticking to his shoes. He shifted uncomfortably, picking at his trousers with the tips of his fingers as though he didn't know what to do with his hands.

"Just relax." The voice emerged from the cloak. It was low and quiet, but Tommy heard it.

The man raised a hand and put it on Tommy's dad's head. Dad's eyes darted around the ring as if looking for an escape. There was no escape. The man in the cloak started to chant, low at first and then higher. There were words in it, but Tommy couldn't catch them; it was as if they were all blended together. He couldn't work out if he was speaking English or some other language. It seemed to go on for a long time. Tommy's dad stood there, quite still, and his eyes were closed, though Tommy hadn't seen him close them. His face looked sweaty, shining in the spotlights now as brightly as the bald bit on his head. The man sitting in front of Tommy whispered something: he caught the word *hypnosis*.

All fell quiet once more. The man in the black cloak drew a deep breath, then he spoke. "Come to us," he said. His voice was not loud but it was powerful and it echoed about the ring: perhaps *beyond* the ring.

Come to us.

After a moment, Tommy's dad opened his eyes. He blinked in much the same way a tortoise might.

The man in the black cloak stepped back and bowed. "Please," he said, "will you introduce yourself."

Tommy's dad looked up at last. He saw the audience, ran his eyes around it. He half raised one hand, let it fall again. Then he threw his head back, stood up straighter, and glared, his eyes suddenly intense. "I," he said, "am Houdini."

There was no preamble, no *great* Houdini or *incredible* Houdini, but Tommy could hear it in his voice: that was who he was. The Great Houdini.

His father looked up and saw the straitjacket. Slowly, he stripped off his shirt. He stood there, the spotlight picking out each grey hair on his chest, and Tommy looked at them. He wriggled in his seat; but nobody laughed.

His father walked around the straitjacket. He stood behind it and reached out both arms as if he was going to dive into it, but instead he waited while the cloaked man removed the garment from the chain and started to strap him in.

Tommy blinked. His dad was standing there in his black suit trousers, his arms crossed over his chest, bound in a straitjacket. He didn't look like a man from an office any longer. He owned the arena with his steely gaze. He looked up towards the ceiling. "Now!" he commanded.

The cloaked man took the chain and secured it to Tommy's dad's feet. Then he stood back and the chain began to withdraw into the air, taking Dad with it. Eventually he hung there upside down, spinning a little one way and then the other. Music rose from beneath the seats, the kind of music that said something was going to happen; then it stopped, and Tommy's dad started to writhe, faster and faster, whipping and twisting his body as though a demon were trapped inside. Then a white strap swung free, wrapping itself about him as he twisted some more, and then there was another and Tommy realised his dad's arms were spinning inside them. Then they were loose and he was pulling the garment from his body, throwing it in triumph down to the sawdust below, flinging it away from him in contempt. He hung there, his body shining with sweat. Tommy couldn't stop staring.

But that wasn't all. Tommy's dad's arms hung loose only for a moment; then he lifted them towards his feet. He did something to the chains and they snapped free. Everyone gasped. Tommy inched forward. Surely, his dad was going to fall. And he *did* fall, he just let go, but he turned in the air, landed neatly on his feet and snapped out a sharp bow.

The audience erupted in applause and whistles and shouts. Tommy heard the man in front of him mutter, "He's a plant," but he didn't care, was too busy clapping and shouting along with the rest, and grinning, he couldn't stop grinning, especially when his dad left the ring and climbed back up the steps and took the seat next to his. Tommy was still clapping as he turned to his dad. "That was brilliant, Dad," he said, and his father kept in role, was so cool about it all, *his* dad, and he just turned to Tommy and gave a single steely-eyed nod.

Later, when the show was over and they were filing out of the big top, Tommy was still grinning. "It was real, wasn't it Dad?" he said.

His dad just looked back at him, quite calm, still being cool. "Of course not, son," he said.

THE NEXT DAY was a Saturday and when Tommy woke, the first thing he thought of was his dad, suspended from a chain, swinging in the air. He grinned and went downstairs and found him sitting at the table, eating cornflakes. His mum was standing by the dishwasher.

Tommy grinned and sat next to him, poured cornflakes from the packet. He usually had semi-skimmed milk but today he chose skimmed, just like Dad, and he started to eat, kicking his legs. His mum brought him orange juice. Dad just ate, looking at the tablecloth.

"Shall we try more escapes today, Dad?" Tommy asked. "Did he tell you, Mum? It was *incredible*." He relished the word, rolling it around his mouth with the cornflake crumbs.

"Don't speak with your mouth full," she said. She looked tired; there were bags under her eyes.

"But..."

"I said be quiet." Mum started loading the dishwasher, clattering plates into their slots.

Tommy looked at Dad, but Dad didn't look back. He wasn't just looking at the tablecloth, he was *glaring* at it. Slowly, he turned and looked at Tommy. "I need chains," he said. "And locks. Where do I buy chains and locks?"

There was something about his voice. He must have been speaking with his mouth full too, but Tommy didn't care. "Yes!" he said. "We can go to the hardware shop."

"Finish your breakfast first," said Mum. "And don't forget to brush your teeth."

LATER, WHEN THEY were dressed and their hair and teeth were brushed, they went to the hardware shop. Dad walked in and stood there, staring, but Tommy asked where the chains were and took Dad's hand and led him to them. Then Tommy's dad seemed to come alive. He walked along the row of chains – gold ones, silver ones, fine ones, thick ones – and he turned and walked back again. He took hold of the fattest silver chain and yanked it between his hands, testing its strength. He grunted. He started to pull it from the reel, faster and faster, spilling piles of it onto the floor. A couple passing them in the aisle tutted and stepped aside, but Dad didn't seem to care.

Someone in staff overalls came by and stopped. "Do you need any help, sir?"

Dad didn't answer.

The lad looked down at the pile of chain. "I'll get you a trolley, sir," he said, and wandered off, shaking his head.

When the chain was in the trolley, Tommy's dad went further up the aisle. They had rope there, twists and twists of it, fat rope and thin rope and bright, colourful bendy rope. He added lengths of that, too, to the trolley. Then he turned and saw the padlocks and he smiled.

"What is it, Dad?"

No answer. Tommy followed his dad as he went to the padlocks, started to throw them, one after the next, into the trolley. Tommy just stood there. He suddenly felt he might as well be invisible.

"Dad?"

His dad stopped throwing the padlocks. He turned and looked at Tommy. No: he *glared*. His eyes were sharp, piercing. There was no recognition in them. Tommy took a step back. "Dad?"

Dad looked down at the trolley, at the things he was going to buy, and his gaze became soft. Tommy swallowed. "It was real, wasn't it Dad," he said.

Dad looked back at him. His look was intense; there were depths in it. It was as though his gaze could lead somewhere else; somewhere *beyond*.

"Houdini," Tommy whispered, but his dad didn't answer. There was no expression on his face at all.

THEY PULLED UP outside the house and Dad started to unpack the boot, winding loops of rope around his shoulder. When he couldn't carry any more, he went inside. Tommy watched as Houdini unloaded the rope into the middle of the lounge and went back for the chains. He came back, dumped the whole slithering pile on top of the rope.

Tommy's mother came downstairs. She stood in the doorway and her eyes widened. "What on earth is that?"

Houdini looked at her. His mouth curved into a smile. "Rope," he said. "Chains." He said each word carefully, each sound distinct and clear. "Locks."

"Well, you're not putting them in my lounge," Mum snapped. "You can put them in the garage. Go on." And she made little shooing gestures with her hands as Dad glared at her, then bent and started looping chains, once more, about his person.

TOMMY WATCHED AS Dad wrapped the chain around and around his legs, and up, over his thighs, around his waist. He was wrapped tight as a cocoon, and soon he couldn't go any higher. He held out the rest of the chain towards Tommy.

Tommy pushed himself away from the wall and took hold of it. Houdini held his arms by his sides, quite still, while Tommy wrapped him the rest of the way. The chain ran out just as it reached Houdini's neck.

Houdini nodded towards the padlocks, but he didn't need to: Tommy understood. He picked up a lock and secured the end of the chain. He told himself it was going to be *incredible*, and his heart was beating fast, but it didn't feel incredible: it felt odd. Dad's balding head shone under the single bulb that struggled to light the farthest corners of the garage.

Dad nodded. Smiled. There was a faint chink of metal as he flexed his arms. Then, voilà! In one movement the chain fell away from him, landing on the floor at his feet. He smiled, took a sharp bow. Tommy didn't clap. He didn't laugh. He couldn't seem to move; couldn't do anything, least of all look away from his father's shining eyes.

"SO, WHAT HAVE you two been doing all day?" Mum was busying herself about the kitchen, cooking the dinner. Steam rose around her. She wiped her hand across her brow, rubbed them on her apron.

This time Tommy didn't answer: his father did.

"Escaping," he said. He wrapped his mouth around the syllables, pronouncing each one quite clearly. "I – escaped."

"Very nice." Mum didn't look as if she thought it was very nice. She wiped her hands again, this time on a tea towel.

"I am leaving." Houdini waved towards the door. He smiled a slow smile, but he didn't look at Tommy and he didn't look at Tommy's mum. He kept his eyes on the door, which stood slightly ajar; a light breeze came through it, stirring the steam that filled the air.

"Not now, you're not," Mum snapped. "Now you can sit down and eat your dinner."

Houdini turned towards her, a puzzled expression on his face. He met her eye and they stared at each other for a long time.

Then Houdini sat down and he ate his dinner. He kept looking up as he did it, not at Tommy and not at Tommy's mum but above them, over them, *beyond* them.

DAD DIDN'T GO to work on Monday, or the day after that. He didn't sit around the house either; he didn't get under Mum's feet. He spent his time in the garage. Tommy knew this because Dad was in the garage when he went to school and he was still in there when he came home. He walked in one evening and found him standing with his shirt off, flexing his wrist backwards and forwards, pulling his hand in towards his arm and then back the other way.

"Flexibility," he said. "Strength. Courage."

"Courage, Dad?"

His dad bent and picked up the end of the pile of chain and held it out to Tommy. Tommy looked at it dubiously.

"Courage," Dad said. It didn't sound like a statement: it sounded like a command.

TOMMY WRAPPED HIS dad in a length of chain. This was new chain, stronger than before. He had grown adept, too, at tying knots in rope: his dad had showed him how. Tommy hadn't known his dad knew how to tie knots, but it seemed he did. He gave Tommy detailed instructions, guiding his hands.

This time, though, it was chain, and padlocks, and handcuffs. Tommy didn't know where the handcuffs had come from. He secured one around his father's wrist, felt the lock snick into place, and he looked up and met his eyes.

"You're not really Houdini," he said. "Houdini lived in America. I know. I looked him up."

Dad looked back at him. After a moment, the handcuff fell from his wrist and clattered to the floor.

"You don't sound American. You sound posh," said Tommy, but his dad only smiled; it didn't look like his old smile.

"Did you know Houdini didn't believe in magic?" Tommy pressed. "I mean, he did *stage* magic. But he didn't believe in real magic. There were these people who said they talked to ghosts, and Houdini went around proving they couldn't. He didn't believe people could talk to the dead. He didn't believe they could come back."

He stopped. Dad was staring at him, and suddenly Tommy felt afraid. He took a step backwards, almost tripped over a pile of rope.

"Get out," Houdini said.

"What?"

"*Out.*" Houdini's voice was white hot; his voice was cold. He shrugged his shoulder and a loop of chain fell to the floor, freeing his arm. He pointed towards the door. "I said get out," he said, and every single word of it was perfectly clear.

THAT NIGHT, TOMMY found a recording of Houdini's voice on the internet. It had first been recorded on wax cylinders in 1914, but there it was, under his hands; he clicked on the file and Houdini's voice filled the room. Houdini spoke quite clearly. He enunciated each individual sound of each individual word. There was only the slight twang of an American accent when he said the word *dollars*.

*   *   *

DAD WAS LIFTING weights when it happened. He had taken to keeping them in the lounge, under Mum's feet, but she hadn't said anything about it, hadn't tried to stop him. She kept to the kitchen these days. Tommy noticed how she would walk out of a room when his dad walked into it. Quite often, Tommy would walk out too.

This time he'd thought his dad was in the garage, practicing. He wasn't sure what he was practicing *for*, only that he was always there. He was building something in there, too: a wooden crate, its proportions a little bigger than a man. Tommy wasn't sure what it was for, but he thought he could guess.

Now he walked into the lounge to watch TV and found his dad was there, raising a dumb-bell to his chest. Dad's chest was naked. Tommy could see the little grey hairs on it, but he could also see that it had changed, was stronger, more muscular. He looked away. His dad didn't move, didn't set down the dumb-bell. He made a little sound in the back of his throat. "Tommy."

Tommy's head whipped around. It hadn't been Houdini's voice: it had sounded like his dad.

"Tommy, I'm in here. I can't get out."

Tommy rushed to his dad, put his hand on his arm. "Dad, it's me," he said. "Where are you? Where?"

Dad's eyes hardened. "Move – aside," he said, and Tommy jumped away from him, and Dad set down the dumb-bell and then he picked it up and lifted it again.

LATER, TOMMY GOOGLED the circus. He had found the old flyer, smoothed it out, read the words through the smudges of ink. The circus didn't seem to have a name. He searched for the dates it had visited, for where it might have gone. He couldn't seem to find it. He examined the flyer again.

Amazing feats, he read. *Amazing feats and mind-blowing escapades.*

He felt tears stinging his eyes. He didn't want amazing feats or mind-blowing escapades. He didn't want to see magic; he certainly didn't want anything hitherto unknown to man. He only wanted his dad back again, the one who wore a suit and went to work and who liked to play Scrabble, and that was all.

ONE DAY, TOMMY'S dad was gone. Tommy looked into the garage to call him in for tea and he found the room empty, the bare bulb a single spotlight shining on a chipped concrete floor. The chains had gone too, as had the rope and the locks. He had vanished, just like that: escaped, leaving not a trace of himself behind.

SOMETIMES TOMMY TRIED to talk to Mum about his dad, but she wouldn't have it. She'd purse up her mouth and sniff, or start talking about something else very loudly, even if she had her mouth full. He'd hear her on the phone sometimes, talking to her own mother, something about *strumpet,* or *hussy,* and he didn't know what those things were, except that they were bad. If he tried to mention it, though, she'd leave the room and slam the door. Sometimes she'd just look at him, and there would be such sadness in her eyes, such an emptiness, that Tommy would shut up all on his own.

There was once, though, when his mother broached the subject. "He wanted to be like Houdini," she said. "He wanted to get away." They were having their supper, and Tommy had been miles away in his thoughts, or wanted to be; but as it turned out, they hadn't been so very far from each other after all.

"No, Mum," he said. "He *was* Houdini."

"Stop that nonsense," she replied, although her voice was kind, quite unlike the way it usually sounded these days. "He wasn't Houdini, he was your dad. But he wanted to be." Her voice went distant. "He wanted to be, didn't he."

"Yes, Mum." Tommy subsided, though he didn't think his words were true, not really. "He wanted to be."

And she went on eating, and she didn't look at him, though she had two livid blotches on her cheeks, just as if she'd been slapped, or as if she'd been crying.

TOMMY'S DAD NEVER came home after that. The years passed and he grew up, started to get into video games and seeing movies with his friends, and after that, girls. He once came across the flyer for the circus when he was sorting through his things, and he let out a 'tch' sound as if he'd been bitten, and he screwed it into a ball. He didn't pause to read it; saw only a string of exclamation marks flying through the air as he threw it into the bin.

THAT YEAR, HE was sixteen. He had met a girl – a nice one this time – and he caught the bus at the end of the road to take him into town. He was going to meet her there, and she would smile and wave and call him Tom, because everyone called him that now, he didn't want to be Tommy any longer. And he went to the back seat of the bus and sat down and propped up his knees on the seat in front. He turned and smeared the condensation on the window with his sleeve.

The familiar streets passed by until they grew wider and busier and the buildings grew taller, and Tommy looked out at them all, looking up at the formless grey sky, wondering if it would rain. It might be nice if it did; he could shelter his girlfriend under his coat, the way they did in films, and it would be funny, and give them something to talk about. Later, they might even kiss.

The bus swung around the last long curve of road before it reached his stop, passing the wide square in front of the town hall, and he sat up straighter and his feet dropped to the floor and his mouth fell open. He wiped the window, once, twice, and pressed his face up against it.

There was an escapologist in the square, standing above everyone else at the top of a flight of steps. There was a big crowd spread below him, and Tommy could hear them even over the throaty engine of the bus, laughing and clapping. The escapologist was all wrapped in chains, a silver coil that went around and around his body, holding his arms fast to his sides. He was smiling. He looked happy. He made a small convulsive movement and a coil came loose and a cheer went up.

Then the man grew still. He was looking towards the bus. Tommy recognised his dad at once; his piercing stare, his balding head, though what hair he had was longer now, growing wild around his ears.

His eyes, for an instant, met Tommy's. Tommy saw his dad squint; he looked as if he was trying to remember who Tommy was. In the next moment, he was gone.

The bus turned the corner and Tommy pressed himself against the window, trying to keep the man in view. He was too late. All Tommy could see, as the bus carried him onward, was a pile of chain; it was all that remained of his father, lying lank and shining and useless on the ground.

THE BABY

CHRISTOPHER FOWLER

Rock and roll and the Dark Arts have always had something of a relationship. It's called the Devil's Music for a reason. However, rather than taking the rather predictable Satanic path with his shocking story, Christopher opts for something far far darker. This is a genuinely horrific tale and shows us the consequences of the corruption of magic

THE DINGY EDWARDIAN pub was called The Grand Duke, but there was nothing grand about the place now. Its windows were covered in peeling gig posters, but half of the bands advertised had since split up, so that only their flyers survived.

Inside, the pockmarked walls and jaundiced ceiling had absorbed a century of cigarette smoke and spilled beer. Bands occupied a rickety stage at the rear of the old saloon bar.

The Duke no longer attracted the music stars of the future. Instead it hosted the bands of the past, those singers who had been granted a brief moment of fame, only to blow their main chance.

Onstage, a shaven-headed DJ in a ragged death metal shirt was selling raffle tickets from a blue plastic bucket. Sasha Field made her way through knots of students to the bar, where her new best friend Tamara was buying drinks. At sixteen Tamara was a full year older than Sasha, and could often get away with buying alcohol in this kind of pub. Tonight her luck was in, so she loaded up on another round of Red Bull vodka shots and lager chasers. Both girls went to the same school, and both had parents who would have been horrified to see where they were now. But that was the point; neither Sasha or Tamara wanted to do anything their parents wanted them to do.

They were here to see a band called Drexelle & The Iconics. Sasha had been raving about them, particularly the singer, but she hadn't stopped complaining since they arrived. The poster had used the wrong typeface for the band's name, they had put the lead guitarist above the singer when *everyone* knew it was Riley who was the real driving force; it was too hot, too crowded to see the stage properly. Tamara was beginning to wish she hadn't come along. And the place was seriously skanky. How good could a band be if it was willing to perform in a venue like this?

"Let's get closer," said Sasha, accepting her drinks and pushing forward. "We can get to the front."

"It's fine back here, we'll only get shoved around if we go further." Too late. Sasha was already on the move and all she could do was follow.

"Where did you get the money for those?" Tamara asked, looking at the yards of pink raffle tickets hanging from Sasha's fist.

"Karen's purse," Sasha replied, stuffing the tickets into her jacket. "She gives me anything I want. It's *so* easy to handle her. All I have to do is say stuff like how much I miss my real mother and she's like, buy yourself something pretty. A total pushover."

"I wish my parents were divorced. Instead they stay out of each other's way. Just as well, really. The thought of them touching each other makes me physically ill."

"Karen will get fed up with him eventually. She'll see what a sad old man he's become."

"Don't you ever hear from your real mum?" Tamara knew her friend was touchy about the subject, but had been wanting to ask for ages.

"She texts me all the time. She's just been really, really busy lately. I'm going to stay with her in the summer. She has a big house in Devon."

Tamara sensed it was probably best to leave it there. "What's the big deal with this band?"

"I keep trying to tell you but you don't listen. You'll see when the singer comes out. It's all about him. He formed the band, he writes all the songs. Drexelle's just a crappy one-octave three-chord player who does what she's told." Sasha downed the vodka shot and chugged some of the lager. Her face looked flushed and feverish in the lights of the stage. Tamara made a mental note to give her some cosmetic tips. In an effort to appear older, Sasha had plastered her face until it had a strange doll-like quality. *Not so hot for fifteen,* she decided. *Why has she slathered her makeup on like that?*

The band members filed onstage to unenthusiastic applause, took their positions and launched into their set without stopping to acknowledge the audience. Riley looked so skinny and craggy that he barely matched Sasha's memory of him. Drexelle had the wasted facial features of a seasoned heroin user. Sasha had been shown pictures of drug abuse at school. She had always known that Drexelle would ruin her lead singer's chances of success. The bitch was jealous of his talent. As soon as Riley started singing, Sasha lost herself in his molten silver voice and knew that she still loved him. When he sang, she was ten again.

The band played four songs in quick succession, and when they finished Tamara noticed that tears streaked her friend's face. Sasha was the only one there who knew all the lyrics. At the end of the set the applause stopped before the band managed to file offstage. The DJ pushed back on and made the announcements for next Saturday's show before drawing the raffle. He could have been reading out his shopping list.

"What do you win?" Tamara asked, trying to see if there were prizes on the stage.

"Tickets for concerts, but I don't want them," said Sasha, the spots from the threadbare lighting rig shining in her eyes. "One of the prizes is that you get to go backstage. It always is. That means you get to meet Riley. Hardly anyone else bought tickets and I bought loads."

"Wow." Tamara couldn't keep the sarcasm from her voice. How cheap was that? Riley had looked as if he didn't know where he was. Drugs and rock – it was all just so *predictable*. "So you don't win, like, a bottle of vodka or anything?" She couldn't see the point of wanting to spend any more time in the presence of the band than was strictly necessary.

"What are you talking about?" Sasha shouted back. "It's the best prize you could ever want. He'll go it alone after this and become one of the biggest stars in the world, he has to, and this is a chance to meet him now, before it finally happens for him."

"I think I'd prefer the vodka," said Tamara.

SASHA SAT ON a beer keg in the freezing brick corridor outside the dressing room, waiting to be summoned. The winning ticket had been held so long in her hand that it had become pulpy with sweat. She felt the heat of the alcohol she had consumed reddening her face, and tried to see herself in the smeary broken mirror on the wall above her head. The dressing room had originally been the pub's outside toilet, but the landlord had covered its roof and turned the side alley into a passage.

After twenty long minutes the door opened and Riley swung out. He had changed into tight black leather jeans and a brown, loosely woven sweater with holes in, and had slicked back his bleached hair. He smelled sharply of sweat, cigarettes and alcohol. "You the girl that won the raffle then?" he asked.

She nodded, unable to speak. The words she had prepared dried in her mouth.

"I've seen you before, haven't I. I never forget a face." He was clearly trying to think, but his eyes looked unfocused and dimmed.

"I was outside MTV for your first-ever live TV performance. I'm–"

"Don't say you're my biggest fan, like some kind of bunny-boiler."

"What do you mean?"

"An old movie, forget it. Drexelle doesn't like it when girls hang around the band. She's not very good at dealing with fans. She thinks they're rivals."

"That's okay, I came to see you, not her."

He tapped long fingers against his bony white throat. "You really did?"

"Of course. You're the talent. She just plays what you write."

"You like my writing?" He leaned back against the wall and folded his arms, studying her afresh.

"I know every song you've ever written."

"Even the bad ones?"

"There aren't any bad ones."

He laughed in surprise. "You're probably the only person who thinks that. Even Drexelle can't remember all the lyrics to my songs. Not any more. Is that it?" He seemed to be looking for the key to her.

"What?"

"You want to be a singer?"

"No," she said quietly, looking down at her shoes. "I'm not good enough for anything like that."

"Then what is it you want?" he asked, a smile forming. "What is it you want most of all?" He reached across and picked up her hand. Her fingers looked absurdly small in his calloused palm, as if they belonged to a doll. "Why are you here?"

"I wanted to meet you," she said simply.

She followed him down the corridor to a strange red-flock wallpapered room behind the stage. Once it had been part of the public bar, but now it was used to store canned drinks and cartons of snacks. He found some glasses and poured her a warm vodka and coke, then pulled the dust-cloth off an old sofa. They sank into the damp cushions beside each other and talked. Riley seemed so different offstage, so intense and connected to what she was saying, even though it was obvious that he'd been drinking. He wanted to know all about her.

"My life sucks," she told him, dropping her head back onto the split sofa cushions.

Riley leaned forward and studied her, placing his arm along the back of the sofa. "How old are you?"

"Sixteen," she lied. "Nearly seventeen. I've always been small for my age."

"Are you still at school?"

"Just for a little longer. I'll be leaving soon. I may not go to uni actually, I may want to start earning so I can move out and get a flat in town." It wasn't quite a falsehood; she hadn't discussed it with her father yet. Talking to Riley seemed to help crystallize her thoughts. "When did you leave school?"

"Me?" He looked shocked by the question. "Jesus, years ago. When we got our first TV break I really thought we were on our way. Turns out we weren't. We only got those chances because Tina's father paid for the demos."

"You mean Drexelle?"

"Tina's her real name."

"I didn't know that." Sasha was amazed. She thought she knew everything. It was all becoming clear. That was why Riley had kept her in the band. He had no choice; her father was picking up the bills. He didn't love her, he just needed her there to keep his career alive. Sasha's heart lifted. She turned and found him staring into her eyes with an intensity that was almost comical.

Without any further thought she raised her face and kissed him. And to her amazement, he kissed her back with a hard, probing tongue that parted her lips and slipped deep inside her mouth.

SASHA TOLD HERSELF she would not cry.

Tamara had gone home without her, leaving her to claim her prize. Now she wished her friend was here to help, but there was no-one she could turn to. She limped out of the filthy alley at the side of the pub and tried to pull her hooded jacket back together, but the zip was broken.

Her jeans were buttoned wrongly and the fly was wet with blood. The heel of her left boot had split, and the top of her thigh was so sore she could barely walk. Now that the booze-blast was wearing off, her head was burning. She had dropped her Hello Kitty purse somewhere, but did not want to go back and look for it.

She tried to understand how it had all gone so wrong, but could not even pinpoint the moment when she had lost the initiative. She had gone from encouraging him to slowing him down, gently resisting, then fighting him off, all in a matter of seconds. It was only when she had looked into his drugged, uncomprehending eyes that she realized the gravity of her situation.

She hobbled around to the front of the building hoping to find the landlord, but the pub was locked up and the lights were off inside. She realized that he probably knew what was going on, and didn't care. That was why the back room had not been locked; the band members were allowed unlimited use of it.

Tamara had asked why the raffle hadn't offered bottles of vodka as prizes. Why should they give away alcohol when the tickets could just as easily be used to deliver girls to the bands? She felt dirty and ashamed, disgusted with her own stupidity. Anyone looking at her now would be able to see exactly what had happened. It was as if she had been branded.

She had allowed a burned-out junkie to force sex on her, lying on a filthy couch in the back of a pub. No – not *allowed* – but she could have fought back harder instead of just begging him to stop. She had lost the most precious thing she owned and had ruined everything.

She could go back and accuse him. She could go to the police and tell them what he had done. But she was underage and they would want to know where she lived, and then they would insist on talking to her father. Nobody would understand what it had been like.

Even Tamara would not speak to her after this. No matter what she told people, it would be her word against his. She had beaten the raffle by buying most of the tickets and had chosen to go backstage – even Tamara would be forced to admit that. She had been seen hanging around outside his dressing room door.

She knew it would be obvious to others that she had been drinking. To accuse him publicly would be to expose herself to an entirely different adult world, one that she would not be able to control.

Although she had dropped her purse, she still had her Oyster card in her jacket pocket and could catch the Tube home, but it was brightly lit down there and she felt sure that the other passengers would stare at her in disgust.

She didn't think of the obvious word for what had just happened. It didn't seem entirely applicable. It wasn't as if he had jumped out on her in the park with a knife in his hand. In her mind, the line that had been crossed was scuffed and blurred. She was afraid that something had been irrevocably altered inside her. It wasn't just her fantasy that had been destroyed.

It was still raining hard outside, but for once she was glad. The obscuring downpour could cloak her guilt and hide her from others. She limped through the backstreets in tears, and even though she knew that it was too far to walk, nothing on earth could make her face the accusing looks in the underground.

Eventually she was forced to catch a night bus. She walked quickly past the other passengers with her eyes fixed on the floor, then slouched down on the furthest back seat. Her MP3 player – another gift from Karen – had been in her purse. She wished she had it now, so she could listen to music and shut her eyes and pretend she was somewhere else.

She returned to find the house in darkness. A note in the kitchen explained that her father had taken Karen out for dinner.

Sasha sat in her room and studied herself in her pink bedroom mirror, trying to gauge the extent of the damage. Her private parts felt raw and bruised, but apart from a thin scratch on the inside of her right thigh and a number of faint blue-grey bruises where his fingers had dug in hard, there were no other outward signs of coercion.

She threw away her torn jeans and pants, knotting them in a binbag, then ran a bath. Keeping the water as hot as she dared, she scrubbed at her body until her skin was red and tender. After drying herself, she put on the quilted pink dressing gown her mother had bought her and dug her old teddy bears out from the back of the cupboard. They smelled faintly of chocolate and childhood, so she arranged them along her pillows. Then she climbed into bed and swallowed a Temazepam stolen from Karen's bathroom cabinet. She fell asleep with *Beauty And The Beast* still playing on her computer. She resolved not to cry anymore; crying was for the blameless.

As she sank into unconsciousness, she tried to bury the terrifying thought that he had used no contraception and he had come inside her.

"WHAT WAS IT all for?"

Her father rose from his desk and walked to the windows. He could not let his daughter see his face, because he was close to tears. "Tell me, what was it all for?"

"All what, Dad? What are you talking about?"

"The private education, the extra tuition, all the effort your mother and I put in to give you a good moral grounding in life."

Sasha thought this was a bit rich coming from a man who had an affair behind his wife's back and then asked for a divorce when she announced she was willing to forgive him. She studied his shoulders, knowing that he couldn't bring himself to look in her eyes.

"I thought they gave you sex education classes precisely to stop this sort of thing from happening."

"I go to a convent school, Dad. The teachers' idea of sex education is to warn you not to have impure thoughts. They don't understand. Sister Prudence says that modesty and reticence are guardians of chastity. She's always going on about hygiene."

"You're just a little girl. The only reason your mother and I put you in that school was to ensure you got the right grades for university. Christ, it wasn't about religion."

"But that's what they drum into you, all day every day."

"You didn't have to pay any attention to that part. All you had to do was concentrate on your studies and be sensible around the mature boys."

"Well I'm not likely to meet any there, am I?"

He swung around to face her, and now she could see the fury in his eyes. "You went out looking for a boy, did you?"

"No, of course not. I didn't want this to happen."

"Then you should have listened to the sisters."

"Listen to them? You listen to them." She pulled the pamphlet from her satchel and read. "'For the Catholic girl there can be no impurity, no premarital sex, no fornication, no adultery. She must remain chaste, repelling lustful desires and temptations, self-abuse and indecent entertainment.'"

Harry waved the words aside. "I don't want to hear anymore of this."

"Neither did I, Dad. 'The follower of Our Lady must be pure in words and actions even in the midst of corruption.' There's no practical advice. It doesn't tell you there are boys out there that'll lie to your face and try to get you drunk just so they can—"

"You're not a complete idiot, Sasha, you're supposed to know that. It's just plain bloody common sense."

"Common sense? He pushed himself on me—"

"—and you did nothing to stop him."

"I tried to talk to him, but wouldn't listen."

"I don't understand why you didn't tell me earlier."

"I was scared. I saw the nurse and she said she would contact you, so I had to talk to you first."

"Well, thank God you're still under fourteen weeks." He was uncomfortable and wanted it to be over. "I'll arrange for you to enter a private clinic and no-one else need know. I can tell the school you've got flu. But before that you're going to tell me who did this to you. You're not leaving this room until I get his name and address."

"I can't tell you that," said Sasha. "I hate what he did to me but I can't ruin his life. It's his baby as well."

"What the hell are you talking about? You were raped, Sasha, he forced you to have sex with him against your will—"

There it was, that disgusting word. It made her feel diseased, marked on the outside so that all the world could see. She needed to reduce its stigma. "It wasn't entirely against my will," she said carefully. "I started out wanting him to, but he wouldn't stop. Look, I'll find him, and I'll find out if he wants us to keep the baby."

Harry threw his arms wide. "I can't believe I'm hearing this. Are you out of your mind? He doesn't want to marry you, he doesn't want anything to do with you, otherwise he wouldn't have done what he did. You think he has any respect for you at all? What, did he think now was a good time to start a family? You were just some silly schoolgirl he picked up and dumped, just like those tarts over in the council flats, the ones who've collected half a dozen kids from different fathers by the time they're twenty-five. You're no better than them."

"Is that what you think?" she asked quietly.

He looked into her eyes and relented. A moment later he had come to her side and was holding her in his arms. "You're my daughter, Sasha. You're my little girl. We have to sort this out. You can't protect him. Don't you see, he's shown he has no respect for you. What he did to you was illegal. It's something no man can do to a girl without her permission. Please, let me help you. We can solve the problem together. Promise me you'll think it over tonight, and we can talk again in the morning. I'll make the necessary arrangements."

She nodded. "All right." It was better to agree when her father was like this. Lying was a survival technique. "What are you going to say to Karen?" She could imagine her stepmother's first reaction. She had gone to the mall to have her nails painted. Hardly a day passed when she wasn't undergoing refurbishment.

"I'm not going to tell her anything, and neither are you. God, that would be the last thing she needs to hear."

"Why can't I talk to her?"

"She mustn't know about this. It was difficult enough when she found out I had a daughter. I can't turn around and tell her that she's about to become a step-grandmother."

"Is that all you care about? What she thinks? Are you going to tell my real mother? No, of course not, because that would mean speaking to her, and you're too ashamed of yourself to do that."

Sasha was angry with herself for losing her temper. It made her vulnerable. She rose and walked unsteadily to the door, praying that her shaking legs would support her until she was outside.

WHAT WE MEAN BY 'Termination.' Sasha re-read the pamphlet with growing horror. There was a full description of the process, illustrated with diagrams of a blankly smiling girl with her legs in stirrups. Despite all the assurances that the procedure was painless, it looked barbaric. She checked the number on her ticket. 38. They were only up to 14. It was all she could do to stop herself running from the room.

"Nervous?"

The young woman who had leaned over to talk to her was smiling pleasantly. She looked exactly like her favourite aunt, who had died at such a tragically early age.

"You shouldn't look at that," she said, indicating the pamphlet. "It will only upset you."

"It's awful," Sasha agreed. The bland pictograms lightened the horror of the situation and only made her think about it more. The idea of cold metal being inserted inside her to kill something: it was like a bayonet slicing into a baby's soft skull, something a Russian soldier might have done to a pregnant woman during the war.

"I know, it's terrible what they do to the little babies. They feel everything, you know. They're torn out and thrown into the bin, and they feel it all. They take a long time to die."

She had a soft American Mid-western accent. Sasha snuck a look at the woman. She was fortyish, dressed in a horrible knitted waistcoat and sweater, in very wide-beamed Guess jeans. Her shiny moisturised face was free of makeup, and her faded blonde hair was tied back to reveal hoop earrings, not real gold. She looked broke.

"I can't keep it," Sasha said, lowering her voice. "I'm at school."

"But can you really do this?" The woman examined her with unnervingly intense eyes. She stared at Sasha's stomach as if X-raying the unborn child.

"I don't have a choice." Sasha folded up the pamphlet decisively.

"But you see, you do," said the woman. "There is another way. One that will take away the little life inside you gently, without any pain."

"How is that possible?" asked Sasha.

"My name's Martitia," said the woman. "Your number won't be called for half an hour at least. I know this place. Let's go and get a coffee."

THE ROOM WAS overheated, the furnishings as nondescript and battered as those in any other low-rent business hotel near the railway terminus. It was the kind of place where you checked yourself in with a credit card and were issued with a pass key without having to see another human being. Where you might die in the night without anyone noticing.

"Make yourself comfortable, love," said Martitia, opening her nylon backpack. "The fifty pounds will just be to cover my expenses. I don't make any money out of this."

"Then why do you do it?" Sasha asked.

"Doctors use drugs and scalpels to conduct an operation that deserves to be more natural and sympathetic to the mother. I'm from a long line of healers who use more spiritual methods. Wouldn't you prefer that?"

"Yes, but–"

Martitia turned to study her with clear eyes. "The decision has to be yours, of course. But isn't that what you want?"

"I wish I could–"

"You can't keep the baby if you can't look after it. I'm sorry to be so blunt, but I want what's best for all you girls. I know the options must seem so black and white to you, to terminate or to keep, but there is another way." The eyes had softened now, misting with her own private grief. "That's why women like me do what we can to help take away your confusion and pain. It's about what's best for you. I imagine you've had enough of people accusing you or telling you that what you did was wrong. Now you need a more practical solution."

"What do I have to do?" asked Sasha.

* * *

THE PROCESS WAS old and not without its risks. It had been passed down among the womenfolk from one generation to another. Martitia told her to sit back and relax, but Sasha was nervous, and in the back of her mind there was a suspicion that she had made the wrong decision in coming here.

"If it helps, you can think of this as an ancient homeopathic remedy," said Martitia, sterilising a needle in spirit. "I need your blood and urine, just tiny amounts of each." Inserting the needle in the crook of Sasha's arm, she withdrew a small amount and emptied it into a plastic beaker, to which she added something pungent from a white paper packet, and a brown liquid. The combining process took just a few minutes. When she had finished, she asked the girl to remove her jeans and pants.

Martitia sang softly to herself as she donned a pair of plastic gloves with practised ease. It sounded like a folk tune, dirge-like and vaguely annoying, the sort of thing old people hummed as they pottered around their flats. "Now, I have to feel inside you, just as far as your unborn baby's head. It won't hurt, but you may feel some discomfort."

"Are you sure that–"

"You mustn't worry about anything. Why don't you just lay your head back on that cushion and close your eyes for a few minutes? I need to put some lubricant on, and it will feel cold. Try to think of something nice. Think of a time before all this happened, when you didn't have anything to worry about."

Sasha tried to relax but she could feel the chill, slippery wetness, the alien hand between her thighs. She thought of her mother, and of Riley singing on the player in her bedroom when she was ten. She thought of innocence and the sheer simple pleasure of not knowing. There was a brown stain on the ceiling, beer or a burst pipe. Martitia was humming again. The sound seemed to pass through her, washing away her apprehensions.

"There, how are you feeling?"

She awoke with a start. Martitia had removed her gloves and was washing her hands in the bathroom basin next door. Sasha raised herself and pulled up her pants, still a little sticky. "All right, I think."

"Well done. That's all for today."

"What do you mean?"

"There are two more treatments, exactly the same as the first. It has to be done over three days."

"You didn't mention–"

"Well, I didn't want to alarm you." Martitia came back into the room, drying her hands. "Just come back at the same time, and now that you know the procedure I imagine we'll be through in about twenty minutes." She went to the desk and wrote out her number. "Here you are, hang onto this. Call me if you need to move the appointment slightly, but it's important that you try to make it roughly the same time each day."

"What happens at the end?"

"At first, nothing. You won't feel any different. Then after about ten days you may feel a slight change – nothing very strong, just enough to make you want to go to the bathroom. You'll pass the – what would have been the baby. That's all. The very same afternoon, you could go swimming or play a game of tennis, although you probably won't feel like it. Every process we undergo takes something from us, but we're strong, our bodies can handle a surprising number of changes."

Martitia could not have been kinder or more solicitous, but there was something about her – the way she fiddled with her neck-chain, the occasional piercing stare – that bothered Sasha. Stepping back into the street she drew a lungful of cold air and felt suddenly safer in the uncaring crowds.

BACK AT THE house she avoided her father and Karen, who were arguing in a distant, weary manner about a weekend to be spent with Karen's family near the coast. She lay on her bed thinking about the baby, its tiny head anointed with – what, exactly? Some kind of ancient remedy that would send it to sleep forever, although she only had Martitia's word for that.

The TV was on with the sound down, some inane grimacing comedians and a singer with too much makeup. Riley could have been given his own spot on TV instead of this rubbish, but the programme makers were as stupid as their audiences. They had no imagination. If Riley hadn't been misled into drugs by Drexelle he would have become famous. He would have kept his beautiful innocence.

And then she realised; the baby was half his, which meant it was likely to be like him, and if she kept it the baby might grow up with a talent far greater and purer than its father's.

Once planted, the thought grew. Other young girls found ways to keep their babies, didn't they? What if she didn't go back to that awful hotel room? She had not given Martitia any way of contacting her. The woman had been completely trusting. She hadn't even been paid yet. And what had she been doing anyway, wandering around the vast waiting room of a hospital drumming up business for her home remedies? She had just wandered in from the street, on the con or simply mad, or perhaps some kind of creepy paedo-lesbian getting her kicks from young girls. And an American – weren't they all religious crazies hellbent on stopping abortions?

Three days of treatments. If she didn't go back it couldn't work, otherwise why would the woman have kept pointing out the importance of returning?

Sasha told herself she would decide in the morning, but she had already made up her mind. She would not go back.

The next morning she folded up the slip with Martitia's number and tucked it under her computer. Then she went back to school as if nothing had happened.

OVER THE NEXT few days she evolved the plan. She would lie to her father and say she had taken care of the problem. Karen would never need to be told of what had transpired. And when her jeans no longer buttoned up and the baby started to show, she would run away to her mother's house in Devon, where no-one would bother looking for her. She would call her mother soon, but not just yet. The time had to be right.

She tried to pretend that her meeting with Martitia had never happened, that she had not been persuaded to accompany her to a station Travelodge so that the crazy woman could fake some mumbo-jumbo in order to feel her up.

The passing days made her nervous, but when her period failed to reappear she relaxed, knowing that her baby was alive. On a rainy Saturday morning her father drove out with Karen, and Sasha sat in her bedroom downloading pictures of Riley. She printed them out and matched them with photographs of babies, trying to imagine what hers would look like. Would it have his incredible eyes? She thought of him, how he had been when he was still innocent, not about the corrupted thing he had become. She decided she had finally made a good match with the photographs when her mobile rang.

"Sasha, I have to talk to you."

She recognised the voice immediately, and almost hung up.

"Please, it took me a long while to find this number. I wouldn't have called, but we had an agreement."

"I'm sorry, I'll pay you the money I owe you."

"It's not about the money, Sasha. Why didn't you come back for the rest of the treatment?"

"I changed my mind."

"But we started the process. I warned you there were risks."

"I'm fine. I'm well. I'm going to keep my baby."

"You don't understand. The process isn't reversible. I explained this to you. Your baby isn't the same anymore."

"What do you mean?"

"It's not really fully alive."

"That's not true. You just want me to come back."

"I want what's best for you."

"You don't even know me!" Sasha cut the call and threw the phone onto her bed. It rang again, and she let it go to voicemail.

HER FATHER WAS spending more time with Karen's family at the coast. Since his daughter's loss of innocence, he was less inclined to spend his evenings with her. She was no longer the little girl he had loved so much. The couple went to Scotland for a week, leaving Sasha alone with the housekeeper, and he had barely bothered to say goodbye.

She wandered about the place looking for something to do. Tamara no longer spoke to her. Although the pregnancy didn't show, it was as if the change transmitted itself to other people, separating her from them. She felt different too; she had experienced something they had not, and it had matured her.

She was about to make coffee and watch a DVD when a sudden spear of pain cut across her groin.

It came in hot sharp stabs about fifteen to twenty seconds apart. As each attack subsided, it left behind an ache that felt like food poisoning. She made her way to the kitchen and filled a hot water bottle from the hot tap, pressing it against her lower abdomen, then lay down on her bed. The pain remained at the same level of intensity, each burst dropping back to a cruel, persistent gnawing. Finally unable to stand it any longer, she went to the bathroom and ran the tap until the water was nearly scalding.

She wanted to lower herself into it but was too frightened to do so, and besides, while the heat might deaden her pain it could also harm the baby. Placing her hands over where she felt the new life to be, she was certain she sensed something tiny shifting about, twitching and nipping, pulling at its life-cord. But whatever was inside her had altered somehow. It felt upset and anxious, but surely it was too small to experience such feelings?

She took two sleeping pills from Karen's bedside table and washed them down with cola. Then she undressed and fell asleep on her bed, hugging her old Edward Bear. It was a little after ten o'clock.

Her dreams were storm-tossed, crimson and violent, not scary but merely disorienting, strange and sad. She seemed to be tilting about on a raft in a hot red sea.

Then she awoke to find the bed streaming with her blood.

It had just turned midnight. The bedside light did not work. The street lights made the blood look black, and when she gingerly lowered her hands between her legs she knew the baby was gone. Using the light from her cellphone she searched through the bloody covers, sure it had somehow chewed through its cord and freed itself, but there was no sign of it.

She saw the trail, though. It led from the bed to the chest of drawers, smeary little prints on the cream carpet, first on all fours and then in tiny pairs, as if it had already learned to walk.

A wave of weakness overcame her, but as soon as she felt strong enough she pulled the dresser out and searched behind it. She found it in the corner, black and shiny with dried blood; an upright foetus with a bulbous delicate head and tadpole eyes, a mouth that would have been comical, so wide and gummy, but it just looked unfinished and unready to be born. She had arrested its development but the magic had allowed it to live on.

The baby was making a noise. It sounded like the folk-song Martitia hummed in the hotel room, but now some of the notes were wrong, and the melody was menacing. She found herself thinking *This is absurd, it's so tiny, what possible harm can it do?* But when it suddenly pulled itself away from the wall and took a faltering step toward her she found herself backing toward the door.

It hissed now, a startling high-pitched noise that resounded inside her head. What scared her most was not knowing what it wanted. She had kept the slip of paper with the telephone number on it. Snatching it from beneath her computer she fled from the room, convinced that the ugly little thing could not possibly travel any distance.

Dropping to the landing steps she punched out the number. It rang eight times.

"This is a strange time to be calling." Martitia sounded half-asleep. "I'm guessing the baby has left your body, hasn't it?"

"It's in my bedroom. I don't know what it wants."

"I can't help you now. You should have come back. It's not human anymore."

"It still has my genes."

"Yes, but in a mutated form. It's between two worlds. It's very hard to understand what such creatures want."

"Can't you do something?"

"I'm afraid not. I can't see you, Sasha. It knows I poisoned it and will only try to hurt me."

"What about me? What will it try to do?"

"It will either love you, or it will hate you."

"What should I do?"

"You must wait for it to tell you what it wants. Neither result is desirable. If it loves you it will try to hide inside you, where it feels warm and safe. It will tell you what to do next, because it is you."

"And if it hates me?"

"It will eat your flesh until it reaches normal size, so that it can continue to grow after you've gone. Soon it will make up its mind. Until then you must try to stay awake. It's dangerous to fall asleep."

"When I went near it, it started hissing."

"Then maybe it's already decided that it hates you. I don't know. It's clever. It knows exactly what you're thinking because it's a part of you. You can try to kill it, but it will know where to hide and how to hurt you. It knows what you really want. It will wait in the dark until you've fallen asleep. You can't run away, because it will always be near you until it gets what it wants."

"And what's that?"

"It will decide for itself. It will tell you."

"It's a foetus, you crazy bitch, how can it talk?"

Martitia sighed as if she'd had enough of the conversation. "It will. It's hard to explain. You see, it isn't really there."

"What do you mean?"

"I told you, it's between two worlds. Yours and his."

"You've seen this before?"

"Only once."

"What happened to the mother?"

Behind her there was a sound of scampering feet.

"What happened to the fucking mother?"

The sound of the baby was coming nearer.

She lowered the phone and held her breath, slowly turning. Behind her, no more than two feet away, the baby swayed in the shadows on shiny wavering legs, its blackened flesh cord hanging down like a puppet's cut string.

She stared down at it and tried to understand what it wanted.

The baby slowly raised its wet tadpole eyes to her and opened its gummy mouth to speak.

Its voice sang inside her head.

It said, *Let's kill Daddy.*

DO AS THOU WILT...

STORM CONSTANTINE

I first encountered Storm Constantine at Fantasycon, when I was but 17 years old. I didn't know Storm or her work at the time, but I picked up a copy of her novel Sign for The Sacred *and was very glad I had. There's a real warmth and complexity to Storm's writing, which the following story beautifully demonstrates. Storm writes movingly about how we empower ourselves and others through symbolic acts.*

FOLLOWING THE STRANGE affair with Brett Lyle it took Leah Metcalfe almost five years to realise the level of his scorn merited action. She might never have done anything, simply allowed the pain to heal and fade, get on with life, as you're supposed to do after a bereavement. She read stories in the media of men who conned gullible women out of all their money – she had always thought them rather careless women – but in her case of conning, Lyle, she felt, had cleaned out her soul rather than her bank account. Or at least he had murdered a little bit of it. She grieved for this sundered part, long after it was polite or sane still to be noticeably doing so. After the vanishing years of moping and longing, which had felt like some nightmarish enchanted sleep, she had eventually become utterly disgusted with the emotions and had put them away, at last awake, and aghast at herself for wasting so much time on what had ultimately proved to be nonsense. Only when her friend Sophie, in whom she had confided during the two years of her involvement with Lyle, brought his name up in conversation during one of their fortnightly lunch meetings did Leah think about him again.

The two women still met each other with an embrace and the greeting, "Blessed be," even though Leah had not been part of Sophie's magical group for several years. She and Sophie rarely spoke of such matters nowadays; their friendship was confined to the mundane. It had been Sophie who'd put considerable effort into maintaining their relationship; Leah was fully aware of this. Perhaps Sophie considered it a charitable act.

A few minutes after they sat down to their lunch, Sophie eyed Leah carefully. "Brett Lyle," she said. "I don't know if this is still a 'no go' area for you, but I thought you should know. It's just burning a hole in me. You weren't the only one, you know. He was still at it after you. Still is."

Leah shifted awkwardly on her seat. The cafe was hot, felt steamy. Outside cold rain hammered the shopping precinct, where women marched about their business. Some had bare legs. Rather unwise, Leah thought, in February. "I'm hardly shocked," Leah said, although just the sound of his name had shocked her.

"Well, of course. I realise that. But... Not everyone is as *aware* as you. Not everyone can get over *things* so easily."

Leah did not really think squandering years of precious life on mourning the loss of a man like Lyle could be described as being aware or getting over it easily, but decided to let this pass. Perhaps Sophie meant it as a compliment. "Why do you mention it? Have you heard something?" Leah realised she was in fact eager to know. She wanted to hear details of another woman's emotional car crash. *Inside, we are all ghouls*, she thought.

"This one is a lot younger than you," Sophie said, sipping her latte, "thought it was for real."

Leah coughed up a laugh. "And I didn't?"

Sophie screwed up her eyes briefly, shook her head. "Sorry, you know what I mean. She doesn't have your *experience*, you know? At least you *did* get over it. I saw the way you were. You did... *incredibly*." She grimaced. "Ack, whatever I say sounds crass."

"Don't worry about it, tell me what you know."

"It's this girl I work with. You've probably heard me mention her: Cassy."

"The one who got burned on a sunbed?"

Sophie smirked. "Yes, *that* one. Complete airhead, but a kind girl. I didn't even know about this *circumstance* until it was too late. We don't talk that intimately, you know. I just noticed something was wrong with her. She was... listless. Totally not like her. So I asked her. And this look she gave me... I recognised it, Leah. Made me shiver." Sophie shivered theatrically to emphasise her words, and Leah found herself freckled by a shiver too.

"She was haunted, *lost*..." Sophie continued. "For a moment she was *you*, and that was even before she told me his name."

"What a chilling coincidence."

"You seem to be taking this very calmly."

"I don't know what I'm taking yet, go on."

"Well naturally, she didn't spill her guts to me immediately. As I said, we're not that close, but she wanted to talk, I suppose, and simply told me 'this guy, he's doing my head in'. I just said something soothing like 'Oh men, bane of our lives, aren't they? Can't live with or without, as they say.' Cassy answered, 'yes, it's just like that,' then walked away from me, right as I was saying something else. At the time I thought it was rather rude."

Leah didn't interrupt or make any noises or gestures of encouragement. She found, in fact, she was becoming increasingly frozen and was aware of a soft whistling noise in her head.

"Cassy didn't get any better, and it started to affect her work. As her supervisor, I was eventually obliged to get her into the office and have a little talk." Sophie paused, clearly waiting for a signal Leah was listening or interested. "Are you OK with this?"

"Of course. Merely waiting to hear."

"You're not completely OK with it, are you? You just can't resist knowing."

"Then just tell me."

"The merest comment on Cassy's recent behaviour had her in tears. She told me she had a disease, and at first I took that at face value and thought she'd got herself into some embarrassing trouble, but even little airhead Cassy can speak in metaphor. I told her to tell me about it, and she did, then. What she described, the mind games, the hot and cold episodes, the yearning to escape, only to be reeled back in, it was familiar. I think I knew even before she found the courage to say his name."

"Lots of people behave like that, men and women alike," Leah said. "That kind of behaviour isn't confined to one man, or even one gender."

"It goes further than that with him, you know it does."

Vampire, Leah thought. "I'm not sure. My views on the man are hardly unbiased."

"Take it from me, it *does*," Sophie continued. "Cassy told me how she'd met him, how he'd seemed like a brother at first. He brought light to her, she said. She fell into love, like someone falling into a vat of acid; to be eaten away, slowly and painfully. They met almost every day – to *talk*. Sometimes, he'd lightly touch her... his eyes would hold her with promises he never said aloud. She wanted more and expected it, even dared to make subtle moves."

"And then the shutters came down."

Sophie nodded. "But of course not entirely, because that's not part of the game, is it? He knows how to drive someone crazy, so he cracked his knuckles and got on with it."

"Poor girl."

"When she revealed his name, I had to... I hope you don't mind, I didn't mention yours... but I told her I'd heard of him and that someone I knew had gone through the same thing. I told her she had to break contact immediately, because it could go on for years, him feeding off her; it would get worse, and never better."

"Did she listen to you?"

"Did she, hell! Did you?"

"And does she know about the wife?"

"Yes. She got the same story as you did, too pathetic and clichéd to be real, but utterly gobbled up."

Leah grimaced. "His problem is, he's bored and wants affairs, but lacks the balls to do anything physical about it. He's more conventional than he likes to think he is. It's no more than that, and some of us are stupid enough to think we can change people."

Sophie raised her brows. "Is that how you've cleaned it up in your head?"

"I believe it to be the truth. I – and also this Cassy – are just as at fault as he is. Neediness, insecurity, the garbage we carry around." Leah made a casual gesture. "Tell her that."

"You don't believe a word of that," Sophie said. "He has magic. He might not know it, but he has, and he uses it. Perhaps it's time for others who have it to take him to task."

"It's none of our business. Everyone is responsible for..."

"Leah, stop it, you've not heard me out. I spoke with Matty about it."

Matty was a mutual friend, who was also a friend of Lyle's. Leah still met him once a month for dinner. Lyle was never mentioned, probably because Matty still felt guilty for introducing Leah to Lyle in the first place. "What did he say?"

"He told me there had been two others, who he knew of, after you. Cassy would be the third. Apparently, the second one got out quick, although the first one was beaten up pretty badly by it. Matty only knew about them because they were part of his and Lyle's social circle and he saw it happening. He didn't know about Cassy. And gods know how many more there are! Lyle sucks the living energy out of people, Leah. It's food to him. Do you honestly think it's OK to know predators like that are hunting vulnerable people and not do something about it? Don't you want to help Cassy? She's helpless, she's... *bewitched*."

"What do you propose to do?"

"Turn a mirror on him," Sophie said grimly. "Throw that leech energy back at him. Make him taste his own self. If that doesn't choke him, nothing will."

"Pointless," Leah said. "He's impervious to magic, believe me."

"You sure about that?"

"Yes, because I threw the book at it. I tried everything to bring harmony into our sick situation, communication, honesty, all that bullshit..."

"Bullshit?"

Leah shook her head. "It was a waste of time. He's impervious."

"And *that's* what killed your faith in yourself," Sophie said, folding her arms and leaning back in her chair. Her expression had become flinty. "You lost your faith in magic, which is why you left the group. That's the truth, isn't it? The real bullshit was the excuse you gave us about how you'd suddenly become too busy to be spiritual."

Leah gestured helplessly. "I don't want to argue about this, we should drop it. I don't want any further... contamination... by even thinking about Lyle, never mind doing some ritual to try and bring him into line, which wouldn't work anyway."

Sophie wiped her hands over her face, sighed. "I remember a woman who believed we were capable of anything. I remember the amazing times we had, the energy we raised, the good we did. That woman was an inspiration. I can't – and don't want to – believe a shit like Brett Lyle could destroy that woman for good."

"I let him happen to me," Leah said. "If you must look at it in terms of magic, let's just say he was a test I failed. And much as I would like to see him gunned down in cold blood, never mind be given a civilised, chastening lesson in self-awareness and responsibility, it's unethical to try and influence another's will. You know that, Soph. We've always abided by that."

"But what about the will of those he targets?"

Leah shrugged. "Like I said, a test. We don't have to fall for it, but some do. And you mentioned the 'second one' who got away quick. She passed the test. There are no doubt others."

"I don't want to believe Brett Lyle is on this earth as a life lesson for vulnerable women," Sophie said. "That's too cruel to contemplate."

"Yes it is. It's bloody cruel. And however many rituals you do, or believe that the universe loves you and wants the best for you, the cruelty is still there. I'm sorry, Sophie. We should have talked about this before. Yes, I lost my faith. Magic is a comforting illusion, like the religions we so scorned, and there's nothing wrong in that, or the aim of groups like ours who want to make a difference. But at the end of it all, most of the positive results must be down to luck, or coincidence. I think focused will *can* move mountains, yes, but perhaps not to order, and not all the time. One thing I learned is that we are truly alone. There is no greater power looking out for us."

Sophie stared at Leah unwaveringly. "He should be tried for murder," she said.

LEAH WAS UNHAPPY at the way she and Sophie parted. She was unhappy that the truth was out, because she didn't want to hurt her erstwhile group mates. She knew she had been a kind of figurehead to them, so for that reason had tried to bow out subtly and slowly. She hadn't wanted them to know she simply couldn't believe in what they did any more. Just thinking about them sitting in a circle, with linked hands, believing they could change the world for the better, made her heart contract with love. It was better to be like them than like she was now.

Unlike Sophie, Leah was self-employed and worked from home. She ran a successful catering business that, aside from weddings and other such big events, offered themed evenings for groups of female friends. In the past, this had included Arabian Nights, Egyptian Magic, Celtic Dream, to name a few. This had been Leah's favourite part of her job. Food and drink had been tailored to the events, which had had a superficially witchy gleam. A friend from her magical group, Ellie, used to come along with merchandise – trinkets, glittering scarves, perfume and jewellery – which the women would browse through and then purchase as they nibbled their exotic treats. As part of the evening's activities, out would come the Tarot cards, and the women would pay a little extra for that. Most evenings, another friend, Sarah, would be there to offer healing or massage. And with repeat clients, once they realised the three women they invited into their homes to pamper them were *witches*, rather different commissions appeared in Leah's in-box. Word spread. She and her friends had been asked to help with sickness, with broken hearts, with money troubles. And to the best of their ability, they did. This was so successful, it got to the point where Leah had had to turn commissions down.

When Brett Lyle had plunged the final knife into her by abruptly exiting her life without chance for discussion or even a decent farewell, the shock of it, never mind the pain, had diminished Leah considerably, and she had taken a break from her work. In fact, she had been unable to concentrate on preparing the food for *any* events, never mind the special ones where she was required to sit and read the cards, or try to help people magically when their lives had taken a turn for the worse. All she wanted to say to them was, "You shouldn't be paying me for this. Life is either crap, great or bearable, and Fate takes a swing at us when it likes. If things are good, enjoy them, if they're bearable, count your luck, if they're bad, poor you. Find a lawyer, a doctor or a psychiatrist. Nothing I can do will change a thing." She had this little speech off by heart, practiced as she lay on her couch in the dim afternoons.

Eventually the emails and calls seeking to hire her died off. At this time, she began to drift away from her magical group also.

After a couple of months, realising that life inevitably continues, as do bills, Leah started looking for work again, and also reinvented the special part of the business, which she regarded as her personal indulgence. Now she offered parties having the theme of a genteel life gone by; afternoon tea on delicate china, such as would have been enjoyed by 'ladies' in earlier decades. She scoured second hand and charity shops for appropriate crockery and cutlery, eventually building up an impressive collection. She experimented with baking recipes she found in old cooking books, and after some careful promotion and free teas in strategic places, the new business shone like the old. Emulating the 'extra services' offered by the previous parties, Leah employed two girls to accompany her and provide facials and manicures. Women of all kinds liked the parties, which proved more successful than Leah had envisaged. But then, she had a gift with preparing food that some would call magical; she *invested* into her business on more than one level, and paid great attention to detail. It might have been a nice touch if, as part of the events, she'd read the tea leaves for her clients, but Leah firmly refused to let herself offer that.

And yet, despite her scepticism and denial, didn't magic still *nibble* at her? When she baked her cakes, working good feeling into the mixture, and sought out the exact special kinds of teas she felt were right, wasn't she still indulging in ritual?

* * *

AFTER HER LUNCH with Sophie, Leah entered her house and, in the hallway, faced the mirror that hung on the wall opposite the door. The glass was faintly smoked, giving a reflection that had always looked to Leah like a scene from a spooky film with a blue filter over it.

"Really, Leah," she said to herself. "When *are* you going to forget what happened? You don't kid *me*, you know."

Shaking her head, she turned to her answerphone on the table beneath the mirror to listen to messages from clients wanting to hire her. She wrote down the details on the pad by the phone. Then came the last one, the third, the fateful knocking upon the door.

"Hello, this is Carol Lyle. I'd like to book a tea party, please, for my birthday in three weeks' time, the 7th. I hope this isn't too short notice, but a friend recommended you. My address is number 8, The Ashes and if you'd like to return my call, my number is..."

At first, Leah didn't realise who it was; she merely wrote down the address and phone number, thinking she might not be able to fit this woman in. And then, as if her reflection was still displayed in the smoky mirror and calling to her, she thought, *Wait... wait a minute!* She went quickly to her office in what was supposed to be the dining room and looked at her cloth-bound appointment book, which lay on the desk. In this she wrote down her appointments in a neat curling script. 7th March. She flicked to the relevant page. As she thought, someone had already booked her for that day; one of her regulars.

Looking at the page, she picked up the phone on the desk, stabbed in a number. "Hello, is that Shannon? Hi, it's Leah Metcalfe here, I'm really sorry but I'm going to have to cancel our appointment for the 7th. Something unavoidable and rather serious has cropped up... I'm more than happy to give you a free party on another date if you'd like one..."

Leah ended the call, punched in another number. "Hello, is this Carol Lyle? This is Leah Metcalfe from 'Tea Cakes'. You called me earlier about a party..."

*   *   *

LEAH HAD NO idea what was urging her on, but decided simply to go with it. It was a coincidence beyond all fathomable coincidences that Brett Lyle's wife had called her on the very day that Sophie had told her about Cassy. *You don't believe, but just go with it... If you're being thrown a bone by Fate, snatch it up...*

Leah had never met Carol Lyle, and only knew what she looked like from when she had once investigated Lyle's Facebook page where he displayed 'jolly' photos of family get togethers. Leah had seen a rather plump, short but attractive brunette, with a wide and innocent smile. She had been smiling in every photo. On the phone, Carol sounded chatty and rather nervous. She laughed a lot.

"I know it is rather short notice," she said.

"That's no problem," Leah replied in her smoothest, most comforting tone. "As luck would have it, there's been a cancellation for the 7th. You must be sure to have all men folk out of the way!" Leah added one of her smokiest laughs. "My parties are girls only."

"Of course, of course," said Carol Lyle. "I wouldn't be getting anything for my birthday if I wasn't doing this myself. Just some girlfriends and my Mum and sister."

"Great," said Leah. "Shall we discuss the menu?"

LEAH CONSIDERED NOT taking her assistants along, but then decided she should not alter her habitual ritual. (*There it was again.*) The party was set for 6.00 pm – an odd time, really. Clients usually opted for an afternoon event or an evening one; not this in between time when people normally ate dinner and then did something else.

Leah prepared the food with especial care. As she conjured her mixtures, she found she had much sympathetic feeling for

Carol Lyle. That nervous laugh, that trusting smile. It seemed particularly cruel for the vampire Brett Lyle to be married to someone like that. *But I suppose she's malleable*, Leah thought. *She won't make a fuss, even when she suspects... she was chosen precisely.*

As she was standing at the door to number 8, The Ashes, (new housing estate, pricey), on a fairly mild March evening, with her assistants behind her, Leah knew why she was doing this. She had to *see*. And when she had seen, she might act.

While they waited for Carol to answer the door, Leah remembered Brett Lyle taking her in his arms, enfolding her as if with wings. "This is how we are," he had murmured. She had felt like a mortal woman seduced by a dark angel. But their kisses had always been chaste. His gaze, however, had never been that.

Leah dismissed the memory, pulled herself together. The door was opening, light spilling out.

Carol Lyle bounced onto the front step. "Hi, hi. Do you need any help with your stuff?"

"No, we'll carry everything," Leah said. "Can you just show us to the kitchen? Amber and Rachel will need somewhere to set up, too, if that's all right."

"Come in, come in..."

Leah stepped over the threshold. This was Brett Lyle's front, this middle class life on an ordinary if upmarket housing estate. This was his lair, to which he always returned; his coffin full of native soil.

It was a comfortable home, although everything was new as if it had only just arrived from a furnishing warehouse. Anyone would have thought the Lyles had recently moved in, except Leah had known 8 The Ashes as Lyle's address when she'd been seeing him. It hadn't been that difficult to discover.

A group of women were sitting in the front room, drinking wine. Leah nodded and smiled at them as she followed Carol Lyle through to the kitchen. Here Carol thrust a huge glass of Shiraz at Leah, even before Leah had set down her crates. "I have white too if you prefer," she said. "Or... juice or something?"

Leah took the glass and swigged. "This is great, thanks."

She set the glass down on the counter and began to remove her cakes and sandwiches reverently from their packaging. Carol, meanwhile directed Amber and Rachel to two of the spare bedrooms where they could work. Then she returned to the kitchen as Leah was arranging an array of heavily iced, liqueur-laced cup cakes on a tiered stand.

"They look *so* beautiful," said Carol Lyle. "I love the decorations."

Leah removed her *piece de résistance* from the crate at her feet. "This is a present for you," she said. "A birthday cake." It was immense, robed in dark chocolate butter icing, fortified with Tia Maria and a lavish pinch of chilli. A mass of black and white fondant roses spilled across its surface in a tangled trail. On each stem, the dark green leaves and thorns had been carefully formed. And the tips of the thorns were red. Half hidden among the petals and foliage was a silvered plaque – again edible – with the words *'For Carol, her birthday'* engraved upon it.

Carol's eyes misted up. "Oh, that's... oh, I really won't want to eat it and spoil it."

Leah laughed. "Take some photos, then eat it. That way you'll have the appearance *and* the taste. Trust me, it's scrumptious."

"Later, then," Carole said. "Thank you, Leah. I didn't expect that."

"My pleasure."

As WELL AS the array of teas, the cakes, the exquisite sandwiches, wine continued to flow. Leah later blamed this for what happened. When the birthday cake was carried ceremonially from the kitchen, now lit with tiny green candles, the women in the room gasped. One of them said, perhaps the mother, "It's amazing, Carol, but rather like a funeral cake! That thing in the middle looks like a gravestone. And whatever made you choose those colours?"

Carol cast an embarrassed glance at Leah. "I... I didn't. The cake was a present."

The other woman laughed. "Really? I hope nobody wants you dead, love!"

"That was a horrible thing to say!" Carol snapped. "No one wants me dead. How could you say that?"

"It was just a joke," the woman said.

"I made the cake," Leah said smoothly, "and my taste veers towards the Gothic. I assure you there's no bad intention in it."

"It's beautiful, and I love it, Leah," Carol said hotly. "Now I'm going to eat a massive piece of it." She brandished the cake knife with a humorous evil leer.

Everyone laughed and Carol cut the cake. Its innards were a dark treacly brown, plump with dates, spiced with cinnamon. Carol quickly dispensed portions round the room, even handed one to Leah. Then, after a moment's silence, all the guests bit into their slice of cake. Leah left hers untouched.

"Oh my god, it's amazing!" Carol cried. "What's in it, Leah?"

One of the other women laughed, wiping crumbs from her lips. "Ah, she's not going to reveal her secret ingredients!"

"On the contrary," Leah said, smiling. "I can tell you that the main ingredients are strength and love."

Everyone laughed again, clearly thinking she was joking.

PERHAPS IT WAS mention of the Gothic, the appearance of the cake, or the woman's clumsy joke that instigated it, but somehow the conversation in the room veered towards the occult. Someone started talking about a friend of a friend who'd visited a fortune teller. "She was accurate to a tee," the woman said. "Knew stuff she couldn't possibly know."

Another woman had just come back into the room, holding her hands out in front of her, since Amber had painted her nails. "I went to one," she said. "Had the cards read. She told me about how I'd have Harry, although I'd no intention of having kids at that point. Was taking every precaution too!"

"I'd love to have my cards read," Carol said wistfully. "I never have."

"Hoping they'll say kids for you too, Carol?" someone asked, giggling.

Carol pulled a sour face. "Fat chance of that."

There was a moment's silence.

"I can read the cards," Leah said. She could have bitten off her tongue, but the words simply came out. Nothing could have prevented them. "I have a deck in my bag." She had never removed them, since the days she'd carried them with her always on purpose.

"Ooh, do me!" someone said.

"And me!" cried another.

Leah glanced at Carol. "The hostess first, I think. Yes?"

Carol nodded. She wasn't smiling now. "In the kitchen?"

"If you like."

DON'T THINK ABOUT *it, just do it*, Leah told herself as she seated herself opposite Carol Lyle at the breakfast bar. She took the dog-eared cards out of their silk wrap and began to shuffle them. They felt familiar, like old friends. A musty scent of the rose oil with which she'd once perfumed the silk drifted around both women. Even though faintly spoiled, the smell wasn't unpleasant.

Carol was leaning on her crossed forearms on the bar. "They look really old," she said.

"They are getting on a bit," Leah said, "seen a lot of use. Here, will you shuffle them too? Just empty your mind of everyday thoughts while you do. Do you have a particular question you'd like to ask the cards?"

"Yes," Carol replied.

"You don't have to tell me of it, just think about it."

"I will." Carol took the cards and closed her eyes. The cards slipped through her fingers obediently.

After a minute or so of silence, Carol opened her eyes and handed the cards back to Leah, who began to lay them out in a simple spread.

"Will you say if it's bad?" Carol asked. "I mean, it must be awkward for you if what they say is bad."

"I'll tell you what I see," Leah said, "but the cards are only a snapshot of now, really. Nothing they say is written in stone. If you like, they are sign posts on the road of life. *You* have the power to change your destiny, but sometimes the cards can help you clarify things in your head, make decisions."

"That sounds like a get out clause to me!" Carol said, laughing. "What if I get the Death one?"

"That card means change," Leah said. "Quite radical change, yes, a rebirth perhaps, but it does not mean you're going to get run over tomorrow."

The cards were laid out, face down. Now Leah was nervous of turning over the first one. Her hand hovered over it.

"Let me," Carol said, and turned the card face up. "The Moon. What does that mean?"

As the cards revealed their story, one by one, Leah wondered whether she was impartial enough to read them accurately. Was she seeing what she wanted to see? A woman deluded, occluded, befuddled? A faithless man? She struggled to voice her interpretation. "You feel you are lacking facts..."

Leah was conscious of Carol staring at her. She knew she wasn't reading very well; it was stilted.

Then Carol announced. "You must know why I hired you?"

"What?"

Carol rolled her eyes, took a swig of the wine by her left elbow. "Come *on*. I do *know*, Leah. At least... My question was, and is, what happened between you and my husband?"

Leah felt her face colour up. This was the last thing she'd expected. "I..."

"And why did you take the job, Leah? You knew it was me too."

Leah made a helpless gesture.

Carol reached out and touched one of Leah's hands. "It's OK, I'm not mad at you. I just want to know."

Leah sighed deeply. "I honestly don't know. Curiosity... A compulsion..." She paused. "Why contact me now, after all these years?"

Carol shrugged. "I just always wondered, that's all. I saw you, this glamorous older woman, and he told me you were just a friend. I always wondered. It didn't seem likely."

An uncomfortable prickle coursed down Leah's spine. "*How* did you see me?"

Carol laughed, rather bleakly. "It's not that difficult nowadays, is it? Your web site, social media. Didn't have to be a private detective lurking round corners. So tell me."

"There isn't much to tell, Carol. I was a fool, that's all. Nothing physical happened between us that you'd call him being grossly unfaithful to you. It was a silly crush that got out of hand."

Carol took another mouthful of wine. "I don't believe you."

"It's true. I never slept with him."

"I don't mean that. I mean it wasn't just a silly crush, was it?"

Leah met Carol's gaze. "No. No it wasn't." She shook her head. "There's no point saying I'm sorry, because I was so *enraptured* I didn't care about you."

"Well, of course. I'm never in the way." Carol frowned. "The problem is, Leah, I still love the bastard. I know he has this thing with women. It's happened many times. But somehow... recently... I don't feel I can hide behind the fancy curtains of this house any more. I feel I'm married to a ghost, who's not really here. He's never been bad to me, always generous, always pleasant. That's what's made it so hard for me. There was nothing for me to put my finger on, except for my hunches, and the women he befriended. He never hides that, you know. He always tells me about them, his *friends*. It's almost like he makes it easy for me to look them up, as if he even *wants* me to. But I never get to meet them, as you'd expect with friends, if they really *are* just that."

Leah nodded. "You're right," she said simply. "They're not just friends, but neither are they lovers. I would call them... victims... prey." She grimaced. "No, let's keep this sensible. He likes the attention. No doubt there's some reason for that, buried in his past. He's stayed with you, Carol. He hasn't exactly strayed. I think to him it's all only a game."

Carol sighed, stared at the counter. "I wasn't sure whether I'd fess up like this to you. I had this urge to meet you, that's all. Someone told me about you, your party thing, and it seemed the right time. Strange, really."

Leah found she didn't want to tell Carol Lyle about the destruction her husband tended to leave in his wake, the tarnished lives. "You want it to stop, of course," she said. "You don't want to leave him, do you?"

Carol looked up. "I want my husband to want *me*," she said. "I wish he didn't need all these... *dalliances*. I suppose I'm scared that one day he'll meet someone who somehow tips him over and then he'll be gone. He can't be happy, can he, if he has to have this *attention*, as you called it?"

Leah paused. "Was there another reason why you wanted to speak to me particularly?"

"I think you know the answer to that. I know quite a lot about you."

"You want it to stop."

"Yes. I think you have a responsibility."

Leah closed her eyes briefly. "OK."

"You didn't eat your cake," Carol said. "Why not? What did you put into it?"

"Strength and love, like I said," Leah replied. "They were for you, not me."

Carol lifted her wine glass, gestured with it. "*In vino veritas*," she said. "It can be a git, can't it?"

'Definitely," Leah said. She lifted her own glass, clinked it with Carol's.

As LEAH WAS driving home, having dropped off her assistants, she noticed that the moon, so clear in the sky, had lost her first slice; the dark was on its way. Leah's mind was empty of busy thoughts, or even analysis. She felt only a pure conviction. Carol Lyle might say she felt haunted by a husband who was barely there, but Leah felt she had seen the true ghost in that relationship. It lived in Carol's eyes, in her nervous gestures, the joking yet bitter reference to having no chance of children. Meanwhile her husband was no doubt off somewhere, telling some woman, perhaps the unfortunate Cassy, how their friendship was special, how it sustained him. His piercing gaze would be holding hers; full of unspoken longings. Words and a gaze that were a trail of delicious crumbs leading only to a spiked pit. Brett Lyle made ghosts of his victims without a single killing. He'd had it all his own way for far too long.

In her house, Leah acted decisively, as if guided by an outer force. In her workroom, she sat down to meditate and fashioned a bullet purely from thought and intention. Into it, as into the most careful of her baking mixtures, she poured a purpose. The bullet was as silver-white as the moon; a lunar dart. Leah did not feel a magical mirror was the answer for Lyle; his armour needed to be pierced. So she fashioned the bullet and gave it to a dark angel with a gun.

CAROL LYLE HAD tried not to think about Leah all the time, but it had proved difficult. On that birthday evening, Carol had taken action for the first time, been someone different. Just that moment of saying to Leah "you must know why I hired you" had been empowering. And then the pivotal moment when Leah had closed her eyes for a second, her murmured word "OK". Carol knew that Leah had meant it. She just didn't know how she meant it.

One week following the party, Brett was home for the evening. He was camped in the front room, shorn of the mask he wore for his female 'friends', playing a video game. In the kitchen, preparing dinner, Carol could hear the blast of machine gun fire and the cries of computer men as they died. These sounds annoyed her; they always did. There was no good reason for him to have the volume turned up so loud. Carol threw a half peeled carrot into the sink, dried her hands and marched towards the living room. She saw Brett sitting cross legged on the carpet, looking like a boy. He did not glance up at her, hunched as he was over the game pad he was holding. On the screen, men exploded in red gouts amid loud explosions that shook the walls. Carol's mouth opened to complain.

And then *he* folded out of the corner of the room. Dressed in black leather, immensely tall, a face pale like moonlight. And he held a gun. Carol saw the blue-black sheen of the weapon as he raised it; almost organic in appearance.

The shot was white, like a sky full of fireworks; it was a sound that had an image. And then her husband's head had exploded; red splashes and gobbets over the TV screen, up the walls, all over her. Carol heard herself screaming, the kind that will never stop, saw the pale-faced assassin glance at her once. He bowed to her, walked backwards through the wall.

"WHAT THE HELL is wrong with you?" Brett was holding her, shaking her, perhaps seconds away from slapping her face.

Carol was utterly disorientated for a moment, then reality somehow see-sawed back into focus. She saw her husband in front of her, unmarked, and clearly not sure whether to be angry with her or amused. "You were shot!" Carol cried. "You were dead!"

Brett Lyle laughed, let her go. "Idiot," he said amiably. "What are you talking about? It's only a game."

Carol stared into her husband's face. She saw a red fleck amid the blue in his left eye. Had that always been there? "It's not always a game," she said in a low voice, "not to everyone."

He pantomimed a double-take. "What's that supposed to mean?"

"You know," she said and headed back towards the kitchen.

"Well, no I don't, actually," he said, in a stiffly offended tone.

Carol wheeled on him, spoke harshly but evenly. "Yes. You do. I'll always be there now, Brett. Remember that. You'll never be alone."

She didn't need to say any more than that, and wouldn't, no matter how hard he pressed her, even when the crazy dreams started happening, when uncertainty seeped into his mind. *Remember what ghosts do*, she would whisper into his sleep. *They haunt you.*

BOTTOM LINE

LOU MORGAN

Magic is power, and there will always be those who wield power for the wrong reasons, or become corrupted by the power itself. Here is a tale of addiction, but it is also a what if? story. Lou asks what would happen if gangsters started to use magic to facilitate their illicit practices. The answer is chilling, but there is also a poignant denouement to this tale that will leave it lingering in your mind for a long while.

THERE'S A DOG in the middle of the road, just running. Right down the centre line, straight as an arrow. One of those little ones: the kind that resemble a handbag on legs and mostly seem to be owned by people who don't actually like dogs all that much. It can shift, though: the way it's going, you'd think the devil was after it.

The car closest to me pulls up; the driver winds down the window.

"Is that your dog? Aren't you going to do something about it...?"

"Does it look like it's my dog?" I can see him looking me up and down, figuring that one out for himself. He obviously decides not, and winds the window back up. A moment later, a blonde woman comes pelting round the corner, waving her arms and clutching a pink lead. The dog's still running. I can sympathise.

I'm tempted to hang around to see how the dog drama turns out, but frankly, it's more excitement than I can handle at this time of the morning. Besides, I'm late enough already, and however relaxed my boss is about life in general, opening up late is more than my life's worth. Before I can do that, I need coffee so I tear myself away from the street theatre and make for the café on the corner. They've got my coffee waiting – same as always, sitting on the counter in its little cardboard cup. It's too milky – again, same as always – and they've forgotten the sugar, but I wouldn't go anywhere else. Partly because this place is the closest to the shop, and partly because I'd have to pay for it. As it is, I get away with a wave of my hand in the general direction of the till and I'm gone.

Opening up the shop isn't particularly taxing, which is just as well given that the coffee's not kicked in yet. Working here... well, it's not particularly glamorous, but at least it's legal. Legal *enough*, anyway, and that's what counts. Mostly I sell marked cards to smartarses who think they're something at poker (and who'll probably end up getting their hands broken with the business end of a hammer) or to kids with tattoos who fancy themselves the next Criss Angel. And don't even start me on the light-fingered little toerags who come in here after school. I nearly lost my temper with one of them last month and Simon had to stop me from turning him inside out. Literally. It would've been messy, granted, but it would have been worth it. Apparently, however, that kind of thing counts as being "bad for business". That's Simon for you. But I owe him: he was the only one who would touch me when I got out and I can still remember the look on his face when I asked him for a job. He was sitting at the counter, stringing cards onto wire for the window display. He put the wire down, and he looked me dead in the eyes and said, "Donnie. Of all the places in the world, with your history, why in God's name would you want to work in a magic shop?"

He had a point. You don't send an alcoholic to work in a distillery, do you? But that's just it. There's magic and there's magic. There's tricks and illusions and sleight of hand... and there's what I do. What I did.

I was a kid when it started – maybe seven or eight. It was little things: handing in homework I hadn't done; the fiver in my mother's purse that wasn't really there... It made me feel clever. It never occurred to me that it *meant* anything, not until I was with my granddad and I booted a football straight through the greenhouse. It was an accident, and I panicked. He heard the glass break – Christ, he saw the ball go through – but when he went to clear up, the glass was gone. The pane had mended itself, good as new. He stood there and scratched his head and frowned, and all the while I did my best to look innocent. I thought I was smart for avoiding a thrashing, but later on, he called me over to sit with him. He always used to sit in the same chair, the one closest to the fire. "Donnie," he said, "I want you to tell me the truth. What did you do to the glass?"

"Nothing, Granddad." I always was a terrible liar.

"Is that so? Well, then." He sat back in his chair and he smiled. "Nothing. Nothing, indeed." And he winked at me, then pointed to the fire. Which had turned blue; the same blue as the sky on the first warm day in spring, or the blue of a pretty girl's eyes. I watched, and the flames turned purple, then black, and slowly back to orange. He laughed, and told me to close my mouth, which was wide open. "You're not the only one who can do tricks, you know," he said, folding his arms.

And that's how I found out. It runs in our family, the magic. *Real* magic. Always the men, generation to generation, back as far as anyone cares to remember – and then some. It runs down the male line, and the first time you use it, your clock starts ticking. My granddad lasted another three years after the day we had our chat. My father, he made it to his fifty-fifth birthday.

Me? I'm on borrowed time.

"Be careful with it," my granddad said. "It's a gift, and it's a curse. No, don't laugh. I mean that. You see, you can do anything you want with it: *anything*. The world's yours. But magic... it eats you up from the inside. It'll take another bite out of you every time you try it until there's nothing left of you but a shell. And once you start..." he shook his head, "You take it from me, boy, once you start, it's mighty hard to stop. Or at least, to stop in time..."

Not that I paid the slightest bit of attention. You don't, at that age, do you? Take Lizzie, for example. Lizzie was a girl I was in school with. I had a bit of a thing for her, and being a nice, sensible sort, she wouldn't give me the time of day. So I gave her a tree. Like you do. Not just any old tree: this one grew overnight, right by her bedroom window, and instead of fruit it was covered in little silver bells. When the wind blew, they sang. At the time, I thought it was the best idea anyone's ever had. In retrospect, it might have come across a touch stalkerish. Didn't matter, as it turned out: within a week, she was going out with one of the football team, the tree had rotted and the bells had rusted, and I promised myself I'd never waste magic on a woman again.

So instead, I took my magic to Rudge.

Rudge is a fixer. He's always got an eye out for magicians, and for a kid with a certain moral flexibility (not to mention, in my case, a growing magic addiction and a general dislike of authority) he can be a pretty attractive option. He gave me a trial, had me work a couple of illusions that I could have done in my sleep, and then he put me to work. My first job was to act as a lookout. No magic, he said. Of course, I didn't listen. and in the process of not listening, I saved everyone's bacon. Rudge was impressed, and it wasn't long before he had me working every job he ran.

I'm what's known in less law-abiding circles as a Ledru. There's a very specific skill set required for that line of work, and we're hard enough to come by. Did you ever see one of those cold-case shows, where the bank's been robbed and no-one can quite work out how it was done? If nobody can crack it, then I'd bet my life on them having used a Ledru. We're illusionists – often prestidigitators too, but that's just part of it. We get you looking one way while the money goes the other. Easy. Back in the old days, when I ran with Rudge's boys, we had a Houdini and a Farla; a Belzoni for muscle and a Banachek as a front man. Then there was me, and the Marvey. But while all the others were your common or garden lowlifes that Rudge so liked to rely on, me and Marvey, we were the real deal. Put the two of us on a job and you couldn't go wrong.

Well. Until Marvey pulled his own vanishing trick and waltzed off with the money.

Rudge didn't take kindly to that. Not at all. The way he saw it, I should've stopped Marvey as soon as I knew what he was doing… which just goes to show how little Rudge understands it. It's *magic*. I didn't know: that's the whole *point*. It didn't matter to Rudge, though: one of his little blue errand boys had me stopped and searched – and lo and behold, who's suddenly got a pistol in his pocket? You'd think I'd have noticed, wouldn't you, but magicians don't usually expect to be on the receiving end of a trick.

Five years, that got me, and that was only because I gave up our Houdini and Belzoni. Farla had already washed up on a beach by that point, and God only knows where Banachek got to. Somewhere a long way away, I hope.

Still, five years is long enough to get yourself straight when the most your magic can extend to is doubling your cellmate's cigarettes just to get him to stop bloody whining. When I went in, I was so far gone on the magic that I didn't care. It was only when I realised I couldn't do any in there – not if I wanted to keep myself in the same number of pieces I'd started out in, anyway – that it hurt. And believe me, it *hurt*. Those first couple of nights, soaked through with sweat and shaking like it was the end of the world… you could've heard me screaming from a long way outside those walls.

The upshot is that five years later, I come stumbling back out onto the streets. I'm clean(ish) bar the occasional little hiccup and the odd free coffee; not enough to get me into trouble, but something to keep my hand in. Simon gave me a chance, and working in the shop does seem to do the job, in a funny way. There's something about the place that keeps the urge, that all-encompassing need, at bay. The props and the cards and the party pieces. If I wanted to, I could pull flowers out of top hats until I dropped, but it wouldn't be the magic that killed me; it would be the sheer mind-numbing monotony.

Five years. Like I said, it's a long time. But that's the thing about Rudge: he's got a hell of a long memory.

I'M CONTEMPLATING THE untold pleasures of a stock-check when the bell over the door rings, and the atmosphere immediately changes. It's like a thunderstorm just walked in. His name is Marcus, he's built like a tank and he's one of Rudge's goons. He's exactly the kind of person I don't want to see. The ventriloquist's doll by the door slowly opens its eyes and turns its head to follow him as he walks across the shop floor towards me.

"Donnie Taylor."

"I'm impressed. You managed to walk and talk at the same time. What's your next trick?"

"You think you're funny, don't you?"

"Not really." I straighten the stack of cards by the till. With characteristic charm, Marcus swings a meaty fist at them and sends them flying.

"He wants to see you."

"Does he? Well, I want a yacht. We don't all get what we want in life, do we?" He turns this over in his mind. His eyes narrow while he's thinking about it, and his lips move as he tries out appropriate responses. Finally, the gorilla speaks. It's worth the wait.

"He wants to see you. Tonight."

"I got that. Tell him I'm washing my hair."

"Taylor..."

"Alright, alright." I hold up my hands in submission. This seems to make him happy. He nods, grunts and heads back towards the door. He pauses to stare down the dummy, which tips its head on one side and blinks at him. I'm half-tempted to make it blow him a kiss, but there's some lines even I won't cross.

Come closing time, he's waiting for me outside the shop, leaning against the wall like he owns the place. He's been there all afternoon, scaring off passing trade – which was probably half the point. Not that he managed to keep the bloody kids away, mind, so that's another tenner Simon'll have off me at the end of the month.

"You ready, Taylor?"

"No, Marcus. I'm standing here for the good of my health."

He considers my answer longer than should really be necessary – I swear, Rudge's boys are getting thicker – and then he makes a sound which could be a laugh. It starts somewhere low down in his chest and gurgles its way up until it sticks in his throat. It's with no small satisfaction that I snap my fingers and seal his mouth shut. It's still there, more's the pity: he just can't get it open. And there's absolutely nothing he can do about it. It's a petty move on my part, and I can feel the magic scratching away at the inside of my skin, but at least I won't have to listen to him mouth-breathing all the way across town.

I beam at him. "So. After you, sunshine."

I HATE RUDGE'S place. I've been there before, a couple of times. He lives up at the top of a tower block in the middle of town, looking down on the rest of us like he's king of the city. I guess in many ways he is. He's not subtle about it, either: he's had some hocus-pocus worked on the balcony so it's lit up like a rainbow. Wherever you are in the city, come night-time, you look up and you see Rudge.

He's not a magician himself, Rudge. We make him nervous:;it's one of the reasons he likes to have a few of us on a leash. "On retainer", he calls it, but we all know what it means. The Vegas lights on the outside of the building? They're just to remind the rest of us of the firepower he's got at his disposal should we step out of line. I don't trust him; worse, I don't trust myself around him. I was burning through magic so hard and fast while I worked for him that I damn near killed myself... and the worst part was that I liked it. So it's with some trepidation that I step into the lift with a still-mute Marcus and press the button for the top floor.

It smells just like I remember it: of money and magic. Paper and ink and fire and forgetting. Already I'm wondering if this was a mistake, but before I have a chance to change my mind, the door at the end of the hall opens. It's not Rudge, of course. He wouldn't dream of opening his own door, and most certainly not to the likes of me. But I recognise the face: how could I not? The last time I saw it, it was yelling at me from the wrong side of a one-way window. It's our Belzoni, and he doesn't look especially happy to see me. He's even bigger than I remember him being: I'd guess his biceps are wider than my neck. He scowls at me, raises an eyebrow at Zippy behind me and steps away from the door.

Rudge is out on his balcony, perched on the edge of a plastic sun-lounger, wearing a Hawaiian shirt and sunglasses. Yes, it's dark, and yes, it's the middle of winter outside... but Rudge isn't going to let a little thing like the weather get in the way of his relaxation. I look round the room, and sure enough, there's a pasty-faced kid slumped on the sofa; his eyes aren't quite focused and he's wearing a vacant expression I've seen too many times in the mirror. Tripping on the magic and keeping Rudge's balcony at a pleasant seventy-eight degrees.

"Donnie!" Rudge is coming through the sliding door, opening his arms like I'm his long-lost brother. "You're a hard man to find!"

"Not exactly, Mr Rudge." It slips out before I can stop it, and I don't miss the twitch at the corner of his mouth.

"Get you a drink?"

"No, thanks. It's hardly a social call, is it?"

"That's what I always liked about you, Donnie. You're all business."

"Speaking of which…?" Being so close to that kid is making me nervous.

"Speaking of which. Yes." Rudge holds out his hand, and someone puts a glass into it. Where do all these flunkies come from? It's not that big a flat.

He takes a swig, and wipes his mouth with the back of the other hand. "To business. When was the last time…?"

"I think we both know you remember when the last time was."

"Ha. Yes. Shame about that."

"About what? The fact your Marvey walked off with the money, or the fact you felt the need to take it out on me?"

"Water under the bridge, my boy. Under the bridge." He waves his arms around, and narrowly avoids pouring the rest of his drink over the floor in his enthusiasm. I catch a waft of vodka and my stomach turns. To be fair, my stomach's turning already. It's not just the smell of the booze, or being stuck in this box of a flat with a man I ratted out breathing down my neck… it's not even Rudge. It's the kid. It's the kid and his goddamn magic. I can feel it crawling all over my skin, looking for a way in. It's distracting, to say the least, but that's what Rudge is counting on. By the time I've cleared my head enough to actually listen to him, he's in full flow.

"… getting the band back together, as it were. The way I look at it, you can finish the job, and we can all move on. No hard feelings."

No hard feelings? He's a piece of work, alright, and if I had any sense I'd walk out that door right now. But I don't.

Something cold and hard presses against the back of my head. I can't see Marcus, but I'll wager it's his finger on the trigger. Rudge is smiling at me.

"You know I could deal with that," I say, jerking my thumb back at the gun. Rudge is still smiling.

"Could you?" He finishes his drink and hurls the empty glass out of the open window, over the edge of the balcony. "I need a Ledru."

"I'm retired."

"Then consider it a favour for an old friend."

He pulls something out of his pocket; tosses it at me. It's a photograph. It spirals down to the floor between us, landing face-down on the carpet.

"There's a man who has something that belongs to me. I want you to get it back. Simple job, in and out."

"If it's simple, you don't need a Ledru, do you? Send the Belzoni."

"And if I thought that would get the job done, my son, I would. But I need a magic man. This one, he knows me, knows my crew."

"Forgive me if I'm reading too much into this, but it sounds pretty personal to me. You know I don't do personal."

"You will this time."

"Is that so?"

"Like I said, consider it a favour for an old friend." And he slides his toe underneath the edge of the photo and flips it over.

Even though it's been three years, I recognise her. I'd know her anywhere – no matter how long it had been. It's my daughter, Grace. The unutterable bastard has just thrown me a photo of my seven-year-old daughter. He's proud of himself too: you can smell it, rolling off him in sweaty waves.

He's also absolutely right. I will do the job, and not because he's trying to use Grace as leverage.

I'll do it because I can't help myself.

The moment I walked into that room, I was lost.

It's not the lingering smell of the vodka, and it's not the stale cigarette smoke hanging around in the corners – I gave up the cancer sticks years ago. It's the raw spark of the magic in here. It's painted into the walls, stitched into the carpets. It's heavy enough in the air that even breathing makes me ache inside from sheer need: that unspeakable, overwhelming vertigo of wanting something so badly you'd break your own mother's neck to get it. Or your daughter's.

I won't be that man again.

I know what Rudge wants. The job's a set-up, just like bringing me here was a set-up. The man he's talking about? It's the Marvey – I can see it in his eyes. And I know how the job'll go. There's only so many ways it can end: with me in a breezeblock box, or a wooden one... or me taking over from the kid in the corner then ending up in the wooden box. If it's not me, it'll be the Marvey. That's why he wants a magic-man.

Who am I kidding? I'm standing here staring Rudge down like I have a choice. Of course I don't have a choice: I never did. If I honestly believed that, I would have given up the magic altogether, not pissed around with parlour tricks. No doubling-up on cigarettes, no free coffees... none of it. But I didn't.

This is it: that moment of clarity they talk about. The one where you step outside yourself and you see exactly where you're headed. The moment I never had until now. Still, no time like the present, is there?

The magic makes the room feel sharper. I need to let it out, need to take the edge off. It cuts and it burns and I can't breathe, and still Rudge is eyeing me and there's a gun to my head and my daughter's face smiles up from the floor. And somewhere far below, people are coming and going and doing whatever it is that they do.

I think of Grace. She won't miss me; she barely knows me. What am I to her, anyway? A stranger she met once or twice; a man in a cold-lit room where the chairs are bolted to the floor and the air smells of boiled cabbage and bleach.

Marcus nudges me with the barrel again, and I remember his mouth. I snap my fingers and hear the gasp of breath as his lips spring open. The rush is almost enough to knock me off my feet, making me see stars. The kid on the sofa groans as magic calls to magic.

Rudge is grinning now: a great big grin plastered right across his face. It almost makes him look friendly. Almost. He thinks he's got me, and I suppose he has. He's got me. But this is going to happen on my terms, not his, and if I'm going down he's coming with me.

Tomorrow morning, Grace will look out of her window and she'll find a tree hung with silver bells that sing in the wind. It won't – can't – last, but it's the best I can do for her.

Tonight, I'm going to light up the sky.

Rudge wants magic?

Magic he'll get.

MAILERDAEMON

SOPHIA MCDOUGALL

Sophia's first words to me were, "I'm magic." This was many years ago, long before I worked in genre, at a fancy dress party in Oxford. It was only after I commissioned her story, that I realised that this was the same Sophia I'd met all those years ago. A lovely bit of serendipity then and never were truer words spoken.

<u>LadyJinglyJones</u> on November 28th, 2012, 12:08 am (GMT):
This, I know how to fix. I only wish I was as good with C# or nightmares. If it happens again tonight, then get up. Go into a different room and do something. Nothing too interesting. *Don't get on the internet.* If you touch your laptop it had better be to clear out your cache or run a de-frag. Then read a page or two of something boring – I've got Wray's Guide to Electromagnetics, though my old professors would weep bitter tears if they knew I was using it that way. Then try going to bed again. Repeat as necessary: if you're going to be awake through the night anyway it's always better to be awake and upright. There's more opportunity for awful things to get into your head when you're horizontal.

<u>Seven Magpies</u> on November 29th, 2012, 12:27 am (GMT):
understand about 60% of what you say as per usual but will give it a go. don't have other room to go into or know what defragging is but suppose can tidy sock drawer.

> <u>Seven Magpies</u> on November 29th, 2012, 10:00 am (GMT):
> hey thanks actually got six hours or so sleep and have very tidy sock drawer. bonus. not seen you around for a bit. RL still poking you? stamp on its toes and say i sent you, i am fighty when nightmares harass my friends.

> > <u>LadyJinglyJones:</u> on November 29th, 2012, 19:14 pm (GMT):
> > Oh, well. You saw my last post-of-angst, things haven't advanced much yet. Efforts remain in vain, etc. Presumably it can't stay like this forever. In the meantime, I sing "Recession—Recession!" to the tune of Tradition from Fiddler on the Roof, and, yes, have nightmares.

> > > <u>Seven Magpies:</u> on November 30th, 2012, 12:12 am (GMT):
> > > do you want to try LEVANTER-SLEET? one good turn deserves another.

> > > > <u>LadyJinglyJones:</u> on November 30th, 2012, 12:38 am (GMT):
> > > > What's LEVANTER-SLEET?

GRACE WAITS A few minutes for her friend's reply – she is a little intrigued by Seven Magpies' sudden discovery of the shift key

– but it's almost one now, and she is exhausted; she's always exhausted. She closes the laptop, leans over to slip it under the bed, and lies down.

She is very confident in the advice she gave Seven Magpies. Knowing what she can expect, sleep ought to be almost impossible for her, and yet she's trained her body so well, or is so desperate, that consciousness spills out of her almost at once.

Then it returns, altered.

Her house is on fire. It's her fault, she left a candle burning. Now she won't be able to claim on the insurance – is the insurance still even up to date?

Grace wakes and frowns in the dark. That was pretty mild, barely even worth waking up over. She thinks her dream-self ought to have been grateful for actually having a house to burn in the first place. She turns over onto her side, draws her knees up close to her chin, and shuts her eyes again.

She slips straight back into the dream.

Everyone was wrong about the fire. It wasn't an accident, nothing to do with a candle. Something is following her. She's in a tiny room, lying on a mattress surrounded by boxes and cases. She tries to move, but she can't. She can't see it yet, but she knows the building is burning. The boxes on every side of her begin to smoulder. She scrambles upright at last as the wall of burning boxes falls in and she knows that all the doors are locked...

She thrashes and wakes. She flings herself over to lie spreadeagled, trying to stifle the uproar of her heartbeat against the mattress.

The burning thing pursues her, starting fires wherever she stops to rest. She could camp out beside the Thames, where perhaps it wouldn't find her, if she could only get there. The streets veer and spiral away from the way she wants to go, and break into flames when she tries to turn back. There were people in the house she left burning. There was a baby she was supposed to look after. Somehow she is there again, back where she started but outside, looking up at the fire pouring from the windows, hearing the screams.

By morning she's had almost eight hours of sleep, with only brief interruptions of wakefulness, and she's limp and shattered under the duvet, as if she's been dropped from a great height. She lies, like an upturned woodlouse, trying weakly to remember how to work her limbs. Nothing comes of it. Tears prick at her eyes. She drags the covers over her face and thinks that being awake is unbearable and being asleep is no better, and this is so far from the first time she's thought that that she can't remember what anything else felt like.

She beseeches herself at length to get up, and loathes herself for her failure to comply. Eventually, reaching under the bed for the laptop feels more or less achievable, a halfway house towards entering the day. Even that requires her to spend a good ten minutes gathering the will-power, luring herself out from under the covers with the remote possibility someone will have emailed her good news.

There's no message about anything she's already applied for. Her in-box is full of job vacancies that will all turn out to have a hundred applicants already.

There is, however, a notification of a new reply from Seven Magpies:

<u>Seven Magpies</u>: on November 30th, 2012, 01:13 am (GMT):

Mr LEVANTER-SLEET is a nine-foot skeleton-demon with a body made of the shadows of plague-pit bones and corpse-candles for eyes and teeth like someone's playing pick-up sticks with meat saws and steel sabres.

"Oh," says Grace, aloud.

She flexes her fingers on the keyboard, and sucks her teeth, rehearsing ways of replying, before acknowledging herself flummoxed. If nothing else, Seven Magpies has surprised her out of paralysis. She gets out of bed and ponders while she makes tea.

Most of the time, Grace finds it easy to overlook this particular aspect of her eccentric friend's eccentricity. She met Seven Magpies three years ago on a fan forum for a series of post-apocalyptic games called *Angels of the Embers*. When the forum split into squabbling factions, they retreated to LiveJournal, where Seven Magpies usually posts *Angels of the Embers* fanart of superior quality, pictures of the tiny Victorian mourning dresses for dolls she occasionally sells on Etsy, and dispatches from the ongoing catastrophe of her personal life. Occasionally, however, she also posts about the spells she has conducted using bones and seaglass and rowan roots; the spirits she has spoken with on the muddy tideline of the Thames. Grace quietly avoids commenting on those posts, (she doubts it speaks very well of her that she always *reads* them, fascinated) except when Seven Magpies mentions eating holly berries and cutting herself to get blood to draw on mirrors, then Grace jumps in to post worried comments about the risk of infection and the number of the Samaritans and how she'll come straight over if Seven Magpies wants, whether just to talk or to walk her to the doctors.

Seven Magpies never takes offence – Seven Magpies treasures kindness, from anyone, for anyone, however expressed. But they have never met in the flesh, even though they both now live in London. Seven Magpies once explained politely that she expects her online friendships to stay online for the foreseeable future, and Grace now only suggests meeting in what seem like emergencies. Yet she counts Seven Magpies as a good friend. She, along with Otherwise86 and From Jupiter whom Grace *can't* meet because they live in Vietnam or West Virginia, occupy invisible, weightless places in the web of people to whom she's close. She certainly knows them better than the people she lives with. It's one of the things she likes about the meeting places of the internet, that it lets programmers discover that they can make friends with witches.

Besides, she understands Seven Magpies' cloistered life a little better these days. All her housemates are already at work, and Grace is glad of it. She likes them well enough, but it's not an arrangement any of them would have chosen freely, and nor is it one she'll be able to afford much longer, as everyone must know. She's taken to hiding in her room from them, and she hasn't seen any of her real friends in months. She tells herself she can't afford it, and that's true, but it's something even more essential, and even more depleted than money that she can't spare.

When she returns to the laptop, she finds that Seven Magpies is awake and explaining further:

<u>Seven Magpies</u>:
on November 30th,
2012, 09:11 am
(GMT):

Mr LEVANTER-SLEET
doesn't like boys,
and he doesn't like
other nightmares but
he does like girls
in trouble, so if any
other nightmares
turn up on his watch
he will tend to stab
them. I find him very
effective.

Grace stares, and even laughs a little, and tries to look at it from her friend's point of view. Can Seven Magpies *really* believe in magic and nightmare-slaying demons? A lot of the time, she sounds so... *reasonable,* that Grace thinks probably it's all just a *hobby,* an elaborate game of pretend that makes Seven Magpies feel better about life.

So Seven Magpies is saying "Play with my imaginary friend, maybe you'll feel better too."

On the other hand, sometimes it sounds as though Seven Magpies believes it utterly.

But even in that case, it's not *really* that different from Seven Magpies saying "I'll pray for you." Grace is an atheist, but not the sort of atheist who gets offended when people offer to pray for her, and she feels bad about having complained to Seven Magpies in the first place: Seven Magpies certainly has it worse.

Politeness, she decides, costs nothing.

<u>LadyJinglyJones</u>: on November 30th, 2012, 09:23 am (GMT):

All right, send me the demon.

<u>Seven Magpies</u>: on November 30th, 2012, 09:25 am (GMT):
i'll
ask
him
to
head
over!

Grace is relieved to have avoided awkwardness, and amused to think she has discovered a new rule of modern etiquette (when offered a demon over the internet, a lady accepts graciously). She gets dressed and heads to the Jobcentre.

The novelty of the exchange enlivens her about as far as the bus stop, but then the dream sours everything again like an aftertaste. God, she hates everything about this. She hates the beautiful gothic houses that overlook the park at the top of Seven Sisters Road and she hates the betting shops and Chicken Feasts at the bottom of it. She hates the perversely bright green of the Jobcentre signs, and the empty ritual of the Jobcentre itself. You have to turn off your phone before you go inside; you can't take in food or drink – not even a bottle of water – as if it's a temple you have to enter in a state of penitential purity.

She waits humbly on a citrus green couch, and tries not to focus on anything. Her heart is pounding inexplicably and the details of everything are dangerous as rocks in shallow water; if she lets her attention run against them she'll overbalance, sink.

After twenty minutes this begins to fade, mercifully, into ordinary boredom. She realises she's forgotten to bring a book, again, and starts to look around at her fellow unemployed. A fair-haired young man is standing by the wall, damp from the drizzle, clutching the usual plastic folder and frowning anxiously into its contents as if afraid he's forgotten something. He must have been afraid of being late, too, for he's slightly out of breath. He radiates nervous energy, so he's probably new.

"Could you sit down there, please?" a security guard says to him, tone and stance announcing that despite the 'please', it's not a request.

The young man looks perplexed. "Sorry?"

"You can sit down there or stand to use the workstations."

The newcomer glances at the touchscreens mounted on

green MDF plinths at the far end of the room. He tilts his head, incredulous. "You mean I'm *not allowed to stand up?*"

The realisation that this is exactly what the guard means ignites a mutinous mood among the jobseekers. Jaws drop, eyes meet, everyone is briefly alive with sarcastic fellow-feeling.

"Watch out!" snarls a large tattooed man, "We've got a *stander* in here!"

"Practically a *terrorist!*" says a thin man in a grey tracksuit.

"We can kneel on the floor, if it'd make you feel safer," Grace offers the security guard, who huffs ominously. The young man forestalls any further escalation by sitting down next to her, though he accepts everyone's indignant sympathies with a shake of the head and a roll of the eyes.

"I'm Luke, what are you in for?" he asks Grace. He's fair, improbably sunburnt for November with a short, square blond beard; he looks like a slender, harried Viking. He smiles at her and Grace feels a very distant twinge of regret that she's stopped bothering with makeup and doing her hair. Then her name is called, which at least introduces her to him, but they don't get much further.

The advisor grieves over Grace's forms. "You always think computer people should be fine come rain or shine, don't you?" she sighs.

"That was the idea, yes. Might as well have done the arts degree after all," says Grace, unsmiling.

She takes a mild, spiteful pleasure in making the woman's eyes glaze over by explaining programming languages, about the differences between Ada and Java and C++ and C# and how everyone wants a year's professional experience in C# these days and of course she's never going to get that if no one gives her a job...

"Nothing's changed," summarises the advisor, eventually.

"No," Grace agrees, and is humiliated at how her voice cracks on the word.

"See you in two weeks," says the advisor, pretending politely not to notice.

*　　*　　*

GRACE WAITS IN the rain for nearly half an hour, trying to summon a bus by chanting its number in her brain, and shivers all the way back. The yearning mantra of *two-five-three, two-five-three* gives way to *home home home,* and when at last the quiet and warmth of her room enfold her again she nearly weeps, at once with relief and with misery that it *isn't* her room, and its safety can't be relied on. The dole does not cover the rent. She's paying it out of her overdraft already. Soon she will have to move, and moving will easily cost two hundred pounds in itself.

She crawls onto her bed, resisting – just barely – the temptation to crawl into it, and opens her laptop.

There's a new email. The conversation about Mr Levanter-Sleet had thus far taken place entirely in comments to Seven Magpies' post about her insomnia, but apparently Seven Magpies has decided the time has come for privacy, though it's hard, from her message, to see why:

Here you go. Hope he can help! – Morgane.

There isn't any attachment.

Grace already knew her friend's name was Morgane (*yes,* her real name, but no, not her *original* name), though she can't really think of her by anything other than her screen handle.

"So you *can* capitalise, when you want to," she says affectionately to the screen, and gets on with the day's work.

She types:

Please consider my application for the position of Digital Architect. I believe I am well-suited for this role.

I am excited by this opportunity to apply for the post of Junior Programmer. I have a proven track record in software engineering and software architecture.

I would like to apply for the post of audio secretary. I am diligent, conscientious and hardworking. I am also educated way above this godawful job, which is probably one reason why you won't reply to this, but you should give me a chance anyway because I find it spiritually fulfilling when people too lazy to type their own letters drone into my ears, and photocopying excites me. Sexually.

She finds it mildly cathartic to write dash off parody entries while thinking out the real thing, though she sometimes panics at the possibility of pressing 'submit' by mistake. She deletes everything after 'hardworking' and does it again properly.

It's only when she scares herself in this way that she recovers any real belief someone might read what she writes. The emails feel as insubstantial as prayer, wisps of incense sent into the sky to appease unrelenting gods.

Nevertheless, she grapples with an online application form for hours, comforting herself a little by sneering inwardly at how cack-handedly it has been put together. At four she remembers that she hasn't eaten lunch but it doesn't seem worth it now. She loses a few more hours looking for cheaper places to live on property websites, googling 'housing benefit' and trying not to cry, then she microwaves a bowl of instant risotto, and at last, gives up.

She closes her internet browser, opens a compiler instead, and starts to play.

She's stopped caring about music, clothes, films, books, games (except, dimly, *Angels of the Embers,* and that's really only nostalgia) food and sex; all that's left are mucking about on the internet and this.

It began as a mess of different projects: she needed to learn new programming languages, and to keep herself from entirely losing the ability to do complex maths. Now, though, it's wonderfully pointless. She sets up a loop of programs talking to each other in different languages, passing a package of data between them, in a pipeline of digital channels that forms a maze, a labyrinth, a collaborative work of art. It's possible to turn the results into visual images and in the end she does this, watching the pixels dance into shapes that are like clouds and river systems but also like architecture. But in a way this isn't where the beauty of it lies for her. It's the complexification itself, existing somewhere between her mind and the computer, the moment when it seems to lift away from both like a bubble into brief, spontaneous life.

She turns out the lights at last, and remembers she has a guest.

"Hullo, Mr Levanter-Sleet," she says, and waves into the empty room.

It takes longer than she's used to to fall asleep. If *this* on top of everything else is going to go wrong too...! But she hasn't forgotten what to do, so she drags herself up and goes and cleans the bathroom. *Girls in trouble*, she thinks as she tries to wipe a smear off the mirror that turns out to be a shadow on the wall behind her. What a mortifying category to belong to.

But when she returns to bed, sleep comes with delicious speed, dark and velvety as it settles over her like a crow on its nest. She does wake once in the night, with a confused sense of the slope of the mattress being wrong, as if someone's resting beside her. But she rolls over and plummets back into sleep, and when she wakes again, doesn't remember it at all.

It's just before nine. After only a short struggle, Grace gets up and is in the shower before it occurs to her to think about her dreams.

She can just remember something about building a very complicated book case, and the colour yellow.

She raises her eyebrows at herself. She hadn't thought she was so suggestible. But she's not about to complain about it.

<u>Seven Magpies</u> sent you a direct message on December 10th, 2012, 22:44 pm (GMT):

so hey did LEVANTER-SLEET do any good?

You sent <u>Seven Magpies</u> a direct message on December 10th, 2012, 23:09 pm (GMT):

I guess he did! Tell him he's a good demon.

<u>Seven Magpies</u> sent you a direct message on December 18th, 2012, 04:04 am (GMT):

i can't tell him anything.

HER LUCK DOESN'T, in any larger way, change overnight. The odd bad dream or two still gets through, but they're more about missing trains and failing exams and less about mass suicides and plague, and when she wakes she says "Tsk, tsk, Mr Levanter-Sleet, you're slipping!" instead of weeping under the blankets.

She starts having coffee with Luke from the Jobcentre after their appointments. His sunburn and his redundancy turn out both to be courtesy of the British Army, and he is amazed – a little *too* amazed, really – to have met a woman who likes playing computer games. They have already discussed the disappointing third *Angels of the Embers* sequel half to death. It isn't quite enough to get her actually looking *forward* to her appointments, but it does work very nicely as an incentive to get through them without screaming or throwing anything.

Still, once or twice things are so bad that she stops moving in the middle of getting dressed and has to curl up on the floor for minutes on end before she can go on.

Then she finds a new comment on her weeks-old 'post of angst.'

<u>From Jupiter</u> on December 20th, 2012, 14:24 pm (DST)

Hey, sorry I'm getting to this late. RL crazy. So, are things still this bad? Because you don't sound well, dude. "I hate being awake and I hate being asleep"????? Just *look* at that, would you? If it was anyone else talking like this, you'd have tucked them under your arm and marched them to the doctor months ago. You have socialised medicine over there. Go take advantage while it lasts.

Grace stiffens, baffled and slightly offended, then rereads her post.

She nearly replies that things are in fact somewhat better, it's only being awake that's a problem now, but then realises that might not be very reassuring.

She types, in the end:

Thank you.

GRACE IS LUCKY with the anti-depressants. Several of her friends online have had awful trouble finding anything that works, and the doctor warns her she won't feel better for at least a fortnight; actually things start to feel less dreadful within a week. She feels mildly dizzy for a day or two, but that soon wears off.

The only other side-effects are the dreams. The leaflet in the box with the pills warns that this can happen, but anything's better than the nightmares – and these are *good* dreams, really. It's only that night after night they grow in detail and complexity, until they're sometimes exhausting. A painted city carved into the walls of a canyon. A tunnel that's also a garden, opening at both ends to whirling stars. Building a cathedral in a desert of blood red sand. Impossible shapes, and music she can't remember when she wakes up. And there's someone beside her yet half out-of-sight, a pillar of shadow with clawed hands that help her build, bright eyes that watch her climb.

She would wonder why it isn't frightening, but the figure is somehow so unobtrusively part of everything else, that she never questions its company, or retains more than the faintest residue of its presence in her brain when she wakes.

*   *   *

SHE SITS WITH Luke on a bench on Hampstead Heath. Bars of shadow stretch over the grass, longer than the height of the bare trees and the level of the chilly red sun seem to warrant.

Luke's started applying for jobs in security, on the Jobcentre's orders. But he's not physically intimidating, despite experience of carrying a gun around, and probably does not convincingly project actually wanting to do it.

"I'm going to be out of the army, I want to be *out of the army,*" he tells Grace. "Not *army-lite.*" He frowns into the middle distance. "I think I'll open a flower shop. Call it Guns and Roses."

Grace feels slightly guilty about telling him she's just had an interview that seemed to go *really well,* though she knows she's being silly. But Luke is delighted for her. So – not quite to celebrate, because she hasn't got the job yet – and not quite to console him because of course he doesn't need it – she buys him a drink. Then she takes him home to play computer games and when they've blown up enough things they get into her bed. Collapsed over him, afterwards, Grace thinks that remembering the reason why people make so much fuss about this almost makes forgetting in the first place worthwhile.

Around three in the morning, she wakes and finds Luke sitting on the edge of the bed, taking long, slow, deliberate breaths. She reaches for his shoulder, finds it damp with sweat and he flinches slightly.

"Sorry," he says. "Just – bad dream."

She strokes his back in silence and thinks, of course, the *army.* They get this, a lot, don't they – he hasn't told her anything, but surely he must have seen awful things.

Or done them, possibly. But then Luke lies down, looking so wan and battered, she's ashamed of herself.

"People were stabbing themselves in the eyes," he whispers.

Grace kisses him and strokes his hair, then lies beside him and drifts straight back into a wonderful dream about a labyrinth in a forest full of flowering creepers and a black shape, stamping sullenly along a parallel path, just the other side of the hedge.

EVEN THOUGH THE interview went so well, even though she was nearly sure she'd got it, when the email comes through she still *knows* it will be a rejection. When it says *I would be delighted to offer you the position of Systems Administrator*, she has to read it several times to be sure she's understood it properly.

It's not exactly what she wants but she'll get, at last, to train in C-bloody-# and the money is decent and she doesn't have to go back to the Jobcentre on Tuesday and she feels she could turn into a bright vapour of relief and float away.

When her first paycheque comes through, she calls friends she's been too miserable to talk to all this time and goes into a cocktail bar in Soho. She still shudders at drinks that cost £8 but orders them anyway – and wonders, too late, if it was unkind to bring Luke here, when he still can't do this, can only accept what she buys for him. He doesn't seem at ease – little to say for himself, pale under the fading remains of the tan.

But on the last Tube home Grace watches their reflections in the black mirror of the opposite window and it's nice, to see them from the outside; a young couple companionably sprawled over each other, half-drunk and half-asleep. She dozes, and imagines she sees two points of pale light reflected above her head; a black shape, blacker even than the tunnel walls, protectively crouched over her.

Luke jolts awake beside her with an embarrassing cry of alarm, shocking other passengers. He flushes and sits up straight, mumbles something about more dreams and people turning into trees, which doesn't sound so horrific but evidently was. The phrase *doesn't like boys* scrolls through Grace's mind before being instantly censored.

* * *

LUKE'S BEEN OUT of contact long enough that Grace is starting, crossly, to suspect she's been dumped. But then his Facebook is suddenly crammed with Get Well Soon messages along with anxious inquiries from people who, like her, don't know what on earth has happened. Grace leaves a similar message and a few voicemails and texts on his phone and eventually, Luke does call her. "Are you okay?" she asks at once, and there's a long silence.

"I've been in hospital," says Luke quietly, and she hears him swallow. "I'll just say it, I guess. I... everything... got away from me and I... cut my wrists. A bit. And..."

"*Fuck,*" gasps Grace. "Luke, *Christ.* I'm, God, I had no idea..." (but *is that completely true?*) "I'm so sorry."

Luke sighs, weary and staticky across the radiowaves. "It kind of crept up on me. I mean, yes, there's the whole Unemployed Ex-Military thing but I just... thought I was handling it all right. But evidently not. So. I'm clearly not exactly in a *relationships* position at present."

"Okay. I mean, anything you want, of course. But, if there's anything I can... if I can *help* at all..."

Luke hesitates. "No," he says carefully. "I really like you. But I don't feel I can be around you." He sounds puzzled at himself. Apologetic.

"Right," says Grace. And again, "I'm sorry."

"You didn't do anything wrong," says Luke.

Grace lays the phone down gently and carefully on her desk. "You vicious bastard, Mr Levanter-Sleet," she whispers, and then runs out of the room and out of the house, away from what has happened and from having *said* that.

THAT NIGHT SHE has horrible nightmares for the first time in months. The next night she puts off going to bed as long as she can, sculpting with code to soothe herself until three in the morning, and that's followed by some of the richest, most complex dreams yet (worlds of staircases and stars; whispering places under the sea).

She forces herself to believe it doesn't feel as if someone is making a point.

Seven Magpies sent you a direct message on March 30th, 2013, 05:12 am (GMT):

I really need Mr LEVANTER-SLEET back.

You sent **Seven Magpies** a direct message on March 30th, 2013, 09:49 am (GMT):

Fine. Take him then.

Seven Magpies sent you a direct message on April 1st, 2013, 03:32 am (GMT):

I've tried and tried.

THEY HAVEN'T UNFRIENDED each other on Facebook, so she continues, feeling mildly stalkerish, to keep an eye on Luke. He doesn't post much over the months that follow, never anything very personal (unless perhaps he does and she's on a restricted access list). She can't tell how he's doing. But he's alive, and he's away from her and she *knows* those facts can't be related.

SHE MOVES OUT of the house-share and gets a place of her own in Archway, still offensively expensive for what and where it is, but it's wonderful to have her own sitting room and to do the washing up in her own damn time. Nevertheless, she's no longer quite so blissfully grateful for employment that she enjoys running to the assistance of every idiot who's forgotten their password. There's a particularly annoying creature in Client Solutions called Jawad, who appears to believe it's charming that he can barely make a computer turn on, besides which he's into amateur theatre and keeps muttering Shakespeare to himself in the office kitchen when he makes coffee. The worst of it is, she has to go to the play; Jawad has got everyone in the office going and the company is very into Team Bonding, so she knows it'll look bad if she doesn't.

The theatre is a black box studio above a pub in Camden, and when she files in among the rest, Jawad is standing alone in the half-dark on the stage, wearing vaguely Victorian military dress, a brace on his leg and a hump on his back. Then the lights come up and Grace braces herself for the worst as Jawad starts telling them that a war has ended and he can't stand peace.

It's some time before Grace even comes back to herself enough to put into words that he's wonderful. The play is wonderful, but the pace flags noticeably whenever Jawad is offstage, which fortunately isn't often. Jawad surges through it all: restless brilliance and sarcasm and rage. By the end the charm's gone, she can *see* his mind coming to pieces and yet, though she knows he *has* to die, she's sorry to see it happen.

"That was amazing. And I never even liked Shakespeare before this, I wouldn't have come if I didn't have to," she tells him in the bar afterwards, still stunned into tactless truth,

"That's the best thing you could say," says Jawad. Now Richard has gone, he seems like someone new. His hair – harshly slicked back for the play, lightly gelled for work – is tousled over his forehead. "I was too shy to even audition for anything when I was at university. So I have to get it out of my system now."

"You should be a *professional*," says Grace.

Jawad shakes his head wistfully, "I admit, I do sometimes dream of the RSC descending in glory to whisk me away. But I have friends who are pros, and it's so hard – I don't think I could live that way. Also it would count as matricide if I tried it, so here we are."

Watching someone act in a play is surely a terrible reason for changing one's mind so thoroughly about a person, but Grace finds she keeps thinking about the bit when he seduced Lady Anne and hoping his computer will go wrong so he'll drag her over to fix it.

Fortunately Jawad remains an utter idiot with his computer.

He gets into another play almost immediately and Grace helps him run lines in the kitchen at lunch. They linger talking on the steps of St Paul's after work and, at last, kiss at the Tube station and Grace goes home, her body humming with excitement and fear.

She is surely no longer a Girl in Trouble, so Mr Levanter-Sleet would probably have wandered off by now, even if he were real. But it's been eight months since Luke, and she doesn't *really* believe in nine-foot skeleton demons made of shadows who don't like boys.

(Though she's off the anti-depressants now, she still has those beautiful, elaborate dreams).

She wakes up beside Jawad one Sunday morning and studies him anxiously as he sleeps, but his face is smooth and quiet, black eyelashes lying still on his cheeks. Nothing happens. Does it? He never mentions nightmares, she never sees him moving restlessly in his sleep. But is he a little more subdued, does it mean anything when he decides he's too tired and busy to go to the next audition that comes up, or the next?

Then one morning he wakes with a groan and puts both hands to his face and Grace asks "What?" while cold rinses through her blood.

"Are you brewing LSD under the bed?" says Jawad. "I always have the most messed up dreams when I sleep here!"

"You didn't say anything," says Grace, almost accusingly. Jawad shrugs. "What was it about?"

"Drowning," says Jawad, and something hollows in his expression. "It's often drowning... and it went on and on and on."

"And this *always* happens when you sleep here?"

"'For never yet one hour in her bed, Did I enjoy the golden dew of sleep'," says Jawad hammily, "'but have been wakened by my hideous dreams.'" Though that wasn't his line, Grace remembers – that was Lady Anne. Talking about the evil king she'd married.

She's suddenly weak with affection for him. All this time he's borne it.

"Would you say," she asks carefully, "that it's getting worse?"

Jawad doesn't answer for a while. When he makes himself smile again she can see the effort, but there's nothing but warmth when he folds her into his arms. "Never mind," he says. "You're worth it."

"Leave him alone. You leave him the *fuck alone*, Mr Levanter-Sleet," she hisses into the bathroom mirror when Jawad is gone. "And you can drag my brain through hell all night long, I don't care, you're not *getting* him."

You sent <u>Seven Magpies</u> a direct message on November 12th, 2013, 22:16 pm (GMT):

I need to see you.

OF COURSE THE lift isn't working. Of course Seven Magpies has to live at the very top of the tower. Grace slogs grimly upwards, past ripped binbags, through a stubborn reek of urine, floor after floor, and rehearses what she's going to say to Morgane when she sees her. *How could you do this to me. Fix it. Fix it fucking now.* Panting she lurches onto the top floor.

The wind soughs in over the walkway, catching at shreds of plastic and paper. There's a deadness and emptiness up here – aging graffiti scrawled on front doors that somehow Grace senses never open any more. She makes her way to the green door she was told to look for, the last door on the highest floor.

"Hello, Lady Jingly Jones, it isn't locked," pipes a voice from inside. It's a high, pure-toned, remarkably posh voice, like that of an aristocratic child.

She pushes open the door and Seven Magpies – Morgane – scrambles to her feet to meet her.

She can't be as young as she looks – from her blog, she's about Grace's age, surely? – she doesn't even look out of her teens. She's frighteningly thin; bare, sapling limbs emerging from a beaded flapper-girl dress that's too big for her. Her hair is bobbed flapper-short, too, though it seems likely Morgane might have done that herself. Her feet are bare and slightly bluish on the grey carpet. She must be freezing.

"Do come in," says Morgane, in her cut-glass accent, gesturing elegantly. A princess in a tower, thinks Grace, and wonders what she's come here to do with her.

The room is tiny, one corner occupied by a grubby kitchenette. There's a sewing machine on a stained coffee table surrounded by cotton reels and swatches of black satin, and there's a pattern of bones laid out on a makeshift hearth of slate tiles in the middle of the floor. But there's also an Xbox by the old cathode-ray television, a laptop lying on a crumpled velvet blanket on the unmade bed. And there's *Angels of the Embers*, stacked with other games beside a tall bookcase that is nevertheless too small to contain all Morgane's books.

"I thought he'd stay for a week and then come home," offers Morgane. She sounds so forlorn that Grace seethes with an unstable brew of guilt and anger.

"He's trying to kill someone," she says.

Morgane titters. "He wouldn't have to *try*."

"He nearly did kill someone else!"

"I did tell you what he was like."

"But I didn't think he was real!"

"Oh," says Morgane. "So you were humouring me. You shouldn't have done that. We're supposed to be friends. I was only trying to help."

Grace deflates. Scrubs her hands over her face and into her hair. She moans, "So what are we going to do?"

Morgane reaches down and lifts a stone from a heap beside the tiles. It has a hole through it which Morgane positions against her eye.

"Can you see him?" Grace breathes.

Morgane nods. "I saw him when you came in together," she says. "This only makes it clearer. I always see them. All of them."

"There are others?" Grace tries to keep from visibly shuddering. "Here? Right now?"

Morgane's voice quivers. "They're too much for me all on my own. Mr Levanter-Sleet is very different from most."

"How?" asks Grace.

Morgane puts down the stone. "He's a lot nicer." She smiles. "Shall we make a start?"

Morgane kneels daintily on the floor, gesturing for Grace to do the same, and says "I'm going to need some blood."

"Somehow I knew you would," says Grace, sighing.

"I'm very hygienic," protests Morgane.

She is, actually, producing a pair of small surgical scalpels in sealed plastic sleeves, and handing one to Grace. "Not yet, though," she says. She clears away the bones and places pebbles at points on the square of tiles, then pours out black sand from a bottle, drawing a pattern.

"Have you always... been like this?" Grace ventures after a while.

"I always saw things," says Morgane neutrally, frowning thoughtfully at her stones and rearranging them. "But was I always a witch? No. That takes a lot of self-training. Now, please."

She cuts her own hand with practiced indifference, and carefully spills the blood into a circle of sand that's joined, by a long winding pathway, to a similar point on Grace's side of the hearth. Grace, reluctantly, mirrors her, and Morgane begins whispering. Grace wonders if it's Latin or something, but then realises it must be English, although Morgane is too quiet for her to catch any words other than, occasionally, "please."

She sits motionless, silent. Grace watches anxiously, sucking at the back of her hand. She assumes she's not supposed to speak but this goes on for so long that at last she asks: "Is it working?"

Morgane opens her eyes. "No," she says, and destroys the pattern in a sweep of her bony arm and collapses into a huddle over the wreck.

"He likes you better," she moans into her arms. "He likes what you do more."

"What *I* do?" Grace asks, baffled, but Morgane shakes her head and moans. Grace watches her weep awkwardly then reaches out with her uninjured hand to pat her hair. It's the first time in three years' acquaintance they've ever touched. "I'm so sorry," she says, "Is there anything I can do?"

Morgane lifts her head and shakes it again, bravely this time, "I'll have to work harder." But just for a moment all the shadows in the room seem wrong.

Grace flees, but from Morgane's plaintive cry of "Mr Levanter-Sleet!" Grace knows she's taken him with her.

And so he must still be with her at New Cross station, and London Bridge, and so it's ridiculous that she feels safer now she's away from Morgane's tower. But then it's not *her* he means any harm to.

She struggles to think. She refuses to accept this effort has been a total failure.

He likes what you do more.

She *emailed* him to me, Grace thinks. However much messing around with blood and sand she did first, that's how he got to me. She didn't know where I lived, how else could he have found his way?

She stares at the pattern of coloured lines on the Tube map.

* * *

"I'VE BEEN THINKING," says Jawad, and Grace tenses. "Maybe... you see, we could both save a lot of money, if... oh lord, that is the least romantic way of putting it. I mean, I miss you so much when you're not there. Maybe we could move in together?"

Grace cannot speak.

Jawad's smile falters, and then, bravely, reappears. "You look less than delighted, so we'll just pretend that never happened, and..."

"Let's get married," says Grace, sharply, suddenly. And then she smiles, takes his hand and says it again, properly.

BEING ENGAGED, PERVERSELY, gives her time away from him to do what needs to be done. She tells him she doesn't want them to live together before the wedding; it will make moving into their new home less special. And she needs to talk to her friends, make plans.

It's really not as if she can tell him the truth.

Thank God none of this happened when she was unemployed. She has to spend a lot of money: a powerful new desktop with its own server and a backup generator, because she dare not take chances – and this is going to do awful things to her electricity bills.

She calls in sick to work, and begins.

She starts by ganking a lot of code from a virtual reality game called *World of My Own,* and cobbles on some from *Angels of the Embers* for old times sake, and sets about layering in complexity – patterns of algorithms and pipelines of data and soon starts to panic – for how does this come close to the places she's visited with Mr Levanter-Sleet?

She remembers the cathedrals, the forests, the music, the stars.

She's programming in a sequence of fractals when it occurs to her that the games she was using as raw material are designed to render a three-dimensional world to human eyes on a two-dimensional screen. But why should Mr Levanter-Sleet be so limited?

It's so hard and it goes endlessly wrong, that late into the night she weeps with effort and desperation. But when at last she thinks that, if everything she's guessed and remembered about Mr Levanter-Sleet is right then she might have made something he could perceive as a six-dimensional space, something alters, she starts to feel a lonely pleasure in what she's doing. She's crafting a palace, hung with tapestries of code, stocked with various flavours of infinity, and no other human being will ever see how beautiful it is.

And then she thinks it might be ready.

She types:

Mr LEVANTER-SLEET, do you want this?

It's past four in the morning. Even suspense can't keep her going any longer. She's been running on coffee and stubbornness for days. She can't even make it to her bed; she collapses in her clothes on the sofa. She dreams of nothing.

In the morning, the computer is thrumming audibly. Grace sweeps the mouse to clear the screensaver and drops into the chair because always, through all of this, part of her knew it wasn't real – she was losing her mind, or compulsively playing a game she'd eventually be able to stop–

But there, on the screen is Mr Levanter-Sleet's reply:

YES

THAT ISN'T THE end of it, of course.

The computer in the garage of their new home has to be left on twenty-four hours a day. She tells Jawad it's for work – there are things – very sensitive things – she has to monitor remotely, and so he *must not touch it*. And it's not as if she can just leave the program and forget about it. She checks it every morning and evening, and every few days she spends at least an hour tinkering with it, expanding, searching the internet for new ideas, adding more toys for Mr Levanter-Sleet to play with.

She'll be doing that forever, she supposes. Mr Levanter-Sleet isn't trapped. He could leave the program whenever he likes. She has to make it worth his while to stay.

Mr Levanter-Sleet is busy in the program.

She can track him, spooling through the algorithms, the fractals; one day she turns on the monitor to find the screen dancing with colours that shift into a hallucinatory sequence of shapes: arches, spirals, fountains and, right before it ends, an explosion of flowers. She feels certain it's a gift for her, and before she can stop herself she smiles, and lays her palm wistfully against the screen, because it's beautiful but she can't really see what Mr Levanter-Sleet does.

She no longer has those wonderful dreams. And she's free to have nightmares again. They don't come often (and Jawad doesn't have them at all any more). But when they do...

(Mr Levanter-Sleet wouldn't *need* to try, Morgane had said.)

Sometimes Grace dreams of scattered plastic and glass and blood, Jawad lying on the concrete floor of the garage, amid the ruins of the computer.

She dreams of patterns, and their necessary conclusions.

She dreams that no one ever obeys an instruction to *stay away from that door, never open that box, don't touch that computer* forever.

BUTTONS

GAIL Z. MARTIN

*Investigators of the supernatural and the strange are something
of a tradition in genre fiction and have included such luminaries
as William Hope Hodgson's Carnacki the Ghost Finder, Jim
Butcher's Harry Dresden and, of course, the X-Files' Mulder
and Scully. Gail's unlikely investigators run a rather esoteric
antiques store and one character's penchant for old buttons
leads to a very interesting case.*

"MORE BUTTONS, CASSIE? I swear, you read those things like a
steamy novel." Teag Logan sailed into the shop and never even
slowed his pace.

Some people read novels. I read objects, especially buttons.
I can glimpse the dizzying highs and shadowed lows of a
stranger's life in a single, beautiful button.

I'm Cassidy Kinkaide, and I own Trifles and Folly, an estate
auction and antiques shop in beautiful, historic, haunted
Charleston, South Carolina. Truth be told, we were also a
high-end pawn shop on the side. I inherited the shop, which
has been in the family since Charleston was founded back

in 1670. We deal in antiques, valuable oddities, and, very discreetly, in supernatural curios. It's a perfect job for a history geek, and even more perfect for a psychometric. My special type of clairvoyance gives me the ability to 'read' objects and pick up strong emotions, sometimes even fragments of images, voices, and memories.

"Shipment from the weekend auction just came in," I called to Teag. "I love Mondays."

"Let me know if you find any sparklers or spookies," Teag answered. "I'll get the mundanes out on display." Over the years, Teag and I have developed our own private language. 'Mundanes' are items that are lovely but lack any psychic residue whatsoever. 'Sparklers' resonate with the psychic imprints of their former owners. I'll set those aside until I can go through them. 'Spookies' reek of malevolence. They go into the back room, until Sorren, my silent partner and patron, can safely dispose of them.

Most people think Trifles and Folly has stayed in business for over three hundred years because we're geniuses at offering an amazing selection of antiques and unique collectibles. There is that, but it's only part of the story, a small part. It's the back room that keeps us in business. We exist to find the dangerous magical items that make their way onto the market and remove them before anyone gets hurt. Most of the time, we succeed, but there have been a few notable exceptions, like that quake back in 1886 that leveled most of the city. Oops.

"This is all from the Allendale house south of Broad Street, isn't it?" Teag asked, coming back in with a steaming hot cup of coffee.

"The house itself was impressive," I answered, "but it was packed to the gills. Old man Allendale was a collector and a hoarder."

"Bad for the family; good for our business," Teag replied. "It's not often we need four full-day auctions to clean a place out, and that was after the family took what they wanted and got rid of the trash."

"The crowds came for the Civil War relics," Teag pointed out, brushing a strand of hair out of his eyes. He's in his late twenties, tall and skinny, with a skater-boy mop of dark hair, and a wicked sense of humor. He looks more like a starving artist than an aspiring art history Ph.D. candidate, but he's ABD (All But Dissertation) at the University of Charleston. Blame Trifles and Folly for derailing his ambitions. One summer's part-time job working with the amazing antiques and oddities that come through this store, and academia lost its attractiveness. Now he's my full-time store manager, as well as assistant auctioneer, archivist, and occasional bodyguard.

"The guy spent a lifetime wandering around battlefields, since he was a kid in the Twenties," I replied. "If you think the pieces we got for auction were good, imagine what the museum took. They got first pick, for the new Edward Allendale Memorial Exhibit." I glanced at the pile I was sorting. Mostly small stuff, like musket balls, belt buckles, old postcards, and buttons. A big glass jar of buttons.

I shifted in my chair, trying to get more of the draft from the air conditioning. Summer in Charleston was brutal between the heat and the humidity, and my strawberry blonde hair was more frizzy than usual. I tucked a lock behind one ear because it refused to stay in a pony tail. One look at me and you could guess my ancestors' Scots-Irish background, with the green eyes and pale skin that had a tendency to burn the instant I stepped out into the hot South Carolina sun.

"Be careful, Teag. We've got at least one Spooky in the pile that came today. I can feel it. I'm getting a very strong sense of something... evil. I just haven't found the damned thing."

Teag looked at me and raised an eyebrow. "Dangerous?"

I frowned. "Dark. Consider it dangerous until proven otherwise."

Teag leaned against the doorframe. "Didn't Sorren say there were stories about old man Allendale? About the house?"

I nodded. "Yeah, but there are stories about most of the old homes south of Broad, and most involve ghosts. Sorren wanted us to take this auction because he was certain there was more to these particular stories."

"Grumpy old man with no close family, hoarder, has a heart attack and dies," Teag recapped. "Happens every day, somewhere."

I tried to split my focus between my inner sense and paying attention to Teag. "Not quite like this. Neighbors complain about a shadow watching from an upstairs window. Reports of strange noises. People say their dogs don't like to walk near the house." I let my hands hover a few inches above the large boxes yet to be unpacked.

"There's a... residue that clings to everything, like old cigarette smoke, but it's not physical, it's spectral. I can feel it. Everything's tainted."

Teag looked at me over his trendy eyeglasses. "If it's so dark, how come we let it go to auction?"

"Sorren and I went down to the auction site while you were busy dealing with the rest of the event details. We tagged everything he and I thought had a powerful enough resonance to warrant a second look, and had it taken out of the auction until we could go through it."

"So what you're saying is, we've got a whole shipment of Spookies, or at least Sparklers," he replied dryly. "Wonderful."

"Sorren says he'll be here after sundown to help us go through everything," I said. "All we need to do is catalog what came in, and let him know if anything in particular gives off a strong vibe."

"If anything gives off a vibe strong enough for me to feel it," Teag replied, "it would probably knock you flat on your behind. You might want to let me open the boxes and have a first look."

"Fine by me. I'm going to start on the buttons." Buttons speak to me more often than most objects. I've always thought it was because they were worn for long periods of time, day in and day out, often close to the skin.

I reached for the large tray I use to sort buttons, and picked up the jar to dump it out. I felt a tingle in my hand, and I knew that I'd be picking up strong images from some of these buttons. Strong... but nothing felt evil. I promised myself I would be careful.

I watched as a river of old buttons spilled out onto the tray. Mid-Twentieth Century and older, I guessed, watching the array of colors and shapes waterfall out of the jar. Some, made of metal, wood and bone, looked much older.

I picked up a pencil and used the eraser end to poke the pile of buttons. Using the pencil insulated me from the full strength of the impressions, but didn't block them altogether. That was helpful when I wanted to keep my wits about me.

Images flashed through my mind on many of the buttons. The echo of a child's laugher sounded in the distance when I touched a plastic, heart-shaped button. A round ivory disk yielded a woman's voice, humming to herself, and an image of rolling out dough in a kitchen. My pencil flicked among the buttons, and in my mind I saw the blackboard in a long-ago school room from a shirt button, memories of a heavy winter storm from a coat's fastener, and the distant strains of an orchestra from a dainty pearl ball. It went on like that for a few minutes, glimpsing fragments of long-ago lives, until my pencil hovered above one particular button.

An image came to me so clear and strong that it transported me beyond the back room of my shop.

Tall grass, dry from the summer heat, slapped at my legs. The air smelled of sweet honeysuckle, mixed with the acrid stench of gunpowder. Not far away, I could hear the thunder of cannons. My heart was pounding and my palms were sweaty. I gripped my rifle more tightly, comforted by the smooth wood of the grip, and the cool metal of the barrel. Hoof beats pounded closer, not just a few men on horseback, but a cavalry unit on the move. Men would die today. The fear that I might be among them seemed to freeze my blood.

"Cassie! Come on Cassie! Snap out of it!" Gradually, Teag's urgent voice intruded and the vision receded. I shook my head, and came to myself. Teag stood over me, worried but not surprised. He'd seen me 'trance out' enough times to know what to do.

"I'm OK," I said, still reorienting. Teag's glare meant he knew damn well that I wasn't all right.

"Do you know which button sent you day trippin'?" He made an effort to sound flippant, but I could hear genuine concern beneath his words.

"That's the one," I murmured. "I'm certain most of the resonance is coming from this button."

Teag frowned as he bent over the tray, then picked up the button and held it between thumb and forefinger. "It's old. Looks military. Might even be Civil War."

"I'm almost certain it's Civil War," I replied, remembering the images I had seen. "The question is, why are the impressions from this button so much stronger?"

Teag sat on the edge of my desk. "Did you pick up on anything when we were at the house? Get any visions?"

I shook my head. "I never went inside, remember? I was working the Oliver estate, and I left the Allendale house in your hands. Other than a peek in the front door, I never got close."

"The crew was uncomfortable working there, particularly after dark," Teag replied. "The lower floors weren't a problem, but they really didn't like the attic." He paused. "A couple of times, when the men were loading the truck, they said they felt like someone was watching them from an upstairs window, even though no one was in the house. And Jorge, one of my best workers, called off sick the last day. He never gets sick, but the day before, he swore he'd been chased by a shadow. I don't think he wanted to go back in there."

"I don't think this button is a full Spooky," I said, daring to let the pencil hover a bit nearer to the worn metal button.

'Spookies' were malevolent items or objects with a dark magical history. I knew better than to touch Spookies. I turned them right over to Sorren, and he locked them up, neutralized their magic, or sent them off for further study. Sorren had been at this for a lot longer; I was happy to leave those details to him. "Maybe just a strong Sparkler. He doesn't feel angry just... terribly sad."

"Wandering around for more than one hundred and fifty years without being able to rest would make anyone sad, and a mite cranky, too." Teag looked around the back room and through the door to the loading dock. "Get readings from anything else we brought back?"

I got up and began to wander among the boxes, letting my hand trail along their sides. I felt the residue of daily life, hopes, fears, hunger and exhaustion, but one box made me stop and examine my impressions. "What's in here?"

Teag bent to look at the label, since only he could read his scribbled writing. "Antique baby items. Very good condition."

"That's because they were never used," I said quietly. "There was a christening gown, embroidered linen with eyelet lace?"

Teag nodded, his eyes widening. "Yes. Very pretty."

"Set it aside for Sorren. The child died right after the baptism. I'd hate to think someone might purchase that and carry the resonance forward to a new baby."

Teag moved the box away from the others. "Consider it done. How about anything to go with that button?"

I had moved among all the new boxes, and none drew me in or offered up impressions that matched those of the button. It's hard to explain, but when I pick up on 'residue' from an object, it's as if that impression has its own special frequency. Nothing else was on the button's frequency.

I shook my head. "Nothing." I paused, thinking. "Of course, I don't know what I would have picked up from what the museum took. Maybe that button came from a uniform that was in the boxes for the exhibit."

"I am not taking you in the museum again. No how, no way," Teag said, holding up his hands. "Do you remember what happened when we accidentally ended up in the 'Plagues and Pestilence' exhibit?"

I shuddered. Yellow fever, small pox, malaria, diphtheria, and cholera all wrote their own bloody lines of the city's history. The impressions from that display were so overwhelming that I passed out and didn't regain consciousness for a full day. Even then, it had taken some of Sorren's arcane know-how to bring me out of it. I was happy to donate money to the museum, but there was no way in hell I'd step foot inside again.

"I remember," I muttered. "But maybe a family member could provide some details."

"Not much family to speak of," Teag said, consulting the file he accessed on his smart phone. "There's a niece who drew the short straw, so to speak, on having to clean up after him. No other living relatives."

"Got an address?"

Teag looked at his watch. "What's it going to be for the rest of the afternoon, until Sorren gets here? Unpack boxes or play 'button, button, who's got the button'?"

"Button hunting," I decided. "I don't think the resonance is dangerous, but I'd hate to be wrong about that." I'd learned the hard way to play it cautious after an unfortunate incident with a trunk full of antique porcelain dolls. I shuddered. That was going to show up in my nightmares for a long, long time.

"OK then," Teag said, mustering good spirits for the hunt. He put the button into a plastic box, and he put the box into his pocket. "It's a pretty day. Let's head out to see the niece. My notes said she works nights, so if we head over right away, odds are good we'll find her at home."

Teag's phone had all the contact information, so he handed it over while he drove. It was a glorious day, though hot and humid, something that comes with living in Charleston. If you didn't grow up here, you either loved the weather, adapted quickly, or packed up and left.

I called Sullivan Michaels, Mr. Allendale's niece. She was surprised to hear from me, but agreed to see us, especially when I hinted that we had found something of particular interest among the 'junk' she had been happy to sell at auction.

Teag made a few turns, and pulled into the driveway of a modest, one-story ranch house. Sullivan Michaels' house dated from the 1950s rather than the 1850s, but it looked neat and well-maintained, a far cry from the run-down state of her elderly uncle's home. Teag and I walked up to the door and knocked.

Sullivan Michaels was a plump woman in her middle years. She looked as if she was just getting ready for work, and judging by her clothing, I was guessing something in the hospitality business, maybe the night manager at a hotel or restaurant. She had a broad, intelligent face, but there was no spark that suggested passionate curiosity. "You made good time," she said, welcoming us into her home. "I set out some sweet tea and cheese straws if you'd like a bite."

I left the cheese straws for Teag, and poured two tall glasses of sweet tea. The dark amber liquid crackled as it flowed over the ice, and I knew that if it had been made to true Charleston standards, it would be strong as a hurricane and sweet as a honeycomb.

"Thank you again for using Trifles and Folly for your uncle's estate," I began. "We were going through the boxes, and we came across something interesting. We wondered if you might know more about it."

On cue, Teag held out the box with the uniform button. Sullivan examined it, and then shrugged. "I'm sorry, but there was just so much in the house, I don't remember things like individual buttons." Despite her words, she kept turning the button this way and that in the light.

"Did your uncle keep any records of where he found the items in his collections?" I pressed.

She gave a weary chuckle. "He picked up a lot at flea markets, and he scavenged other people's estate sales. When he was younger, he walked battlefields, poked through abandoned houses, and meandered through the woods near where the armies had fought." She paused. "But for all that, he was almost obsessive about noting down what he got and where he got it. Usually he jotted a note on a scrap of paper and put it with the item. I passed everything to the museum that went along with the items they wanted."

"Did your uncle leave any journals or diaries, something that might have recorded his ramblings?" I tried to keep my tone light, but my inner sense told me we were onto something, and that Sullivan held the key.

Sullivan looked uncomfortable. "He kept a journal throughout his adult life," she said. "Stuffed them full of newspaper clippings, photos, even letters. I haven't looked through them, and I don't know if I'll even try." She sighed. "We weren't very close. My uncle kept mostly to himself and had a rather sour disposition. He'd probably come back to haunt me if he knew I'd donated his belongings to a museum rather than holding out for top market price."

Her comment sent a chill down my spine. Hoarders and misers were the most likely to retain an otherworldly attachment to their worldly goods. "I know I'm asking a great deal, but would you be willing to lend me the journals, just for a little while? We try to know the provenance of all the pieces we sell at Trifles and Folly, and something as trivial as where a button was found or purchased means so much to our clients."

"My uncle's life revolved around acquiring items for his collections," Sullivan said. "I'm guessing you'll find little more than a journal of his shopping trips, but good luck hunting." Sullivan looked at turns guilty and relieved. I could guess why. She probably felt a bit guilty turning over a man's private papers to a total stranger. At the same time, I wondered if, subconsciously, Sullivan picked up a disquieting resonance from the old man's things.

"I'll go get the journals," she offered, and jumped up. Teag went to help, and a few minutes later he emerged with two mid-sized cartons.

"One more question, Ms. Michaels," I said. "Would you mind if we went back into the house, just to see if there's anything we missed, like a button or two?"

"I can't imagine that you'll find anything but you're welcome to go. Just drop the key off when you're finished."

Teag put the boxes into the trunk of his car, and we started back to the shop. "You've got a feeling about those journals, I can see it in your face."

"The button is a clue, but by itself, it's not dark," I replied. "But the more I think about it, the more I'm sure that something Edward Allendale brought home with him for his collections turned into a nasty surprise."

"There are an awful lot of journals. It's going to take forever to go through them all."

"I have a hunch that the button will narrow it down for me."

"Which is why I don't think you should do it alone." Teag might be a few years younger than me, but he acts more like the big brother I never had. "Let's take them back to the shop, order in pizza and a six pack while we wait for Sorren, and work our way through the journals."

I tried not to look as relieved as I felt, but I knew Teag was wise to me. "OK, twist my arm," I laughed. "But are you sure you don't have something better to do?"

"I could footnote my dissertation," Teag replied dryly. "Other than that, no."

Within the hour we had the journals spread across my office. Good ol' Edward had been a compulsive journal writer, and the slim tomes stretched all the way back to the 1930s. We ate, and as the afternoon shadows lengthened, we tackled the stack of books after setting them out in chronological order.

"Where does your hunch tell you to start?" Teag asked.

"The early years," I answered without having to think about it. "I'll take the oldest ones. He's got more than seventy years' worth of books; more than enough for both of us."

I cheated, and didn't start with the oldest volume, but instead I turned my senses inward, and waited to be led. Eyes closed, my hand came to rest on two of the journals. The leather bindings were scuffed and cracked, and the pages had yellowed. Inside, scrawled in a young man's handwriting, entries had been inked with a fountain pen.

June 14, 1939 Spent the day down along the river. I know General Beauregard's troops marched through here, or close to this spot. The man who owns this land says it's been in his family since the war years, but no one ever did much with it. He thought there were a few skirmishes hereabouts. Wouldn't I love to find something they left behind!

I read on, caught up in the old entries. I had braced myself for negative impressions from the journals, but from this volume, I sensed only curiosity and enthusiasm. As soon as I picked up the next journal, the feeling changed. There was a darkness to the journal's resonance. Something had changed Edward Allendale between 1939 and 1940. I had a feeling our button had something to do with that shift.

I flipped through it, scanning the dates. Then I realized something. The first half of the book still had the positive feel of the first journal, but toward the middle, a heaviness hung over the pages. I flipped back and forth, trying to find out where the feeling shifted, and this passage caught my attention.

July 17, 1940. I just don't seem to be able to leave off walking along the river. I think there's something here to find, almost like I'm supposed to find it. I can barely sleep at night, thinking about when I can come back and poke around some more.

On the next page, it felt as if a dark curtain descended. I knew I'd found what I was looking for.

July 18, 1940. I saw a little cave I'd never noticed before. It was shallow and filled with rocks, but I found bits of an old uniform, mostly gone to mold except for a button, a gold coin, and some yellowed bones and a skull. I'm certain one of our boys in gray made this his last resting place. I left the bones, but I took the button, the coin and the skull. I'll figure out who to tell about it. Maybe they'll give old Johnny Reb a memorial parade, and pin a medal on me for finding him.

"But you didn't tell anyone, did you, Edward," I murmured. I riffled through the pages of the journal, and two yellowed letters fell out. I bent down, curious.

"That's odd," I said. "These letters are much older than the journal." I looked to where the journal had opened, and read another entry.

September 5, 1940. I think I may have figured out who the Johnny Reb was in that cave. Mr. Johnson at the Historical Society has been letting me go over the lists of the missing and dead from the battles fought near where I found the skull. I could narrow it down some from the type of button, and today I think I found my man. Some of the dead soldiers' families bequeathed items to the Historical Society. Mr. Johnson let me go through those, too. When I found the letters, I knew it had to be the man whose bones I found. His name was Jonah Macaulay. I kept the letters for safekeeping, and I'll give them back to Mr. Johnson along with the skull and other things once I can figure out how to get old Jonah his final rest.

"Find something?" Teag asked.

I showed him the entry, glad to get the book out of my hands. The darkness that found Edward Allendale had started closing in around me. "It changed him," I said. "Before he found those things in the cave, he was just a young guy looking for treasure. But the sense of him shifts from the time he found that grave."

"So Edward stole the letters, huh?" Teag said when he finished reading.

I nodded. "I think he was used to bending the rules, and maybe by this point, the items he found were already getting a hold over him."

I fingered the old parchment, but by themselves, the letters had no special resonance. Carefully, I unfolded the yellowed paper. Bold pen strokes told me that the handwriting probably belonged to a man, and the signature confirmed it. "Jonah Macaulay," I murmured.

"So what's in those letters?" Teag's eyes shone with the love of the hunt.

I struggled to make out the faded lines. "They were written by Jonah to Elsabeth Bradley, and it appears they were engaged," I said, working my way through the cramped paragraphs.

"*My dear Elsabeth,*" I read aloud. "*The sentiment of your gift pleases me, but I am concerned when you speak of its origins. I know that your people come from New Orleans, and many things are done differently there than in Charleston, but I would be a bit more comfortable with the gift of a small cross or even a medallion of one of the saints, like those the Catholic soldiers carry. Nevertheless, I know the intent of your heart, and you may be assured I will carry your token with me into battle, as did the knights of old.*"

"She gave him something as a good luck charm," Teag said, staring at the button. "And it made old Jonah uncomfortable."

I unfolded the second letter, and noticed immediately that the writing was different. Smaller, graceful, meticulous penmanship hinted that the writer of this letter was female. "That's interesting," I said. "There's a note in pencil on the outside of this letter, saying it was found with the kit bag of a missing soldier."

I scanned down through the letter. "Here it is," I said, feeling a thrill of triumph. *"Darling Jonah. How I pray for this war to be over, and for you to return safely. I know you sent me back to my parents in New Orleans for my safety, but I now feel doubly parted from you. I cannot sleep for fear that something might befall you. I implored my maid to take me to the French Quarter, where a Creole woman sells amulets that bring good fortune. Please do not think me unChristian, but I fear my prayers alone may not be enough to bring you home again. The Creole promised me that if you keep this gold coin near your heart, you will not die. I beg of you, my love, do this for me. Ever yours, Elsabeth."*

"I learned long ago that the devil is in the details when it comes to contracts." Sorren's voice made me jump. He stood in the doorway, and I realized that we had been at the journals long enough for the sun to have set.

"You heard?" I asked, clearing journals off a chair for Sorren to have a seat. Sorren looked to be in his late thirties, but I knew he was older. He had dark blond hair, blue eyes flecked with gray, like the sea after a storm, and a slim, wiry build. Once upon a time, he had been a jewel thief in Antwerp, but that was before the Alliance had recruited him. Now, he put his talents to better use, keeping dangerous magical objects from falling into the wrong hands.

"I heard enough to make me suspect that perhaps Elsabeth should have been more careful with the way she phrased her request," Sorren said. His gaze rested on the old letters.

"If you keep this gold coin near your heart, you will not die," I murmured. I looked up, meeting Teag's gaze. "Could an amulet keep Jonah's spirit from crossing over?"

"Your phone message left a good bit out," Sorren interrupted. "Perhaps you could recap a bit for me." After all this time, his voice still held a trace of a Dutch accent.

Teag and I took turns filling Sorren in, ending with the discovery of the journal and the letters. Sorren listened quietly, but I could see the spark in his eyes that said he was mentally cross-referencing everything we told him against his considerable knowledge of magical lore.

"So Elsabeth asked a Voudon to make an amulet for her beloved," Sorren said. "That kind of magic should not be dabbled in. It's powerful, and the spirits that give the Voudon power, the *loas*, do not make simple bargains."

I moved around the room, letting my hand hover over the journals, decade by decade. "Something isolated Edward, filled him with despair. I can feel how it grew over the years. By the end, it consumed him."

Sorren nodded. "Edward found Jonah's skull – and the button and coin – in a cave. Caves are liminal space, thresholds between our world and other realities. That would have heightened the power of the spell on the coin, and lying there for more than a century would have strengthened it even further. Then Edward happens upon the bones and takes them home with him, to a home built on land reclaimed from the sea – another sort of liminal space. He brings it into a home that already had a history of haunting, so other spirits had found an easy passage from their world to ours."

I shook my head as the horror of the situation became clear. "Jonah, or the coin, fed on Edward's life energy, until Edward weakened and Jonah grew stronger."

"I fear Jonah has been a tool of the coin's curse for many years now," Sorren replied. "If anything of Jonah still remains, it's what is left after the coin drew the power it needed to fulfill the spell."

"We didn't see a skull or a gold coin in the house," Teag said. "But before the house passes on to another owner, we're going to need to find them, or Edward won't be the only victim."

Sorren nodded. "The coin – or rather, the curse on the coin – is strongest in liminal space. So you'll have to go in daylight, avoiding the threshold times."

"Noon, midnight, dawn, sundown," I replied. "And nighttime."

"Exactly. And my magic makes me liminal space," Sorren added quietly, meeting my gaze. Magic had kept Sorren alive long beyond a normal lifespan. "So I won't be able to go with you on this one. My presence will only make the curse stronger." He paused. "Don't worry, Cassie. Teag and I will still get the items to the Alliance. I just need you to find them."

"How do we get it out of there?" I asked. "I don't dare touch it, and I don't want to put Teag in danger."

"Agreed," Sorren replied. "Give me a couple of hours. I need to pay a visit to an old friend."

Sorren left the shop, and Teag and I passed the time cleaning up the pile of journals and unloading a few of the boxes I could assure contained nothing except 'mundanes.' Before long, we heard a knock on the door and rushed to let Sorren in.

"I went to see a friend of mine, one who knows something about Voudon. Mama Nadedge," he said.

"Why didn't you take us with you?" I asked, intrigued and a little put out at being left behind.

Sorren chuckled. "Mama Nadedge died many years ago, Cassie. Her spirit lingers, if one knows where to look. I asked her guidance, and this is what she gave me." He withdrew a piece of paper marked with a complicated, stylized pattern of crossed lines, stars and a heart, something I recognized as a *veve*, a Voudon symbol.

"I took these to a jeweler I know, someone willing to stay open late for a good cause," Sorren said. "He made these for you and Teag." Sorren reached into his pocket and withdrew two silver disks engraved with the same pattern as the paper, each on their own silver chain.

"I know enough about Voudon to know each spirit, or *loa*, has its own *veve*. Whose is this?"

Sorren smiled. "Very good, Cassie. This is the *veve* for Maman Brigitte. She's the spirit who reclaims the souls of the dead and helps them cross over. Believers say she's powerful, and she appears as either a bride or a veiled old woman. She is very near the top of the *loa* hierarchy, which means that whatever spirit placed the curse on Jonah's coin is less powerful than Maman Brigitte."

"At least, we hope so," I muttered under my breath, taking the amulet and slipping it over my head.

THE NEXT DAY, when we reached the Allendale house, I let Teag go on ahead to unlock the door and turn on the lights. I lagged behind, turning my senses inward, listening for the button's owner. There was a presence here. I followed Teag to the attic.

"Teag, let me hold your jacket, please," I said.

I was hoping that having the button close to me would heighten my senses. It did. As soon as I held Teag's jacket, the connection with the button grew stronger. As Teag began to wander around, looking at the attic walls for hiding places, I let my senses focus on the box, let it draw me toward one particular corner.

Against one wall was a large, empty armoire. I stood in front of it, wondering why the button had steered me here.

"I emptied that myself," Teag said, coming up behind me. "We went through it completely. There aren't any hidden compartments, no extra drawers." He shook his head. "We left it here because frankly, no one could figure out how to get it down the stairs."

I looked down toward the floor. "Casters," I said, pointing. "It can be moved. Did you look behind it?"

Teag shook his head. "It was pretty clear no one had moved it for decades, and it's flush against the wall. Never occurred to me."

I went to one side and put my shoulder against the armoire. "Come on. Let's see what's behind it." Teag joined me, and we started to push. The heavy wooden armoire didn't want to roll, but finally, the casters creaked and we inched the heavy box down the wall.

"There!" I said, and pointed. The wall behind the armoire was filthy, covered in dust and a shroud of old cobwebs. Down where the wall met the floor a piece of wood covered a hole and above it, a thin dark crack separated two wide boards.

Teag pulled out a pair of work gloves from his messenger bag, along with a screwdriver. He knelt next to the opening, and began to pry at the wood. I could hardly think straight, because the sensations from the button in my pocket had gone off the charts.

The attic walls melted away, and once again I saw the sunlit battlefield I had glimpsed before through the eyes of the button's owner.

Fear coursed through me, making my heart pound. All around me, I heard the sharp crack of rifles and in the distance, the steady, deadly pounding of cannons that shook the ground beneath my feet. The uniform I wore was gray, or had been once. Now, it was faded from the sun, stained where it had been splashed with the blood of other men, brown from the red clay dirt. Just as I raised my rifle to my shoulder, I heard another loud crack, closer this time, and staggered backwards as if someone had shoved me. My own shot went wild, with the rifle barrel pointed toward the sky as I nearly fell. When I put my hand down to my side, my fingers came away stained with blood.

"It's open!" Teag shouted in triumph, setting the board to the side. A dark hole gaped in the wall. From that hole, Teag drew out a small bundle wrapped in old rags. He unwound the rags and withdrew a yellowed skull. He jostled it, and the lower jaw fell away, revealing a gold coin that had been placed in the mouth.

I stared at Teag and the bundle, then my gaze shifted behind him, to the wall. The thin dark crack had grown wider, and from it, a shadow slipped out like smoke.

"Get back, Teag!"

Teag followed my gaze, but I could tell from the look on his face he didn't see what I saw. Still, he acted, scrabbling backward, clutching the skull and coin. The shadow grew larger, briefly taking the form of a man and then shifting, with tendrils that unwound themselves like a black kraken uncoiling. Behind me, one of the light bulbs flared and then burst with a crack like a gunshot. I searched my senses, and knew that the dark crack was a fissure between more than the attic siding. The Allendale house had been rumored to have been a hotbed of paranormal activity for long before Edward brought home his battlefield treasure. Now I knew why. The dark space was no ordinary splintering of old boards, no settling of the foundation. It was a threshold between the world of the living and the place of the dead.

"Get out of here." I could barely make words come from my throat. The dark shadow was growing larger.

"The hell I will," Teag said. "Maybe it wants the button."

But I could feel what the darkness really wanted; it wanted fresh meat, warm blood, and the life that animated our beating hearts.

My gaze went again to the crack between the boards. I reached for the amulet around my neck for moral support, and pressed the smooth silver disk against my palm.

An image formed in my mind of a woman in an antique bridal gown. A heavy lace veil covered her face. I could sense an aura of power around her.

Leave the shadowed one to me, my child. Send the curse where it belongs, and close the rift.

How? I wondered. How do I close the rift? I looked again at the dark crack, a thin opening, or a small rip. Or a buttonhole.

"I've got an idea," I said, eyeing the skull Teag still held and the distance between me and the wall. "Can you get the coin out of the skull's mouth?"

Teag juggled his macabre charge. "I think so. Dammit! Someone wired it in here."

"Try not to handle the coin if you can help it. Put it on the floor, where it's easy for me to get it," I instructed, keeping my eyes on that damned shadow.

A coin in the mouth of a corpse, a penny for the ferryman, I thought. Perhaps at some point, Edward Allendale had tried unsuccessfully to send his unwanted visitor to the great beyond.

"Got it," Teag said

I reached into the pocket of Teag's jacket and my hand closed over the plastic box with the button, and I fumbled with the latch to open it. The box gave way, and the button tumbled into my palm.

For that instant, the contact with the long-dead soldier was complete. Darkness washed over me, drawing the warmth from my blood. Anger and despair filled me, and my gut contracted with the pain of a rifle wound that was more than one hundred and fifty years in the past. Then another presence filled me, and the image of the bride grew brighter and brighter, becoming a light that flared and forced the shadow to retreat.

Now! The voice shouted in my mind. I dove across the floor, grabbing the coin with my right hand and clenching the button in my left. I skidded toward the wall, and used my momentum to thrust both the coin and the button through the crack.

Maman Brigitte's light struck the shadow man, just as I forced the coin and the button into the darkness. I heard a scream, although I could not tell whether it came from the shadow or whether it was my own.

The darkness vanished, and I slumped to the ground, too spent to move. In my mind, I saw the image of the bride again, bending over the rift, sealing it with her veil. Teag grabbed my wrist, yanking me to my feet, and together we barreled down the stairs and out of the house. We reached the other side of the street and looked back, half expecting the house to disappear into a vortex or tumble to the ground. It did neither, although for an instant, a light flared brilliantly from the attic window, then went dark.

"Want to bet no one sees a shadow at the window again?" Teag asked. I looked down. He was still holding that damned skull. He caught the direction of my glance, and shrugged. "Poor guy is long overdue for a decent burial. Without the coin, it's just a skull. I have an old friend who works at the mortuary. I'm betting he can make sure old Jonah gets a proper burial."

Teag might have said more, but my head was swimming, and I swayed on my feet. He reached out to steady me as I passed out, but there was someone else as well. In my mind's eye, I saw the veiled bride standing over me. She bent down, and touched a finger to my amulet, and the metal disk felt warm on my skin. As consciousness faded away, so did her image, but I had the feeling she approved.

I woke on the couch in my apartment over the shop. Consciousness returned slowly, and with it, warmth. I felt a presence, safe, reassuring, and it carried a honeyed compulsion to rest. I opened my eyes, and found Sorren, looking down at me, concern clear in his features. He helped me sit up enough to sip some sweet tea, and then eased me back onto the pillows.

"Rest," Sorren said, and his voice felt like balm poured over a throbbing wound. "When you're feeling better, there's a new situation to discuss."

"Oh, goody," I murmured, but as I drifted off to sleep, I knew the truth, and so did Sorren. Trifles and Folly was far more than just another antiques store. It helped make the world a little safer, one haunted item at a time. I couldn't walk away from that, not when my gift could make a difference. Not for all the damned buttons in the world.

NANNY GREY

GEMMA FILES

Secrets can run in families, and secrecy and magic are two very old – some would say ancient – bedfellows. Gemma has taken the theme of women and magic and woven it into a dark and erotic tale. It's a warning to the curious, but also a story about how power accrues over time and what dreadful price one must pay for its use.

OH LOW ESTATE, *my love my love,* the song's hook went, or seemed to, through the wall of the Ladies'. Bill Koslaw felt it more than heard it, buzzing in his back teeth through the sweaty skin of his jaws as he pushed into this posh tart – Sessilie, he thought her name was, and the rest began with a 'K' – from behind with her bent over the lav itself, hands wide-braced, each thrust all but mashing that great midnight knot of hair against the cubicle's tiling. And he could see her lips moving, too, half-quirked in that smile he'd literally never seen her lose thus far: *Oh low estate, the threat is great, my love my love (my love)...*

Tiny girl, this Sessilie K., almost creepily so. She looked barely legal, though he'd touched a cupcake-sized pair of breasts beneath that silky top of hers as she pulled him inside the Ladies', nipples long enough to tent the material and one apparently bar-pierced, set inside a shield like a little silver flame which pricked his hand when he'd tried to flick it, drawing blood. And: "Oh, never mind that," she'd said, that smile intact, opaquely unreadable even as she'd leaned forward with her hips hiked high, flipping her skirt up to show her thong already moved neatly aside for easier penetration.

"Bit cruel to your knickers," he'd commented. "Bet those cost a pretty penny."

"No doubt," she'd replied, bum still in the air and both legs wide-spread, aslant on her too-high heels, completely shameless. "But then, it all ends up in the fire eventually. Doesn't it?"

Punctuating it with a bit of a shimmy, like: *well, get a wiggle on. Don't waste my time, groundling; better things to do, you know. Better classes of fools to fuck.*

That airy contempt of hers, especially when delivered in those plummy tones, engorged him. But...

He should be liking this better than he was, he reckoned. Some sort of aristocrat, perpetually drunk and perpetually talking, always with her credit card out like it was glued to her palm and no apparent impulse control to speak of; what *wasn't* to like, for Christ's sake?

Just her, he supposed. Her, and almost everything about her.

He slid one hand up to ruck her blouse over her shoulderblades, and flinched from what he encountered there. Something halfway between a grey-on-grey tattoo of uncertain design and a brand with scabby edges, so rough it took on a Braille-like texture beneath his fingers. As though if he knew how, he could read it, but only in the dark.

"That a birthmark?"

"Oh, we all have one."

"Your family?"

"Some of them too, yes."

"Who was it you meant, then?"

"Oh, Billy, silly Billy. Does it really matter?"

And here she rammed back against him unexpectedly, throwing him off his beat. Singing once more, this time out loud, as she took control of their rhythm: "*Ohhhh low estate, the threat is great...*

(my love)"

"Am I boring you?"

"No, no. Do carry on."

"What's that, then?"

"Quite like this song, is all. I'll stop if you'd like. Wouldn't want to, mmm... put you *off*."

She shot him a glance back over her shoulder, with that, and reached back down between her legs to run one long nail over the seam of his sack – inch-long nails she had, white with black tips like some odd parody of a French manicure, each with a small black bedazzlement down where the cuticle should be. Pressing just hard enough to make him jump, so she could clamp around him and milk him so fiercely it began to hurt as she tossed a loose forelock out of her eyes and winked at him.

Winked.

Jesus wept.

That, right there – as he grunted and came, listening to her give out a rippling laugh in reply, her own orgasm seeming very much like an afterthought – probably marked the exact point at which Bill stopped feeling anything like bad about always having planned to slip her a Rohypnol and rob her house, later on.

BILL HAD COME to London on a Kon-Tiki packet, planning to round-trip Europe before moving on to the next leg of his pre-Uni world tour. But that'd all been put paid to when this arsehole, Gary from Tasmania, decided he'd cheated him out of the proceeds from reselling a bag of weed they'd both gone in on and took off with his stuff in revenge – passport, money, tickets, the whole deal.

Now it was three months later, and Bill still hadn't quite worked himself up to the point where he was willing to tell the Old Man what had happened – just kept on moving from place to place, bed to bed, sofa to sofa. Squatted here and there, took under-the-counter jobs, and tried to build up some sort of pad. Going to clubs had become about the next ride home, the next overnight, and then – slowly but surely – about whatever he could pick up around the flat or the house, or wherever, before they woke up. Small items of value, gold and silver, electronics; stuff non-specific enough to pawn or fence without being traced, but nice enough they'd bring a fair turnaround.

Girl like Sessilie, wherever she lived, it had to be just *full* of stuff like that – a spread of hockable trinkets peppered in and between the *Lock, Stock & Two Smoking Barrels*-type stuff: antique firearms, paintings and knick-knacks with nice pedigrees, etcetera. That was the assumption, anyhow.

He'd long since learned to trust his instincts when it came to such matters, and it had paid off, literally. Hadn't been wrong once, thus far.

So: "Shouldn't there be somebody home, this time of night?" Bill asked as he half-walked, half-lifted her up the stairs. The place was dark, like 19th-century dark; it was the sort of towering three-story house that should really be lit with oil-lamps, not cunning little sodium bulbs on dimmer switches. "Place is a bloody tomb."

Sessilie's constant smile skewed a bit to the left, those horrifying nails making a slithery noise on the banister as she dragged them along its curve. "Oh, there's very little staff left, you know – family holidays, all that. Most of them have already gone down to air out the summer house, for when I'm done with End-of-Term."

"What about your parents?"

"Hmmm, be *quite* the surprise if *they* were here; they've both been dead since I was eight."

"...sorry."

"Oh, no need. Papa crashed a car and killed himself, but Mama held on a few days in hospital, at least. And ever after, it's just been me and Nanny Grey."

As she spoke this last name, Bill almost thought he heard something drop in the dark above them – on the next landing, maybe, or higher up yet. A stealthy noise like a single clock-tick, or the sound of a hairpin falling to the floor. Not footsteps, not exactly. But the dim stairwell and its adjacent hallways took on an air of waiting, of watchfulness, even though absolutely nothing which might be qualified to fill such a role evinced itself.

"You... still have a nanny?" Bill asked, pushing Sessilie up onto what he thought was the second floor, where she laid a finger against her lips and shook her head, drunkenly. Then tottered over to a side-table in those ludicrous heels, their clacking muffled by a thick oriental rug, and took out a long candle the colour of bone that she fitted onto a nearby holder with an absurd little flourish, before rummaging in her purse for a cigarette and lighting it. She took a long drag, then pressed the tip against the candle's wick, which flared into life.

"*Governess* would be the proper term. That's what Nanny would say, anyhow. Such an old *bulldog*, Nanny Grey. So protective! She's always been with our family, you see..."

And here she paused, wavering back and forth, her eyes unfocused – yet still retained presence of mind enough to stub the smoke out in the candle-holder's dish and blink over at Bill, rather sweetly. "'Scuse me," she said. "I feel... rather off-colour, all of a sudden. Might I rely on you to get me to bed?"

Slowest-to-take-effect Rohypnol in all creation, Bill thought, amazed by her stamina. *Ought to check my supply, once this is over with...*

"My pleasure," was what he said, though, giving her a leg-out bow, fairytale prince-style. To which she tittered and made him a practiced curtsy, so well-learnt she barely even stumbled; he slung a hand under either armpit and caught her up with ridiculously little effort (so light, her bones like a bloody bird's), letting her fold into him, apparently too tired to yawn. Sleeping bloody Beauty.

The bedroom in question, which she directed him towards with a series of chest-muffled murmurs, looked almost exactly the way he'd pictured it would – big canopied bed, choked with pillows and fluffy plush dolls: cute versions of un-cute animals, emo anime characters. He set her down in their embrace, and watched her curl into a foetal position, tucking a particularly infectious-looking teddy-bear – the size of a two-year-old, chenille-furred and shedding worn lace in leprous swathes – down tight between those hungry thighs.

Strange little girl, he thought. Well, he was right to want to be rid of her, and not just for the obvious reasons; best to get to it, then flee this damn place. Nothing so big should be so empty, so *quiet...*

And there it was again, from somewhere: that *sound*. A dog's nails clicking on the floor, one leg at a time. A mouth opening, pop-gasp, only to shut once more, without even an exhaled breath.

Get going, son. Grab what you can find, and scarper.

If only he could tell which direction the sounds were coming from.

Closer, now. To his left; no, right.

Bill shut the door behind him with excruciating slowness, tensed for the latch's click, and once he heard it, turned left so hard he thought he might twist an ankle. The candle – left abandoned, with only Sessilie's crumpled cigarette-butt for company – gave just enough light to navigate by, and Bill took the stairs upwards in loping strides, two by two by two. His heart hammered fast in his throat.

The third floor was smaller than it had seemed, from below. Just a door on either side, master bedroom versus guest-room, or maybe office. Forcing himself not to wonder what might be on the other side, Bill twisted the closest knob and slid in sidelong, trying to keep it open just the bare minimum allowable to admit his frame.

Within, he crept across the floor, tai chi tread, heel rolling straight and narrow to toe with every touch-down, to at least keep the creaks even. This had to be where Sessilie's dearly departed Mum and Dad once slept – hung with tapestry like some set for *Hamlet*; a strange mixture of blue velvet and purple trim that shone all the darker in what little moonlight leaked in under drawn blackout shades. Dark like club lighting without the natter of crowds and the underfoot thunder of feet, pulse of music seeping in from everywhere at once as though it were a swarm of tiny biting flies.

(*oh low estate*)

(*the threat*)

(*my*)

Bill felt his way forwards, in search of drawers, cupboards, some sort of indication that anything had ever been kept in this damnable room besides memories and a place for wrinklies to shag. Something pushed forward under his fingers, a slick surface impossible to hold onto. Something hit the ground with a crunch, right in the midst of a bright stripe of moonlight: a presumably happy couple trapped under a fresh lattice of cracks, taken someplace sunny enough their faces were almost impossible to make out in detail, except that the man might have had Sessilie's hair-colour, while the woman's smile cut the exact same angle as her darling daughter's...

Bill froze, waiting in vain for another of those... no-sounds; those weird, unidentifiable lack-of-noises, but none came. So he just kept staring down as though hypnotised, finding himself trying to make out what that was there, on the inside crook of dead Mrs. K's arm, just angled so the camera barely registered it; grey on grey, uneven edges. It couldn't be... no, stupid idea.

No one gets a tattoo – or whatever – just like their Mum's, you twat.

Not even someone as odd as Sessilie, surely. Or... that *was* it, goddamnit. And *that*... he realized, at pretty much the very same instant...

... was the *noise*.

It's right behind me.

Before he could tell himself not to, he'd already turned.

At first, he genuinely didn't recognize her without all that high-gloss cack on her face. She'd taken her hair down, proving it to be far longer than it had seemed when knotted up – brushing her thighs in one thick, glossy, dead-straight fall, shiny-black as her own nail-tips. She'd changed, too, into an actual honest-to-God cotton nightie with long, ruffled sleeves and a button-down front, whose collar went up to her jawline. With skin thus mainly hidden yet feet left bare, she looked both younger than before – enough to make him seriously question his own judgement, in terms of where he'd chosen to stick his tackle – and sexier than ever in a still freakier way.

"Do you like the rest of my home, Billy?" she said, fluttering her lashes. "It's a bit of a dump, but one does what one can. Still, it must've exerted quite a pull on you, for you to go stumbling around here in the dark while you thought I was asleep."

"Well, uh... I was just looking around for..."

"The loo? I do know how you appreciate a nice bathroom, after all. One on every floor, dear; two, sometimes. One wonders how you missed them."

Oh, does *one?* That tone of hers was maddening; not simply the way in which she spoke, but the sentiment – or lack thereof – behind it. And so difficult to listen to as well. Slipped away whenever the ear tried to fasten on it, pig-greasy with happy idiocy, as though nothing said 'like that' could be worth paying attention to, even with only half an ear.

Which was why he found himself trying to focus on the light she held, instead, using its soft flicker to steady himself. "That's from... downstairs, isn't it?"

"Why yes, it is. Funny you should notice."

"Why? I was there when you lit it."

"'Course you were, I knew that. But, you see – this is rather a *special* candle."

She took a moment to run her finger over its uppermost quarter, hot wax slopping onto her in a way that anyone else would find unbearable, and made an odd little fiddly gesture that seemed to make a perfect little approximation of somebody's features emerge from the unburnt portion. Not just somebody's, though – for as she did, Bill heard a fold of tapestry pull back, revealing a long, narrow oval of mirror, and glanced automatically towards its surface. There, hanging inside like a drowned corpse under glass, he recognized himself; his blood congealed, the air itself becoming slow, difficult to move through. He could barely think, barely breathe; his chest heaved painfully, a landed fish yearning for water.

"Whuh..." was all he could say by way of reply, and Sessilie smirked.

"Oh, it's an *awfully* amusing story. You see, when one of my Mama's great-great-whatevers was clapped in durance vile over having been accused of merry-dancing with Old Sir 'S', she smuggled this candle into the clink to make a dolly out of it. And where she put it, I can't possibly say; a very secret place indeed, if you take my meaning. But..."

With a frighteningly massive effort, Bill managed to half-turn himself back towards the door, though his feet seemed snared in treacle, his Achilles tendons shot full of novocaine. He fell to his knees, clutching for Sessilie's ankles, but she skipped back out of range as though playing hop-scotch, content to let his own weight carry him down onto all fours. And even then, practically parallel with the floor, he couldn't manage to keep 'upright'; everything hurt, impossible to support. His hands gave way, knees bowed inwards, joints unsteady.

"It's special, you see," Sessilie went on, "because it can burn all night, and still never quite be consumed. The wax grows back like flesh, so that every new woman of my blood may re-shape the face to their liking, light it, and use it like a Hand of Glory to trap our enemies. Though it has other uses too, of course. Summoning the one who first gave it us, for example, and who is sworn to do our bidding just as we, in turn, swear to eventually pay for that long and faithful service."

Behind her, a stirring. A wind ruffling those tapestries as *something* passed behind them, dropped pin-quiet, clicking dog's nails-distinct. A lip-pop with every step.

"As for *you*, meanwhile," Sessilie added, "how long d'you intend to make me wait, exactly? And after all this trouble I've gone to, on your behalf."

The answering voice seemed to come from everywhere and nowhere at once, soft as fallen leaves. Saying, without haste: "A moment's rest is always pleasant, my lady. You do keep me so very busy."

"Really, Nanny, you're *very* lazy, all things considered; greedy, too. But then, Mama always warned me you were. *Rule with an iron hand,* and all that."

"Yes, my lady. Your lady mother was a perceptive woman, with – very good taste."

"You aren't being impertinent, are you, Nanny?"

"Only a trifle, my lady. Will you deny me that, too?"

"No, Nanny. You may be as impertinent as you like, so long as you do what you're told."

"Yes, my lady."

She rose up then, manifesting from what might have been the bottom of the tapestries, the dark under Sessilie's parents' bed, or a pile of rags in the corner. Thirty at the most, slim and straight and taller than Sessilie yet bent, willow-graceful; coloured white and black and grey like Sessilie's room, with the occasional hint of red at her mouth, her ears, her distressingly long fingers. The dress she wore might've been modelled on Sessilie's nightgown but copied in negative, its fabric less cotton than bombazine, giving off a distinctive swish of underskirts as she stepped forward in her neat little black patent shoes.

The click, the pin-drop, that was the sound of each movement – not a creak, not a sigh, nothing human. As Bill goggled at the realization, she dipped her head as though he'd spoken out loud, projecting: *Yes, I fooled you. I am sorry to play such games. They are the only pleasures left to me, I'm afraid...*

(*Well – almost. I do not mean to lie. Lying is the provenance of your species, not mine.*)

(*But we will talk further of such things, soon enough.*)

"Where'd you... come from?" He asked her, barely able to raise what voice remained to him. She simply regarded him silently while Sessilie frowned, tapping her nails so that the candle-holder rang dully. Replying, impatiently–

"Really, Billy, don't you *listen*? I told you already, she's always here. This is Nanny Grey."

IT WAS A dream – had to be. How else could they have moved from one room to another, on whose walls an array of photos gave way to prints, giving way in turn to portraits, etchings, watercolours, oils? And somewhere in each composition – lurking patient and anonymous, behind or beside the centrepiece arrangement of well-dressed men, women, girls and even some boys who all shared Sessilie's dead-straight ink-fall of hair, her grey-blue eyes, her cruelly slanted smile – a version of Nanny Grey was present in her long black dress, her sensible footwear, no matter what the era.

"Nanny is my governess, as I said," Sessilie told Bill as she pressed him back onto what felt like a nest of sheets. "My servant, my lady-in-waiting. She's my helpmeet, the head of my household; she keeps all of this running, and whatever she does, she does at *my* pleasure." Raising her voice slightly here, a coiled lash, brandished rather than used: "Isn't that so, Nanny?"

"It is, my lady."

"Since – oh, I forget the year. Thirteen-oh-oh something, Mama said…"

"1346, my lady. When the very fount of your blood was almost cut off in full flower, for – was it treason? Yes. You Kytelers are treasonous by nature, I believe. And to kill one's husband, then, no matter what provocation might have preceded such a desperate act, was considered just as bad as conspiring to kill the king himself. They burnt women at the stake for it just as surely as for witchcraft, soaked in oil and pitch with no hope of merciful strangulation, whilst crowds screamed and pelted them with garbage."

"Better by far to turn to the Devil than God, under such circumstances," Sessilie chimed in, with an air of quoting something learned by rote. "Or easier, anyhow."

"Down there in the dark, yes, amongst the rats and bones. A bad place for any pretty woman to end. But then again, that *is* where your ancestor Lady Alyce eventually found me, after all – where we found each other, more accurately."

"Quite. But the promise behind our contract isn't enough to satisfy Nanny, you see, not always. And though it's *such* a bother to arrange for boys like you to come visit every once in a while, Nanny does *so* much work on our behalf that she really must be kept happy. It's only good manners."

"I do value good manners, you see. Courtesy, common or otherwise. The little gestures."

"'Manners maketh man', and all that."

"A party-dress on an ape, that's all they are, when everything is said and done. But since there's no alternative, they simply have to do."

"Given it must've been God who deeded you to us in the first place, directly or in-, do you think perhaps we might be part of *your* Hell, Nanny?"

"I often ask myself that very question, my lady."

"But to no avail?"

"None, my lady."

"That's prayer for you, Nanny."

"Yes, my lady."

Nanny Grey eddied forward with one long white hand on her breast, head bent down submissively. And when she looked up, eyes pleasantly crinkled, she smiled so wide that Bill could see how her teeth were packed together far too numerously for most human beings, bright as little red eyes in the wet darkness of her mouth. While her eyes, on the other hand, were white – white as real teeth, as salt, as a blank page upon which some unlucky person's name had yet to be inscribed.

"Little master," she murmured. "You wished a tour, I believe, and no one knows this house better than I. Come with me, please."

"I don't–"

"Oh, it will be no trouble; what my lady orders, I do. For as she told you, this is the bargain between us – the terms of my employment."

"Yes, and I do hope you were finally paying attention, silly Billy. Because with so little time left, I'd hate to have to repeat myself."

Sessilie leant down then, pressing one ear to Bill's chest, in a vile parody of post-coital relaxation. But when Nanny Grey laid one of those too-long hands on his forehead a moment later, he felt his heart lurch and stutter as though he were about to have a heart attack, pounding double, triple, quadruple-time. Sessilie must've heard it, for she gave yet another of those rippling laughs, and he wanted nothing more than to be able to rouse his limbs enough to tear her soft white throat open with his thumbs. She drew back and pouted.

"I'm going to tell you something now, Billy," she said, "because I actually quite like you, all things considered. One day, when I turn Nanny over to *my* daughter the way Mama turned her over to me, she will take me wherever she's taking you – wherever she took my Mama, and hers before her, so on, etcetera. Back to the first of us, great Lady Alyce in her shit-filled cell. So there; that might help."

Bill swallowed hard, barely scraping enough air to whisper: "It... really... doesn't."

"Mmm, s'pose not; shouldn't think it would. But then, I did only say 'might.'"

He sank down further then, excruciatingly slow, into a deep, deep blackness. Only to hear them still arguing, as he went–

"Do this, Nanny Grey; do that, Nanny Grey. Eat up, Nanny Grey. You'll expect me to digest him completely as well, I'm sure, just to save you the trouble of having to cover up your own indiscretions."

"Well, I could simply take him away now, if you'd prefer – but what on earth would be the use of that, considering? There are limits to even your perversity, I'm sure."

"Really, it's you Kytelers who are the lazy ones. Never doing anything for yourselves... what sort of example do you think that sets, for everyone else?"

"Oh, pish-tosh, Nanny. Why should we have to make the effort, when we have *you* to do it for us?"

"... crazy..." Bill told them both, through stiffening lips, to which Sessilie only smiled, as ever. While Nanny Grey raised a single perfectly-arched eyebrow, expressionless as a cast pewter mask, and murmured, in return: "I had *wings* once, little master. You'd be disappointed too, I'd venture, if you found yourself where I find myself now."

"Poor Nanny. Quite the come-down, wasn't it?"

"A fall, yes, both long and hard. And at the end of it–"

"Me," Sessilie supplied, brightly. "Wasn't that nice?"

A pause, infinite as some gigantic clock's gears turning over, millennial, epochal. Deep time caught in the shallowest of all possible circuits, and only digging itself deeper. After which Bill heard the thing that called itself Nanny Grey reply, with truly terrible patience–

"...even so, my lady."

DUMB LUCY

ROBERT SHEARMAN

Shearman is a magician. I don't mean in the traditional sense, but there is something about the way that Robert uses words and imagery that makes him quite unlike any other writer working today. 'Dumb Lucy' shows Shearman at his best: a poignant, heart-breaking tale that has hints of the work of Russell Hoban and Walter M. Miller Jr about it, but the magic is undoubtedly Shearman's own.

THERE WAS LITTLE magic left to those dark times. The world seemed cracked somehow, too weak for the magic to hold; latterly, as he'd performed his tricks, he'd begun to doubt they would work at all, he'd stood before his audience behind his patter and his sheen and a beaming smile that was well-oiled and ready practised, and he'd felt himself starting to sweat, he'd felt the fear take over – the magic wouldn't hold, the magic would fail. Lucy never seemed to notice. Lucy never seemed to get nervous. And he supposed that if Lucy couldn't see how frightened he was, then neither could anybody else. The magic *had* held. Still, it worried him.

They hadn't performed for a month. It would be better, he supposed, when they reached the town. The villagers wanted nothing to do with their conjuring. They had no coins to waste on such a thing. But he had strong arms, they said, he could work alongside them in the fields – and the little girl, she could join the other children, there were always berries that needed picking. Sometimes the coins they earned were enough to buy them shelter for the night, and sometimes not.

And in the meantime they'd keep on walking, trying to keep ahead of the darkness. Because what choice did they have? He pulled the cart behind them. It would have been much quicker without the cart, but then they couldn't have performed their magic. She walked by his side, and matched him step for step, and kept him company, though she never spoke.

"Is this the town?" he said one day, and Lucy of course didn't answer, and he knew already that this couldn't be the town, it wasn't big enough, it was little more than a street with a few houses either side. But maybe it might have grown into a town, one day, had the blackness not come.

One of the houses was marked 'inn'. He put down the cart, and beat upon the wooden door with his blistered hands. There was no reply, but he knew that someone was inside, he could hear breathing just an inch away, someone trying very hard to be quiet, someone scared.

"Please," he called. "We mean you no harm. We're two travellers, we just want a room for the night."

"This is no inn," a woman's voice came back. "And the people who called it one are long since gone, or dead most like. There is no room for you here."

"If not for my sake, then for the little girl's." And at that, as if on cue, Lucy lifted her head and flared her dimples, and opened her eyes out wide and innocent. It was an expression she could pull at a moment's notice, and it had been a useful trick in the old days, to gather about a sympathetic crowd, to persuade the crowd to part with coins. He saw no signs that anyone inside could see them; there must have been a secret window somewhere, or a crack in the wood, because next time the woman spoke her voice was softer.

"D'ye have money?"

"We are, at present, financially embarrassed," confessed the man, but he puffed out his chest, and his voice became richer – somehow Lucy putting on her pose beside him gave him a little swagger too – "But we propose to pay you with a spectacle of our arts. We are magicians, conjurors, masters of the illusory and the bizarre. We have dazzled the crowned heads of three different empires with our legerdemain, the only limits to what we can surprise you with your own imagination. I am the Great Zinkiewicz, and this, my assistant, Lucy!" And at this he delivered a sweeping bow, directed at where he hoped his audience was watching him.

There was silence for a few seconds.

"You can come in anyway," the woman said.

The inn was dark and dirty, but welcoming for all of that, and warm. The woman showed them both to the fire, and the magicians stood before it, and baked in it, and the man hadn't realised how cold he must have been. But now the heat was on his skin he realised there was a damp chill inside him it would take more than one night's shelter to rid.

"My cart?" he said.

"It's safe. No one will touch your cart."

"It contains everything we own."

"No one will touch your cart."

The man nodded at that, turned back to the fire, turned back to Lucy. Now that they were at rest, he realised once again what an incongruous couple they made. For all that he spoke like the gentleman, his clothes were ripped and mud-spattered, there were ugly patches in his grey beard and his face was bruised. Burly and broad shouldered, he stood nearly seven foot tall. Lucy, by his side, somehow still looked refined. The mud of the fields had never clung to her quite, and as ruddy as his face was, hers was as pale as milk. She seemed dwarfed next to him, she seemed small enough to be folded up and put away in a little box – exactly, in fact, as one of their tricks required.

"There's no food for you," said the woman. "But there's a room upstairs, just for the night; you and your daughter are welcome to it." So, she thought Lucy was his daughter. Perhaps that was for the best.

There was noise on the staircase, and the man looked up, and realised why the woman had taken pity on them. Grinning at them in wonder was a little girl, surely no older than Lucy. And she was a proper little girl too, the man could see that; she had somehow managed to keep her youth, unlike Lucy who just pretended. She was dressed in pink; there was some attempt still to curl her hair.

"My daughter," said the woman, and she said it gruffly enough, but the man could see she was trying to hide her affections, he could sense how she burned with love for the girl, he didn't need his magic arts to tell. He was glad for them. He wondered if there was a father. He knew better than to ask.

Her mother said, "We have guests, make up their bed."

The little girl's eyes widened. "Like in the old days?"

Her mother hesitated. "Yes," she said. "Like in the old days."

The innkeeper and her daughter ate their bread and cheese. The innkeeper wouldn't look at her visitors, but the daughter couldn't help it, she kept stealing glances in their direction. The man knew not to make eye contact yet, not to ask for a single crumb of food. Lucy just stared into the flames, as if fascinated by something she saw there.

"What's your name?" the little girl suddenly asked her.

"She's called Lucy," said the man.

"How old is she?"

"How old are you?"

"I'm seven."

"Then Lucy's seven too."

The little girl liked that. And the magician looked at her directly, and held her gaze, just for a few seconds, and he caused his eyes to twinkle. Lucy never looked up from the fire.

"The magic you perform," said the mother. "It's an entertainment?"

The man nodded gravely. "Madam, many have told us so."

"But it's not *real* magic? I wouldn't have real magic in my house."

"I assure you, it is nothing but tricks and sleight of hand. There is a rational explanation for everything that we do." The woman nodded at that, slowly. "We would be happy to give you a demonstration."

At this the little girl became quite excited. "Oh, please, Mama!"

The woman looked doubtful. "But what good can it do?"

"It cheers the soul somewhat. It amuses the eyes. If nothing else, it makes the night pass that little bit faster."

"Please, mama!" The little girl was bouncing up and down now. "I do so want the night to go faster!"

"No magic," promised the man. "Just a little trick. So simple, your child will see through it. I give you my word."

Words counted for nothing in those days, but the woman chose to forget that. "All right, if it's just the one." And then she smiled wide, and the man could see how beautiful she was when she did that, and how much younger she looked, and how like her daughter, and how she wasn't that much older than her daughter, not really, nor so different either.

Lucy rose from the fireplace, stood as if to attention. The man said, "We'll get changed into our costumes." The woman told him there was no need for that. The man said, "Please, madam, you must allow us to present ourselves properly, presentation is what it's all about!"

The magicians went outside to the cart. They changed into costume. No one was in the street to see, and besides, there was no moon that night, it was pitch black.

When they went back to the inn, the little girl clapped her hands at the sight of them, and her mother's smile widened even further. What a pair they looked! The Great Zinkiewicz wasn't a tramp, how ever could they have thought him so! – he was a lord in a long black evening coat, and his blistered hands were hidden beneath white gloves, and the top hat made him taller still, my, he towered over the room! And he looked smoother, softer, he was charming. Lucy was in a dress of a thousand sequins, and when she moved even the slightest muscle the sequins seemed to ripple in the firelight.

"The Great Zinkiewicz will ask his beautiful assistant to give him a pack of playing cards." His beautiful assistant did that very thing. Zinkiewicz held the pack between his thumb and forefinger. "I shall now ask a member of the audience to confirm these are just ordinary playing cards. You, little madam? Would you do me the honour? Would you be so kind? Would you tell everyone, we have never met before?"

The little girl giggled. She inspected the cards. She confirmed they were very ordinary indeed.

"I shall now ask you to pick a card. But don't let me see it. Don't let my assistant see it. Trust neither of us, keep it secret from us. Yes? Good. That's good. Now, put it back in the pack. Anywhere you like, good."

He handed the pack to Lucy. Lucy fanned the cards in her hand, held them out. The Great Zinkiewicz produced a wand, and tapped at the deck once, twice, three times. "Abracadabra," he said.

"What does that mean?" asked the girl.

"I'm glad you asked me that. I don't know. No one knows. That's what's makes it magic."

"All right," said the girl. She seemed unconvinced by that, so he winked at her.

He took back the cards from Lucy. He shuffled them. He removed one. "Now," he said. "Is this your card?"

"No."

"Oh." Zinkiewicz pulled a face. He looked at Lucy. Lucy pulled a face back. It was so perfect an imitation, and was so unexpected, those blank passive features suddenly contorting like that, really, you had to smile. "Oh. Well. I'll try again. Hmph. Is *this* your card?"

"No!"

"This one, then?"

"No!"

"Then this one!"

"No!" She laughed, she could see something good was coming.

"Well then," said Zinkiewicz. "Well, I'm stumped. Lucy, do you have any idea?"

And Lucy sighed, a big mock sigh, why was she saddled with such a dunce for a partner? She walked up to the little girl. She reached behind the girl's ear. She seemed to tug at it, gave a little grunt of exertion. And then out she pulled a piece of card, and it was all rolled up tight like a straw. She opened it, presented it to Zinkiewicz.

And, as if taking credit for the magic himself, Zinkiewicz then presented it to the little girl, with a bow and a flourish.

"Yes! Yes, that's the one!" She clapped, so did her mother.

There were a few more tricks performed, for as long as it took for the fire to burn out. And, at length, the innkeeper offered the magicians some bread and cheese. Zinkiewicz thanked her, and they ate.

"I know how you did the trick," said the little girl.

"Oho! Do you, indeed?"

"Yes."

"Well, we have to keep these things secret. You better whisper it in my ear."

The little girl laughed, looked at her mother for permission, and the mother nodded, laughed too. So the man got down on his knees, and the girl bent close, putting her lips right up to his ear, and whispering softly, and covering her mouth with her hand so no one could see. She told him the secret, and the man rolled his eyes, slow and despairing.

"You've seen right through me!" he wailed. "You'll become a magician too, I'll be bound, like my Lucy!"

But the little girl had got it wrong. The man had broken his promise. There had been real magic tonight, he had felt it flow right through him, he had felt the old confidence back, and it had been good. There had been no fear at all, it had been so very good. And the innkeeper and his daughter need never know. Lucy would know, but she'd never say.

"Does she ever say anything?" said the woman suddenly. "Is it just part of the act, or...?"

The man shook his head, put his finger to his lips, as if it were something mysterious he wasn't allowed to divulge. But the truth was, he had no idea.

THEY SAT UP late that night, into the small hours, the magician and the innkeeper. The children had gone to bed. The woman fetched an old bottle of Madeira wine, she said she'd been saving it for a special occasion. Maybe this was one.

He said to her, "Aren't you going to run away?" And then he blushed bright red, because he supposed that would sound like an invitation to accompany him, her and her kid, and he didn't want that.

"We're going to stay," she said. "We've decided. We're happy here. There's nowhere out there that's better. And maybe, maybe they'll leave us be."

The man nodded, and finished his glass, and went to bed.

IN THE MORNING, the magicians left. The woman gave them some bread for their journey. The little girl gave Lucy a hug, and Lucy didn't quite know what to do with it, but the girl didn't seem to mind she wasn't hugged back.

They never saw the innkeeper or her daughter again. In the weeks to come, as the blackness overtook them, the man would suppose they were dead.

*　　*　　*

FOR THERE WAS little magic left to those times, not since the demons and angels had gone to war. No one had seen a demon and lived. And yet some said they were monsters, giants, dreadful to look upon, so terrible that if you so much as glimpsed one your heart would stop in terror. And others said they looked just like us. They looked just like us, except if you got close you'd find out their eyes were sharper than ours, and redder too, maybe; and they had little bumps on their head, just small, not quite horns, but maybe, no, horns, small – they could be hidden beneath hair, or a big hat; and when they spoke sometimes fire and brimstone would come out their mouths. But they looked just like us. No one had seen an angel either, but they were just as deadly, and they looked just like us too, like every stranger coming into town, like everyone you do not recognise. There were no wings, nothing so easy or giveaway, no holy trumpets playing to herald their arrival. Some had halos, but they were very ordinary halos, a little grey, a little rusted. The angels and the demons, they could be everywhere, anywhere, all about us. And yet no one had ever seen one. Not seen one, at any rate, and lived.

No one could guess why the demons and angels were at war. But it wasn't about us. They didn't care about us. And wherever they met in battle a blackness would descend, and it would engulf everything, and nothing could escape it, and it was spreading across the land.

The world seemed cracked, somehow, too weak for any magic to hold; or happiness; or faith; or love.

Still, he pulled his cart onwards, and sometimes he faltered, and Lucy never faltered.

One week away they found a road sign directing them towards the town, and it wasn't even damaged, it was in one piece, and the man felt his spirits lift.

Four days away they found the old road itself, and there were some holes in it, and it wasn't strictly straight, but it was still easier going for the cart.

One day they arrived at the town. There were bridges and churches and statues and shops. The road was choked with old discarded vehicles. There was litter. There was a theatre. They went into the theatre. It was big and imposing and the roof was still on.

The man took Lucy's hands, and he made her look at him, directly, into his eyes. And he said, "Listen. We don't have to stop. We can keep going. We can just outrun the blackness. We can keep going."

And Lucy didn't even shake her head. She pulled free, began to unpack the cart.

It was all in good condition, considering. The Sword of a Thousand Cuts had rusted, but that could be put right with a good dose of varnish. A trick mirror had fractured, but just a little, it needn't spoil the illusion too much. The Cabinet of Vanishments was soaked with rain water, and one of the doors had warped slightly with the wet, and they sat it upside down on the stage to let it dry out. But it didn't matter. It didn't matter, they didn't use the Cabinet any more. They only kept the Cabinet for show.

The man unrolled the pack of posters. He walked over the town, stuck his posters up against the sides of buildings, walls, the disused telegraph poles that stuck out of the ground like dead tree stumps. Really, he stuck them up against anything that was still standing. He didn't see anyone, but they saw him, he knew; he knew that once he'd moved away the people would come out from their hiding places and see what he had to sell. They were old posters, he'd stuck them up and pulled them down from any number of towns upon his tours – he looked younger in them, photographed in his full costume, in days when he filled out his clothes better and his smile was more fluent – 'The Great Zinkiewicz Entertains!' it said, and beneath, 'With His Glamorous Assistant, Lucy!' – but this was the *old*

Lucy, the Lucy from before, buxom and beaming, almost as tall as he was, standing proud in her sequined gown and her feather head dress, gesturing towards him in the picture in a display of pride and awe. His assistant, his best friend, his wife, back before he'd lost her, and the blackness had swallowed her soul. How he missed her.

By the time he got back to the theatre the sun was already starting to set, and he could sense that the townsfolk were on the move; in spite of themselves they wanted to be dazzled and entertained. Little Lucy was already in her dress. He put on his white shirt, black trousers, white gloves, black hat. He stood with Lucy in the wings as he heard the auditorium fill, and he felt a sudden sickness in his stomach, performer's nerves. And he wanted to run away, and he wanted too to do what he was born for, and stand in front of the crowd, with all those eyes on him, all expectant, all hungry, all making him the centre of their diminished worlds for a couple of brief hours.

"Break a leg," he muttered to Lucy, and together they stepped out into the lights.

The lights shone in his eyes, he couldn't see his audience, couldn't see how large they were, how apprehensive. He gave his smoothest smile and hoped it passed as confident. He spread his arms out wide, as if inviting everybody in for a special hug.

"I am the Great Zinkiewicz," he cried, as if challenging anyone out there to deny it. No one did.

The patter went well. He felt he had a real rapport with Lucy that night, their little rehearsal at the inn those weeks ago had sharpened them both. He was garrulous, the bigger the tricks he performed the more grandiose the metaphors he used to describe them, he'd never use one syllable when five would do. And beside him Lucy in all her blessed muteness struck such a comic contrast; she'd never open her mouth, she'd talk to the audience in her own way, she'd roll her eyes, she'd shrug, she'd flop her arms once in a while as if to demonstrate the physical heaviness of having to work with such a braggart.

The audience began to chuckle. This was one way in which little Lucy always scored over her glamorous original; his wife had often tried to top his jokes, and she'd never been a funny woman, it had never worked.

So they chuckled, then they laughed outright. At some of the tricks there were even admiring gasps, and there was lots and lots of applause.

There was no real magic. Not tonight, it seemed. But that didn't matter.

And at some point the mood shifted. The applause seemed thicker somehow, not crisp like clapping should be, thick like syrup; the laughter... what, more ironic? Crueller, even? He didn't know what had caused it. Had it been him? It might have been him. Because the fear was back. Everything had been going so well, and he couldn't believe the signs as the fear first stole over him – a coldness in his heart, a slight loosening in his bowels – no, he thought to himself, why now? He heard his jokes for what they were, and they were just words, pointless words; he felt how forced his smile was, could feel just how far it stretched across his face and no further; he began to shake, and sweat. He could see himself, one man caught in the lights, pretending that there was still something magical to the world when all about him was darkness.

The darkness, the darkness had come. The proper darkness, solid, weighty, and it lumbered across the theatre towards him. And he could hear his audience die, every one of them, and the demons came in, or was it the angels, or was it *both*, were they both here together, had they put aside their differences and stopped their war and come to see the show? His audience were lost, the angels and demons were in their seats now, crushing down their corpses. And the darkness, all the darkness, all about, unyielding, and pure, and the only light left in the world shone down upon him and Lucy.

His patter dried. He stumbled over his words. Stumbled over his feet. He panted, he licked his lips.

From the void came a voice, a single voice, and it was sharp like gravel, and he didn't think there was anything human in it at all.

"Give us a good trick, magic man. And maybe we'll spare your life."

IT WAS IN just such a theatre that the Great Zinkiewicz had first seen the darkness. It had not been a good show. The audience weren't attentive, he thought some of them were drunk. And Lucy was talking too much again, in spite of what he'd said to her the night before: it was all in the rhythm, he kept explaining to her, gently, the act only could work in a very exact *rhythm*. "I just feel there's more I can offer," she'd said. "I just stand about looking decorative, and getting sawn in half, and stuff. I'm worth more than that." And he had promised he'd try to find a better way to include her in the show, and they'd kissed, and then made love. And, do you know, he thought he'd probably even meant it.

As they'd trudged towards the grand finalé, he'd given her the signal, and she'd nodded, gone into the wings. And out she had wheeled the Cabinet of Vanishments.

"Behold," said Zinkiewicz. "The Cabinet of Vanishments! Now, my wife will vanish before your eyes. When she gets locked up in my special box, and I tap upon the door, and say the magic word – yes, you all know it, abracadabra! I don't know what it means, no one knows what it means, if we knew it wouldn't be magic – I'll say the word, and my wife will be gone!"

He'd felt at last a flutter of interest from the audience.

His wife had said, perkily, whilst wagging her finger at him, "And just you make sure I get back in time for tea!" Audience death once more. Jesus.

He closed the door on her, and he felt a relief that she was out of sight. And a sense of something else, deep inside, some new confidence. Or power.

He tapped on the door three times with his wand. "Abracadabra," he said.

He opened the door. She'd gone. There was some half-hearted applause.

He closed the door again. "Now to bring her back," he said. "I suppose!" And there was some laughter at that, and he thought to himself, you see, Lucy, one *can* improvise comedy, but only if one's a professional.

"Abracadabra," he said. He opened the door. The cabinet was empty.

He closed the door. He turned to the audience, smiled, but he felt it was a sick smile, and he could feel himself beginning to sweat.

"I'll try again," he promised them. "Abracadabra!"

Still nothing – but no, really *nothing* – and this time it seemed to Zinkiewicz the cabinet was not merely empty, it somehow seemed to have no inside at all. Black, just black, a darkness. That would spill out into the world unless... unless he slammed the door shut.

He did. He held the door closed. He felt it, he felt something beat against it, thrum against his fingers. He didn't dare let go. He didn't dare hold on either, he didn't dare stand so close, because he knew that for all its fancy design and name the cabinet was just a bit of plywood a few inches thick, it wouldn't be enough to contain what was growing within. And at the thought of it he pulled away, as if he had been burned – and for a moment he thought he had, and he stared down at his fingers, expecting them to be charred and black. They weren't. They weren't, but he stared at them anyway – and for too long, he could hear behind his back the audience stir from stultified silence and begin to heckle.

He turned back to them. He didn't know what to say. His tongue felt heavy, sick, and yes, his fingers, they still *burned*. "I'm sorry," is what he came out with. "I'm sorry."

And behind him he heard it, and he knew now he wasn't imagining it, there was a knocking from within the cabinet, something impatient to be released. And then there was a voice to it – "Hey!" Muffled, but still sounding perky, so annoyingly perky. "Hey, let me out! Is it time for my tea yet?"

There was some polite laughter, they thought it was part of the act. He opened the door. There was Lucy. He took her hand to help her out, she had to bow so her feather head dress wouldn't get caught, and her sequins sparkled as they came out from the dark. They made their bows together. They went for two bows, although the applause didn't really warrant it.

That night in their digs they had argued. She told him this wasn't what she had expected from their marriage. It wasn't just the act any more, it was the entire *marriage*. She was bored with the constant travelling. It wasn't as exciting as she'd expected. She thought they'd be on television by now. "Do you still love me?" he'd asked. She'd thought about it. "I don't know," she'd replied.

She turned away from him in the bed, and he wanted to reach out towards her, but he was too proud, or too frightened he'd be rebuffed. And he lay there in the darkness, and it seemed to him that it was a darkness so profound, and he wished they'd left the bathroom light on, or had the curtains open, anything, the darkness was beginning to hurt his eyes. And he felt that surge of power inside him again, and he knew she was right, he should be better than this, it was all supposed to be better.

He didn't know her any more. He didn't know her. Their magic was gone.

And he realised all the darkness in the room was her, it was her, it was coming from her. He could feel it now, it was pouring out of her. With every breath she made she was spitting more of it out, and it lay heavy on her, and it lay heavy on him, and it was going to suffocate him unless he stopped it. He'd lost her. He'd lost her. She'd been swallowed up whole.

He got up. She didn't stir.

He packed the truck with all the props he needed for his magic act, his costume, the takings from the last three weeks of performance. He drove off into the night.

Within a few days the truck ran out of petrol. There hadn't been a petrol station. There was barely even a road any more. He abandoned the truck. He found a horse cart amongst the rubble that lay about, so much rubble, things thrown away and no longer wanted. He loaded the cart. He picked up the handle. It was so heavy. He had to be strong. He walked.

The world was cracked, and the darkness was pursuing him, and he had to outrun it. And in some towns there was talk of war.

He did a few tricks for coins and food. Most of his tricks didn't work without an assistant.

Some nights, if the ground was dry, he slept underneath the cart. He could pull the canvas covering down for added warmth or shelter. One morning he woke to find a little girl was curled up, at his feet, like a dozing cat.

"Oi!" he said. "Wake up!" The girl did, stretched, looked at him without shame or curiosity. "Who are you?" he demanded. "Where have you come from?"

She didn't answer.

And he didn't ask again, because he felt somehow if he did she would go away.

When he pulled the cart along, she walked beside him. And the next town he reached, he played his act, and she was there. She knew the tricks just as well as he did. And she had her own sequined dress, it fitted perfectly.

The distance between towns seemed greater and greater. Sometimes they'd walk for weeks before they'd reach a new one. And when they did, the people were hostile, or hid from them altogether. The paths were hard to walk, the ground rough, chewed up even, and no matter how much it rained the mud beneath their feet seemed so hard and sharp and unyielding. "I can't go on," he'd say to the girl, "I don't see why we're going on," and he might cry, and then the girl wouldn't look at him, as if she were embarrassed. One day he dropped the handle of the cart. "I've had enough," he said, "if we must walk, I'm not carrying this any more!" Without missing a beat she went to the cart, tried to lift it herself, tried to drag it behind her. She was such a little thing, but she managed it; he could see her grit her teeth with the effort, and then force one foot on in front of the other, so slowly, too slow – she was going to pull the cart no matter how long it took. Shamed, he went back, relieved her. She smiled at him then, just a little smile, and it was of triumph, but it was not unkind. On he walked. On she walked, always keeping pace.

He called her Lucy, it was what it said on the posters. And sometimes as she slept beside him he thought he could see something of his wife in her face. Sometimes he liked to pretend this was his wife, but small, and silent, from the years before he'd met her. And sometimes he didn't need to pretend, he knew it was true.

"GIVE US A good trick, magic man. And maybe we'll spare your life. You, and that brat of yours."

He tried his best. But the cards kept slipping through fingers damp with sweat.

"Haven't you got anything better?"

He pulled a rabbit out of his hat. He pulled a hat out of a rabbit.

"Last chance, magic man."

He didn't know what to do. He looked at Lucy for help.

Lucy didn't seem afraid. She seemed as blandly unaffected by this as she was by everything else. And for a second the man rather envied her. And for a second he was rather frightened of her too.

She held his gaze for a moment, then turned, and left the stage.

He thought she'd abandoned him. And he couldn't blame her.

But she came back, and when she did, she was wheeling on the Cabinet of Vanishments.

"No," he said to her. "No."

She shook her head at that. She set it down centre stage. She presented it to the audience. And so, he went on with the act. He cleared his throat.

"I shall say the magic word, abracadabra. I... I don't know what it means. No one does. What it means, I." His voice cracked. "Maybe that's why it's magic."

There was laughter. Real laughter, or were they mocking him?

He opened the cabinet. There was no darkness in there, the darkness had all got out long ago.

And Lucy gestured that *he* should step inside.

"No, I'm the magician," he said.

She ignored that. With a bow, with a flourish, she once more waved him towards the box.

"No," he said. And this time he was quite firm.

She stared him down for a little while. Then she leaned forward, and he thought she was going to speak at last, he thought she was going to whisper something in his ear. He bent down to listen. She kissed him lightly on the cheek.

"Get on with it," came the voice from the audience.

They got on with it. Lucy climbed inside the cabinet. She looked so tiny there suddenly, you could have fitted five Lucys inside, more maybe. He closed the doors on her. One didn't shut properly, the rain water, the warping – and there was laughter again, and this time they were definitely mocking him. He had to hold the door to keep it flush.

"Goodbye," he said to her. And he liked to imagine that inside she mouthed a goodbye to him too.

He tapped on the box three times with his wand. "Abracadabra," he said. He stepped away from the box, the warped door swung open and revealed that the cabinet was now empty.

"Can you bring her back?"

"Yes," he said.

"Bring her back."

"No," he said. "I'm not bringing her back. Not to this place."

They came up on to the stage then, and took him by his arms, and bent him over backwards so his spine hurt, and held him tight. He saw that they were demons and angels, both – that they had little lumps for horns, and lapsed haloes, both.

"Bring her back," they said.

And he felt such a power surging through him, the magic was back, even in a world as cracked as this. And he thanked them, sincerely – he thanked them that they had helped him give his best performance, that they had made his act at last mean something. The fear had gone. The fear had gone forever, and they could now do what they liked to him.

THEY BIT HIM, and punched him, and pulled at his skin and hair. And he didn't cry out, he laughed, he barely felt a thing, he was so full of magic now, he was invincible. This enraged them still further. They shut him inside his box, and they set fire to it, and he didn't cry out, not once, and he looked deep into the flames and fancied he saw in them what Lucy had found so fascinating, and it didn't hurt, not very much, right up until the end.

AND LUCY TURNED about, and opened her eyes, and there was noise, and people, and the buildings stood intact, and the smell in the air may not have been clean but at least it wasn't sulphur.

Her sequined dress was ripped, and spattered with mud.

There was a pack of playing cards in her hand.

There was a tongue in her head.

She began to speak, and the more she said the better she got, and the better she got the louder she became.

She fanned out the playing cards to the world.

"Roll up, roll up," she said. "Prepare to be dazzled by the Great Zinkiewicz!"

For a while no one paid any attention. But then, even in a world so cracked, the magic began to hold.

ABOUT THE AUTHORS

Dan Abnett is a multiple New York Times bestselling author and an award-winning comic book writer. He has written more than forty novels, including the acclaimed *Gaunt's Ghosts* series, the *Eisenhorn* and *Ravenor* trilogies, volumes of the million-selling *Horus Heresy* series, *The Silent Stars Go By* (the 2011 Christmas Doctor Who novel), *Triumff: Her Majesty's Hero*, and *Embedded*. In comics, he is known for his work on *The Legion of Super-Heroes, Nova, the Guardians of the Galaxy* and the Vertigo series *The New Deadwardians*. A regular contributor to *2000 AD*, he is the creator of series including *Grey Area, Kingdom* and the classic *Sinister Dexter*. He has also written *Insurrection, Durham Red, Judge Dredd, The VCs* and *Rogue Trooper*. He lives and works in Maidstone, Kent. Dan's blog and website can be found at www.danabnett.com and you can follow him on Twitter @VincentAbnett

Storm Constantine is the author of over 30 books, both fiction and non-fiction, as well as numerous short stories. Her fiction titles include the best selling Wraeththu trilogies and stand-alone novels, *Hermetech, Thin Air,* and the Grigori Trilogy. Her esoteric non-fiction works include *Sekhem Heka* and *Grimoire*

Dehara: Kaimana. Storm lives in the Midlands of the UK with her husband and four cats.

Award-winning horror author **Gemma Files** is currently best-known for her Hexslinger novel series (*A Book of Tongues, A Rope of Thorns* and *A Tree of Bones*, all from ChiZine Publications), but has also published two collections of short fiction (*Kissing Carrion* and *The Worm in Every Heart*, both from Wildside Press) and two chapbooks of poetry. Five of her stories were adapted by *The Hunger*, an erotic anthology TV series co-produced by Tony and Ridley Scott's Scott Free Productions. She lives in Toronto, Canada with her husband and son.

Christopher Fowler is the multi-award-winning author of over thirty novels and twelve short story collections including *Roofworld, Spanky, Psychoville, Calabash, Hell Train* and ten Bryant & May mystery novels. He recently wrote *Red Gloves*, 25 new stories to mark his first 25 years in print, the *War of the Worlds* videogame for Paramount with Sir Patrick Stewart, and won the Green Carnation prize for his memoir *Paperboy*. He currently writes a weekly column in the *Independent on Sunday* and reviews for the *Financial Times*.

Will Hill is the author of the critically-acclaimed *Department 19* series, which have been translated into eight languages and sold in more than fifteen countries around the world. The first book in the series was the best-selling YA debut hardback of 2011. He grew up in the north east of England, and now lives in east London with his girlfriend.

Alison Littlewood is the author of *A Cold Season*, published by Jo Fletcher Books, an imprint of Quercus. The novel was selected for the Richard and Judy Book Club, where it was described as "perfect reading for a dark winter's night." Alison's short stories have been picked for the *Best Horror of* *the Year* and *Mammoth Book of Best New Horror* anthologies for 2012, as well as featuring in genre magazines *Black Static*, *Crimewave* and *Dark Horizons*. Other publication credits include the anthologies *Terror Tales of the Cotswolds, Where Are We Going?* and *Never Again*. Visit her at www.alisonlittlewood.co.uk

Sarah Lotz is a screenwriter and pulp fiction novelist with a fondness for the macabre and fake names. Among other things, she writes urban horror novels under the name S.L. Grey with author Louis Greenberg and a YA zombie series with her daughter, Savannah, under the name Lily Herne. She lives in Cape Town with her family and other animals. She can be found at slgrey.bookslive.co.za, deadlandszombies.com and sarahlotz.com.

Gail Z. Martin's newest series, The Ascendant Kingdoms Saga (Orbit Books) debuts with *Ice Forged* in 2013. In addition to *Ice Forged*, she is the author of The Chronicles of The Necromancer series (*The Summoner, The Blood King, Dark Haven* and *Dark Lady's Chosen*) from Solaris Books and The Fallen Kings Cycle from Orbit Books (*Book One: The Sworn* and *Book Two: The Dread*). For book updates, tour information and contact details, visit www.AscendantKingdoms.com

Sophia McDougall is a novelist, playwright, artist and poet. She is the author of the bestselling Romanitas trilogy (twice shortlisted for the Sidewise Award for Alternate History) set in a contemporary world where the Roman Empire never fell. Beside modern Romans, she has also been known to write about fish robots and ghost Nazis. You can find her at sophiamcdougall.com

Born in Wales in the UK, **Lou Morgan** studied medieval literature at UCL and now lives in the south of England with her husband, son and obligatory cat. Her first novel, Blood and Feathers, was published by Solaris Books in August 2012, and her short stories have appeared in several anthologies.

She has a weakness for pizza, and for cathedrals (but probably not at the same time) and can be found on Twitter at @LouMorgan... usually when she's supposed to be doing something else.

Audrey Niffenegger is a writer and artist who lives and works in Chicago. When she was a child she was convinced (due to an unfortunate encounter with a faux biography) that Sherlock Holmes was a real person. Years later she was perplexed to realise that his creator, Arthur Conan Doyle, believed that fairies were real. Some years after that she discovered The Doyle Diary by Charles Altamont Doyle, Arthur's father; it is a sketchbook he kept while he was an inmate at an insane asylum. 'The Wong Fairy' owes a great deal to The Doyle Diary's introduction and detective work by Michael Baker. It is always gratifying when reality is stranger than fiction; many thanks to Mr. Baker for inspiring this story.

Thana Niveau lives in the Victorian seaside town of Clevedon, where she shares her life with fellow writer John Llewellyn Probert, in a gothic library filled with arcane books and curiosities. Her stories have appeared in *Best New Horror 22* and *23*, *Terror Tales of the Cotswolds*, *The Black Book of Horror 7*, *8* and *9*, *Death Rattles*, *Delicate Toxins* and the charity anthology *Never Again*, in addition to the final issue of *Necrotic Tissue*. She has just published her first collection, *From Hell to Eternity*.

Robert Shearman is probably best known for writing that episode that brought the Daleks back to the revived series of *Doctor Who*, but he started out as a theatre and radio dramatist, writing strange comedy plays for the likes of Alan

Ayckbourn, about people falling in love with their younger selves, or imaginary friends magically coming to life; his two series of the interactive BBC radio series *Chain Gang* both won Sony Awards, with a third series due in 2013. He has written three collections of short stories, *Tiny Deaths, Love Songs for the Shy and Cynical,* and *Everyone's Just So So Special,* and collectively they have won the World Fantasy Award, the British Fantasy Award, the Shirley Jackson Award and the Edge Hill Short Story Readers Prize; individual stories have been selected by the National Library of Singapore for the Read! Singapore campaign, and nominated for the Sunday Times EFG Private Bank Award. A fourth collection, the horror-themed *Remember Why You Fear Me*, is published by ChiZine in Canada later this year. His ongoing quest to write one hundred new short stories can be found at justsosospecial.com. He is currently writer in residence at Edinburgh Napier University.

Melanie Tem's recent and forthcoming stories include 'Corn Teeth' (*Asimov's*, Aug 2011), 'The Classmate' (*HorrorZine* anthology edited by Jeanie Rector) and 'Timbrel and Pipe' (*Dark Fantastic* edited by Jason V. Brock & William Nolan). Her play *Comfort Me with Peaches* was produced in May 2011 at the Academy Theatre in Pennsylvania. She is currently at work on a science fiction story set in a world in which writing and music have been lost, as well as a novel that, so far, defies categorization.

Steve Tem's newest collection is *Ugly Behaviour* (New Pulp Press), gathering the best of his noir fiction. This will be followed in 2013 by *Celestial Inventories* (ChiZine) collecting his recent contemporary fantasy, and *Onion Songs* (Chomu) collecting his more off-beat and experimental work.

Liz Williams is a science fiction and fantasy writer living in Glastonbury, England, where she is co-director of a witchcraft supply business. She is currently published by Bantam Spectra

(US) and Tor Macmillan (UK), also Night Shade Press and appears regularly in *Realms of Fantasy, Asimov's* and other magazines. She is the secretary of the Milford SF Writers' Workshop, and also teaches creative writing and the history of Science Fiction. Her novels include *The Ghost Sister* (Bantam Spectra), *Empire of Bones, The Poison Master, Nine Layers of Sky, Banners of Souls* (Bantam Spectra – US, Tor Macmillan – UK), *Darkland, Bloodmind* (Tor Macmillan UK), *Snake Agent, The Demon and the City, Precious Dragon, The Shadow Pavilion* (Night Shade Press) *Winterstrike* (Tor Macmillan) and *The Iron Khan* (Morrigan Press). Forthcoming in 2012 are *Morningstar* (Morrigan) and *Wordsoul* (Prime). Her first short story collection *The Banquet of the Lords of Night* is also published by Night Shade Press, and her second, *A Glass of Shadow*, is published by New Con Press. Her novel *Banner of Souls* has been nominated for the Philip K Dick Memorial Award, along with 3 previous novels, and the Arthur C. Clarke Award. Liz writes a regular column for the *Guardian* and reviews for *SFX*.

Also edited by Jonathan Oliver

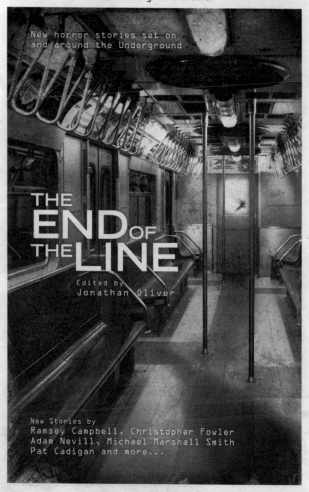

UK ISBN: *978 1 907519 32 1* • US ISBN: *978 1 907519 33 8* • *£7.99/$7.99*

The End of The Line *collects some of the very best in new horror writing in a themed anthology of stories set on, and around, the Underground, the Metro, the subway and other places deep below. This collection of 19 new stories includes thoughtful, disturbing and terrifying tales by Ramsey Campbell, Conrad Williams, Christopher Fowler, Mark Morris, Pat Cadigan, Adam Nevill and Michael Marshall Smith amongst many others.*

 WWW.SOLARISBOOKS.COM

Follow us on Twitter! www.twitter.com/solarisbooks

Also edited by Jonathan Oliver

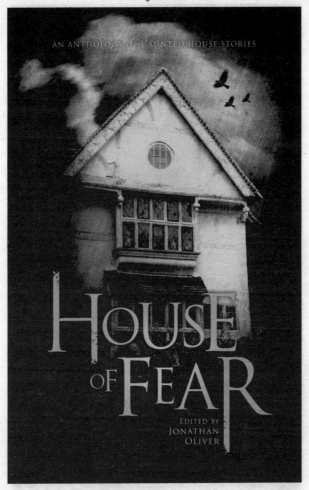

UK ISBN: 978 1 907992 06 3 • US ISBN: 978 1 907992 07 0 • £7.99/$7.99

The tread on the landing outside your door, when you know you are the only one in the house. The wind whistling through the eves, carrying the voices of the dead. The figure briefly glimpsed through the cracked window of a derelict house. Editor Jonathan Oliver brings horror home with a collection of haunted house stories featuring Joe R Lansdale, Tim Lebbon, Christopher Priest, Rober Shearman, Sarah Pinborough and others.

UK ISBN: 978 1 907519 95 6 • US ISBN: 978 1 907519 94 9 • £7.99/$7.99

Imagine a place where all your nightmares become real. Think of dark urban streets where crime, debt and violence are not the only things you fear. Picture a housing project that is a gateway to somewhere else, a realm where ghosts and monsters stir hungrily in the shadows. Welcome to the Concrete Grove. It knows where you live...

 WWW.SOLARISBOOKS.COM

Follow us on Twitter! www.twitter.com/solarisbooks

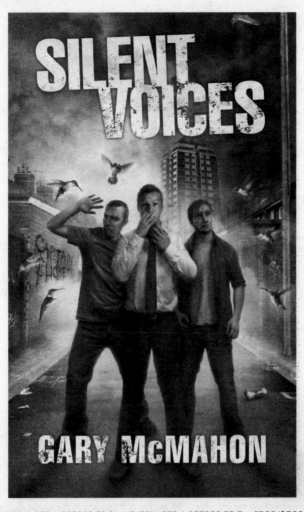

UK ISBN: 978 1 907992 78 0 • US ISBN: 978 1 907992 79 7 • £7.99/$7.99

Twenty years ago three young boys staggered out of an old building, tired and dirty yet otherwise unharmed. Missing for a weekend, the boys had no idea of where they'd been. But they all shared the same vague memory of a shadowed woodland grove... and they swore they'd been gone for only an hour. Welcome back to the Concrete Grove. The place you can never really leave...

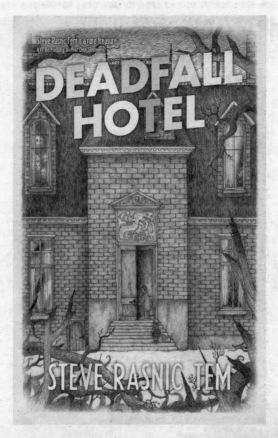

UK ISBN: 978 1 78108 018 4 • US ISBN: 978 1 78108 019 1 • £7.99/$9.99

Alice isn't having the best of days – late for work, missed her bus, and now she's getting rained on – but it's about to get worse.

The war between the angels and the Fallen is escalating and innocent civilians are getting caught in the cross-fire. If the balance is to be restored, the angels must act – or risk the Fallen taking control. Forever. That's where Alice comes in. Hunted by the Fallen and guided by Mallory – a disgraced angel with a drinking problem he doesn't want to fix – Alice will learn the truth about her own history… and why the angels want to send her to hell.

What do the Fallen want from her? How does Mallory know so much about her past? What is it the angels are hiding – and can she trust either side?

 WWW.SOLARISBOOKS.COM

Follow us on Twitter! www.twitter.com/solarisbooks

UK ISBN: 978-1-907992-01-8 • £7.99 // US ISBN: 978-1-907992-00-1 • $8.99

a nightmarish otherworld of fathers and sons, hopes and dreams, love and death.

Regicide
Nicholas Royle

 WWW.SOLARISBOOKS.COM

Follow us on Twitter! www.twitter.com/solarisbooks

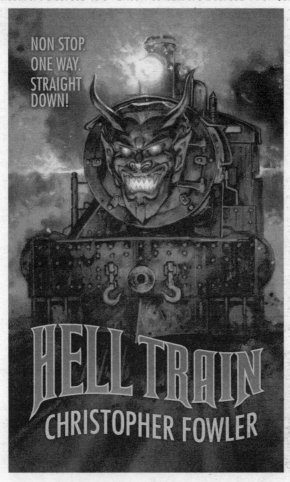

NON STOP.
ONE WAY.
STRAIGHT
DOWN!

HELL TRAIN
CHRISTOPHER FOWLER

Bizarre creatures, satanic rites, terrified passengers and the romance of
travelling by train, all in a classically-styled horror novel!

'The very British spirit of Hammer Horror rises from the grave in
Christopher Fowler's rattling, roaring yarn.'
- Kim Newman, author of *Anno Dracula*

 WWW.SOLARISBOOKS.COM

Follow us on Twitter! www.twitter.com/solarisbooks